CW01590247

SMALL PLACES

Matthew Samuels

ISBN: 979-8-740376-36-3

For more information, address: mail@theabditory.co.uk

FIRST EDITION

www.theabditory.co.uk

For content and trigger warnings for all my books, please check theabditory.co.uk/content-trigger-warnings

For Ros, with all my love

Chapter

I

The antique shop is a jumbled mass of aging knick-knacks. China animals sit next to old glassware, shoulder-to-shoulder with rusted toy cars and maps from years gone by. Rows of coins, arranged by date, form a neat display next to a stack of dolls. In the corner of the shop window, jaundiced by the yellow film stretched across the glass, sits a large mace of sorts, curiously blunt tubes protruding from only one side of the bulb at the top, looking more like a giant key than a weapon. It's an antiquarian's dream; days, if not weeks of exploration for the right eyes and mind.

It's not remotely of interest to a ten-year-old. In particular, it's not remotely of interest to the pair of ten-year-olds stood outside it, both wondering where the patisserie, which used to inhabit the space, has gone.

"Where's the cake?"

I'm embarrassed to admit that this is how I remember it all starting, my bemusement slowly turning to frustration.

"When did this happen? Why is it *here*? Why do old people like this stuff?" I continue, childish annoyance bubbling out of me. "Can't they just buy new things that don't smell like a cat lady's house?"

Sam shrugs and peers deeper into the shop.

"I dunno Jamie," she says. "Old people, old things. Maybe it reminds them of when they were young?"

I blow my cheeks out and shake my head. "Maybe. Come on, let's go."

"Now then, what do we have here?"

I spin around, instantly feeling guilty as I recognise the deep, authoritative voice of Sergeant Michaelson, the local police officer.

"Hi," I manage to squeak, as I take in all six foot two of his uniformed self. He might as well be a giant.

"Well," he says slowly. "What were you two planning? We've had a rash of thefts recently and I don't know what else a couple of troublemakers would be doing at a shop like this."

"Nothing!" Sam manages, and the Sergeant comes down on one knee, subjecting me and my friend to a hard stare.

"Hmmmm," he muses, his dark eyes boring into me. I take a step backwards only to find the very solid glass of the antique shop still exactly where I'd left it.

Suddenly, the bell above the door of the shop tinkles as Mrs Jones, the owner of the store, comes out and looks at us.

"Oh Sergeant," the fifty-something, greying blonde says lightly. "These aren't the children I meant. This is Tanya's boy and Sarah's girl; they're harmless."

I bristle at the idea of being harmless – it doesn't seem like a good thing to be. Sam glares at the woman, but I think that we're both unsure of how to react when there's a policeman who might have real handcuffs with him and could take us to prison. Actually, that might be interesting; then we could stage a daring escape from prison and become famous.

While I'm thinking, Michaelson rises up slowly and puts his hands on his hips, looking over at Mrs Jones. I take the opportunity to survey the array of gadgets on his utility belt: a sturdy-looking truncheon, a boxy handheld computer, two pairs of handcuffs, a walkie-talkie, what looks like a torch and a load of other bits and pieces. I'd love to have a go with the walkie-talkie, but I daren't ask.

"You're sure about this?" he asks.

"Oh yes," she says. "It's those teenage boys that loiter by the supermarket – you know, the ones who tear around on their bikes. They're the problem, not these two. They're much too young – and if I know their mothers, they've been well brought-up."

"I'm not too young," Sam pipes up in a reedy voice. "I'm ten. That's old enough."

Mrs Jones laughs politely. "Of course, dear," she says. "I just want the Sergeant to know that it's a case of mistaken identity."

Sam scrutinises her, not quite knowing if she's being poked fun at.

"Well, I do apologise in that case," Michaelson rumbles. "I was simply looking out for our village's latest retailer."

Jones smiles at him. "That's very kind of you," she says. "Thank you. And you two are welcome to come in and have a look around another time – there are a few things that belonged to my great-grandfather, and he always told me they were magical."

She giggles, looking embarrassed in front of the policeman, but he grunts tolerantly. We both stare at the ground, not really sure what to do.

"Well then," she says. "Why don't you two run along so that I can talk to the Sergeant?"

I exchange glances with Sam. She rolls her eyes and huffs, then flicks her head in the direction of the lane where my parents live. I nod, and we run off down the road, a laugh of pure relief escaping from me a few seconds later.

"That boy though..." I hear the Sergeant say as we trip down the pavement.

"Really, please!" Mrs Jones says in a placatory fashion. "I know it's not a common hair colour, but it doesn't make him a *criminal*."

I barely register it through my giggles. A second later, Sam joins me and for a few moments we can't stop laughing.

It's a warm, sunny July day and there aren't many people around the village; I'd guess that most of them are in their back gardens or the beer garden of the one local pub. Unfortunately, there's next to no chance that my parents will be there; my mum's been working a lot to make up for my dad losing his job. He's been doing odd bits of work around the village, but there's not really that much to be done, so he's been around the house more. His cooking stinks, and he's been asking me to do loads of chores, which is one of the reasons why I was killing time with Sam by the antique shop.

"What do you want to do now?" Sam says, interrupting my train of thought.

I skid to a halt outside our neighbour's garden. Their lawn is immaculate; a sprinkler is keeping it watered and for a moment I'm tempted to see if I can dash across to it and back again without getting wet.

"I'm thirsty," I admit. "Want to come in for a drink? If we're really quiet, maybe we can get out again before my parents notice."

"Sure," she says. "Why are they fighting this time?"

I shrug and turn towards home. "I don't know. Mum's been working a lot. Dad's being strange. I swear he fixed the Davis' fence last week."

Sam looks at me askance. "Weirdo. What's strange about that?"

I bite back a retort. "I told you two weeks ago that's why I couldn't come out for water fights – dad and I fixed the fence together. And they look at each other funnily when they think I'm not watching. Do yours do that?"

Sam thinks for a second as we walk up the badly paved path leading to the small house. "Not really. They ... you know ... do it a lot."

"Ugh!" I recoil and then start giggling uncontrollably. Sam fakes throwing up, then we hurriedly hush ourselves as we reach the front door, slipping through with exaggerated stealth.

The hall is cool and dark; I start down it but Sam takes a moment, her eyes still adjusting. I can hear my parents in the study, I think, so the kitchen should be safe.

I beckon Sam onwards, and she tip-toes across the laminate floor quietly. The door into the kitchen isn't one of the squeaky ones, but I'm still careful as I usher Sam in.

Like mice, we slip across the room past racks of herbs and spices, breakfast cereal boxes and bowls left out for washing up. I find two glasses in the cupboard almost out of reach and, filling them with squash, we gulp down big mouthfuls until we're both panting because neither of us paused for breath.

We stand looking guiltily at each other and then freeze.

"Oh no," I whisper.

"God I'm tired," I hear my mum say, her voice getting closer. "I don't see why you can't get more work at the pub."

The other door to the kitchen bursts open, bouncing off the countertop.

"Shit!" she cries, jumping as she sees us, hand clasped to her chest. "Jesus Jamie, you scared me … uh, sorry."

Adults keep apologising to me today. It's getting weird.

She takes a few steps into the kitchen as my dad follows a moment later, looking harassed. He's an accountant and lost his full-time job a few months ago, and mum seems to be a bit tired of him looking and not finding anything new.

Despite his lousy cooking and chore-giving, I love having him around more. His hair's thinning, his checked shirt is fraying and his jeans have definitely seen better days. But he's my dad. He gives great hugs, smells … reassuring … and I've inherited his love of reading.

"Oh, hi Sam, Jamie," he says, looking at us. "Hot day, huh?"

Sam nods and I flush, embarrassed. Thankfully, I'm saved by the phone ringing, and my dad, also seemingly thankful for the interruption, goes to answer it. There's a quiet exchange of greetings, then a pause.

"Ah, no, now's not a great time Jack," he says. "I'm sorry, is there anyone else who can…?"

He looks over and sees my mum looking daggers at him.

"Look, I'm sorry, it's just that …"

Another pause.

"Ok, could I send Jamie?"

I glance at Sam, confused. Where am I being sent, and why?

"Sure, he'll be over in a moment."

He hangs up the phone and awkwardly heads back into the kitchen.

"That was Jack, from three doors down. He needs some medication that Beckett picked up the other day. I told him that Jamie could help – Jamie, you don't mind helping Mr Abbott, do you?"

Honestly, I'm glad of an excuse to get out, even if it means going to Mr Abbott's house. He's kind of ok, although he always tells me really long weird stories, which I used to love as a kid, but now I'm older it's embarrassing. Well, sometimes they're kind of fun, but he takes them so seriously. And his house smells like old person, although I guess he is an old person, so that makes sense.

Anyway, I nod. "Come on Sam, let's go."

She rolls her eyes when only I can see, and we dash out of the room.

"Thanks kids," I hear my dad say distantly, but we're halfway out by then.

We skip down the garden path again and across to Mr Abbott's house, pausing outside the front door. Most people leave their doors unlocked around here, but I still feel weird about just going in and I can tell that Sam feels the same.

"Are you sure about this?" she whispers. "Do we have to go and see him, like, in bed? That's disgusting."

"He's sick, Sam," I say, although I'm doubting myself as well. I think Mr Abbott is a distant friend of the family, from when my dad worked in London with his brother, but I've never really been sure of the connection. And honestly, it's just scary going into an old man's house. I'm glad Sam's here.

"Ugh, fine then," she says, and pushes the door open, grabbing my arm and pulling me along with her.

I blink as we step into the hallway; it's brightly painted. My parents have never really been motivated to decorate, so our house has stayed the same shade of off-white that it's always been. It doesn't bother me, but Mr Abbott's house is dazzling by comparison, the hallway boasting a strip of sparkling sky blue that races along a white wall. Seaside pictures, complete with a ship's wheel, are hung along the walls, and despite my hesitancy, it feels light and airy, not heavy and close.

We both jump a little as there's a cough from up ahead.

"Jamie?" a weak voice calls from somewhere beyond. "Is that you?"

"Yes Mr Abbott," I call back as loudly as I can, although to my embarrassment I can hear a definite quavering in my voice. "I'm coming."

Glancing hesitantly at Sam, I head down the corridor and into the lounge. Sighing loudly, she follows me into the front room, which is mountain-themed in a stark contrast to the nautical hallway. Huge prints of the Rocky Mountains, the Grand Canyon and Norwegian fjords litter the room. There are bookshelves in between, filled with travel books, fiction, fairy stories and a multitude of classics everywhere.

In the brightest corner of the room in an easy chair, his back to a bookshelf, looking out of the window across the lawn, is Mr Abbott. He's swathed in blankets despite the heat, and looks terribly tired. The blankets are drawn all the way up to his chest, a thick mustard-coloured jumper just visible above it. There's a mug of something next to him; it looks and smells like chicken soup.

"Thank you for coming," he says hoarsely, before coughing and clearing his throat noisily. I remember him being around quite a lot when I was smaller; a big bear of a man with a hearty laugh. "I won't keep you inside on a day like this, but ..."

He has another bout of coughing, making Sam take a step backwards, a slightly disgusted expression on her face. Mr Abbott wipes his mouth with a handkerchief and clears his throat again.

"I'll be quick," he says. "I need you to go and get some medicine that Beckett – Mr Andrews to you – was collecting for me. He lives in Huntsman's cottage by the Manor. Do you know it?"

We both know it. We've been fascinated by the old Manor house for years, always wanting to steal in, the high iron gates always thwarting us. I've probably spent hours with my nose pressed between the rails of the gate, staring at its façade, wondering who lives there, what they do, and whether they host elegant balls and parties. There's a small cottage just outside it where a man lives; until today I'd not known his name. It's towards the outskirts of town, and although I've seen him around, smoking outside the pub, I've heard my parents say that he keeps himself to himself, whatever that means. I guess it means he doesn't talk to other people.

"Ok," I say, finding my voice. "I know where that is. Um … Mr Abbott … are you ok?"

Slowly, he smiles at me. Even that looks tiring for him and I suddenly feel sorry for this old man, a wave of goodwill somehow outweighing my desire to get back outside.

"Ah, thank you for your concern my friend," he says, his voice creaking. "Well, unfortunately, even Mistress Mel can't help an old fellow like me, but she's trying her best. Now, you take this to Mr Andrews and he'll give you something to bring back, ok?"

He picks up a small velvet pouch from the coffee table next to him and holds it out. I take two steps forward and he drops it into my outstretched palm.

"We'll come straight back," I assure him, suddenly feeling sad.

"I know you will," he says. "Thank you both very much."

"Come on," Sam hisses at me, taking my hand and pulling me back out along the corridor until we're safely outside and further down the road.

"I don't *like* him," she says. "That was *weird*. Was he dying or something?"

Normally I'd be scared, but despite some of his stories being a bit creepy, most of my memories of Mr Abbott are kind ones, well-meaning ones. He'd always give well-intentioned gifts: beautifully illustrated books, maps of fantastical places, a pocket-knife that still sits on a shelf, out of reach until a future birthday.

"I … I think he might be," I say shakily, and Sam falls silent.

We walk down the road a way and I try to think of something that might cheer her up. "Maybe Mr Andrews will let us go into the Manor?"

Sam scoffs. "Doubt it. He's just the groundsman and doesn't even live in the Manor. It's not his, he'd just get in trouble."

Sam and I have played together almost since we were born, but sometimes she can be a bit mean.

But being completely honest, it's a small village and there aren't many friends for a white-haired boy with parents who always argue and don't really get into village life. The few times we've fallen out, I found myself playing alone for a couple of days. That got pretty sad, pretty quickly.

Most villages in the English countryside revolve around either the pub or the church, and my parents aren't religious or big drinkers. Dad would occasionally go down to the pub with Mr Abbott, until he got sick and we got poor. We're a bit short on friends of the family and none of our nearby neighbours have children – they're all retired pensioners unwinding in the countryside.

"Well, you never know," I manage, but Sam just snorts softly. She keeps walking with me though, so that's the important thing. I feel awkward, but try to enjoy the summer's day; it's warm and everything smells like wildflowers and cut grass. I run my fingers along the rough brickwork of boundary walls, playing at avoiding the thorns of the raspberry bushes growing rampant on the side of the path, occasionally picking one of the sweet fruits and popping it into my mouth.

On the other side of the village, houses begin to thin out and finally fade from view. The last hundred metres before the Manor is farmland; maybe they own it? I don't know – I don't even know who 'they' are.

I feel a surge of unease as we near the small bungalow just outside the Manor gates. Much like our garden, it's a bit overgrown, weeds and bramble bushes growing everywhere, the path to the front door barely clear. There's a wooden sign standing in front of the crumbling brickwork, with 'Huntsman's Cottage' printed on it. It looks like it's fallen over and been replaced a lot.

I take a deep breath and scurry up to the front door, looking for a bell. There isn't one, so I reach up for the knocker, which is in the shape of an archer's bow, and knock as loudly as I can. Next to me, Sam flinches at the sound, but doesn't say anything. I can tell that she's uncomfortable, even if she pretends not to be. Sometimes I think she covers up being afraid with just jumping into things, and it's got us into trouble a few times.

I hear heavy footsteps tramp through the house, then the door is flung open. A solidly-built, sandy-haired man dressed in jeans and a checked shirt – in much better repair than my dad's – looks down at us.

"Hello there," he says, looking puzzled. "Can I help you?"

"Ah, hi," I manage. "Um ... Mister Abbott sent us ... for his medicine. And we have to give you this."

I proffer the small velvet bag, which Mr Andrews takes in a large hand. He's not as well-muscled as some of the men I've seen on TV in action films, but he's closer to them than anyone else I've seen in real life.

He peers into the bag and says something softly that I don't catch, before closing it back up.

"Ah," he sighs. "I'd forgotten about Jack's medicine, I must admit. He asked me to go and get it from Mel."

He pauses. "At the Manor, of course. Wait, aren't you David's boy?"

My father's name is David. I nod, uncertain of what this means.

"Pours a good pint that man. Reliable. You probably are too."

"He's got white hair," Sam bursts out. "Don't you think that's weird?"

I feel myself flushing crimson with embarrassment. I might be about to cry. Being humiliated in front of other kids is one thing; you can fight them or tell them about the time Sam peed herself on the way back from the swimming pool. Adults are another thing entirely. You've got to be well-behaved or they tell your parents. Or worse, march you home and then tell your parents.

"No," he says kindly. "No, I don't. Not when some of my friends have hooves, wings or scales. To me, you look perfectly normal and boring."

Sam wrinkles up her nose like she's smelt something bad. "Scales? Like, snakes?"

Mr Andrews sighs, handing the small bag back to me. "You'd better come in. I'm afraid that I'm in the middle of a rather delicate job right now. Would you mind going a little further and collecting the medicine yourselves?"

Sam looks at him suspiciously – and maybe rightfully so. I've always been a bit bad at the whole 'stranger-danger' thing, largely because I know, albeit by sight, most of the people in the village and what to expect from them. When Sam goes away, or we fall out, I spend a lot of time sitting on walls watching the world go by.

"Come on," he says. "Mr Abbott wouldn't have sent you here if he didn't trust me, would he now?"

Sam thinks for a second, then nods in agreement. Whatever else she thinks of Mr Abbott, he definitely falls into 'nice old codger' territory, rather than 'potential threat', so I guess that gives his friend here the benefit of the doubt.

Mr Andrews leaves the door open, walking down the hallway and closing the doors to the sides. At the back, I can just about see a kitchen, or at least a room with a large sink in it. Sam gives me a look, then grins and saunters into the house, looking nonchalant. Taking a deep breath, I trail along behind her, closing the door behind me and instantly regretting it; it closes with a firm 'thunk', bringing images of dank prison cells to mind.

I swallow and try to push that from my mind, hurrying after Sam into the kitchen.

And it's not quite like any other kitchen I've been in. New appliances sit alongside old ones, a toaster next to a mortar and pestle, mid-grind by the looks of things. Herbs hang drying on wires along the ceiling and walls, a blender or juicer sits on the side, still dirty with chunks of something green. Mugs are piled high in the sink, and a large chest freezer takes up most of one wall. There's an empty fireplace that looks like it once had a spit or a rail above it for a cookpot, ornate black metalwork surrounding it. My eyes are drawn to the small decorative doors on either side; maybe that's where you collect the ash from?

The whole room smells deeply meaty, like a hundred hams have been roasted in here, alongside Christmas turkey and steak. I feel like there should be a dog curled up by the fireplace, ready to flush grouse from somewhere, like in a book that I read at school a few years ago.

"Right, so you'll have to step through the magic door," Mr Andrews says, before pulling the blind on the back door down and turning the key in the lock a few times, which makes Sam take a step backwards.

"Don't worry," he says, walking back over to the other side of the kitchen and knocking on a green tile once, then twice, then three more times. "Just walk over to the little door to the left of the fireplace and everything will work out. Follow the main track to the junction in the woods, then turn left. Mel's hut isn't far along. Tell her I sent you and give her the bag."

I'm confused, but he's an adult and knows best, so I start walking up to the fireplace. The world grows around me, slipping upwards, getting bigger, the walls taller, until the door at the side of the fireplace seems like a normal size, not six inches like it was before. I daren't look around for fear that it might all vanish, so I reach out and turn the handle, opening it and seeing bright light beyond. I take two steps forward and suddenly I'm through.

Chapter
2

My first impression is that the air in the Manor grounds is somehow fresher than regular air. Sweeter. I blink hard a few times in the bright sunlight, taking a tentative step forward. I'm in a clearing, a path in front of me leading into dense woodland. Huge oaks reach into the blue sky, leafy and thick. I can hear the scurrying of creatures, a squirrel looking quizzical on a branch for a moment before running off into the trees.

I panic and look back, relieved to see the back door of the bungalow right behind me. I can see Mr Andrews moving around inside, by the mortar and pestle. A moment later, Sam is beside me.

"Hey," I say. "That was weird."

She looks around, squinting. "So weird. Why couldn't we just go through the regular door?"

"Maybe because it was cool?"

Then she laughs, all arguments forgotten, and I

join her a moment later. "So cool. Wait until we tell the others at school about this. Come on, let's see what else is around."

She starts down the path and I run to catch up with her, not wanting to fracture our delicate friendship.

There's something here ... something I can't quite put my finger on.

I look around, playing for time. Purple flowers litter the forest floor, contrasting with the bright green grass. I take another deep breath, filling my lungs with the sweet, thick air. I feel ... amazing, suddenly noticing all the little insects scurrying around on the leaves, how elaborate the birdsong is. I could practically skip.

"Sam," I say tentatively. "I don't think this is the kind of place that we should tell ..."

Then there's a deep rumbling sound, stopping me mid-sentence. Sam freezes and her head whips around like a scared deer. I'm frozen in place, but I manage to glance back down the path, incredibly thankful for the sight of the bungalow not too far down the track.

"What the hell is that?" she whispers, as a loud crash sounds, accompanied by the sound of splintering wood. "Let's go back!"

I shake my head. "No way!"

"Seriously?" she hisses, her face contorting. "That could be a bear or a panther or something. We could *actually* die!"

"We *promised*," I plead. "Sam, *please*."

She shakes her head and I wonder if she's going to pee herself again. Unsure of where I'm finding the courage, I lower myself down as much as I can without actually being on my hands and knees. I try to watch exactly where I'm stepping, as well as keeping an eye on the surrounding foliage, before starting down the trail again.

Ten steps on, I look back at Sam. She hasn't moved.

"Come *on*," I hiss at her, and she glares at me, but eventually starts moving. There's another crash and I think I see trees to the right moving. The birds have all gone silent. I focus on just putting one foot in front of the other. Step by step by step.

There's another bassy rumbling sound, like a fire engine revving, and I feel like I might pee my pants instead. I'd give anything to be at home listening to my parents argue right now. My familiar, loving parents - why did I ever leave the house?

I see a fork in the path up ahead and gesture sharply to Sam, who looks like she's about to cry. She scowls, then looks relieved, and we both break into a run, a higgledy-piggledy, panting, crying sprint until we nearly collide with a wooden house in another clearing.

I set my back to it, panting, hands on knees, trying to catch my breath and looking around, wondering if we're being followed. Sam collapses onto the grass next to me, breathing hard and definitely crying a little bit too.

"That … that was awful, Jamie," she says, looking up at me. "Is it still coming?"

"I don't ... think so," I say, feeling queasy.

Then the door to the hut creaks open and we both scream. In our defence, the old woman poking her head out of the door is definitely a witch, or at least she's dressed the part, although why you'd dress for Halloween in midsummer is anyone's guess.

"Shhhh," she says, her hideous face contorting into something vaguely resembling a sympathetic look. She's got a hooked nose, beady brown eyes, tanned, leathery skin, a long chin and is actually wearing a witch's hat and long black robes.

"Quieten down," she says. "You'll make the Ypotryll angry. I won't tell you twice."

Sam's gulping, panting tears suddenly stop, and she pushes herself up, staring at the witch.

"Who are you?" she says defiantly, hands on her hips. I stand up and take a step away from both of them.

"Who am *I*?" the witch replies. "I'd ask the same of you, given that you're the ones tumbling onto my doorstep."

I take a look around, the woods now silent around us. The house is actually a bit larger than I'd thought; it's less of a hut and more like a large, single-storey chalet. It's definitely made of wood, but there's a stone chimney, smoking slightly on the other side of the building.

"Um," I say, quietly, remembering my manners. "I'm very sorry ma'am. We didn't mean to cause trouble. Mr Abbott sent us, and well, um, Mr Andrews as well. Are you Miss Mel?"

Her face splits into a wicked grin, revealing a jagged line of uneven teeth. I steel myself. She must be an actual witch, and actual witches do terrible things to children, or so I've read.

"Uh, we brought this for you, from Mr Abbott," I manage, Sam trembling beside me.

I fish the velvet bag out of my pocket, offering it to her with a sweaty hand. She hooks one long, bony finger around the tie loops at the top, and I shudder at the sight of her black-painted fingernail. I recoil slightly as she leans in, then catch myself doing it.

"Well," she says thoughtfully. "So, the old man is still clinging on then? I suppose I shouldn't turn you into toads after all. He needs all the help he can get, and they're not so good at carrying medicine, toads. Wait here."

With that, she vanishes back inside, the door slamming behind her, showering me with moss. I sneeze and look around, hoping that the noise hasn't attracted ... whatever she called it. The thing. The big thing.

"Jamie," Sam hisses. "We should go. *Now*."

"Just ... just a moment longer," I beg her. "This is important."

"God," Sam whispers, praying furtively. "Please keep us safe from the witch. I swear I'll be good. I'll load the dishwasher every night and I won't complain, ever."

There's a rustling and the door opens again, the witch reappearing in the doorway.

"Here," she says, tossing me a small package. I fumble,

almost dropping it on the grass, but manage to pin it against my knees. I get a better grip on it and stand upright, blushing. "You tell him to mix a spoonful of that with hot water – not boiling, mind you – and take it once a day, every day. There's no cure for cancer, but that'll give it a good run for its money, and it didn't come cheap. Mind you, he's paid for it and then some, you tell him that as well. Now, repeat that back to me, both of you."

I glance at Sam. "Uh, a spoonful in hot water," I say.

"Not boiling," Sam fills in, her voice trembling, but she rallies and makes it even and confident. "Taken once a day, each day."

"And he's paid for it," I finish.

"Good children," she says, cracking another, kindlier grin. "Now run along back to the huntsman and don't dally."

Neither of us moves an inch, and the witch – Melusine – narrows her eyes at us.

"Did you want something else? Perhaps *one* of you would like to try being a toad?"

"Are you really a witch?" Sam asks with a little sass, and I stare at her, aghast.

Melusine cackles almost exactly like witches do in the movies. It's wild, high-pitched and somehow crackly. The forest clearing seems to dim a little and I wonder how much more bladder control I can muster. My knees start to shake and I wonder why I didn't agree with Sam to get out of here when we had the chance. Then Mel stops and looks directly at her.

"Yes," she says quickly, snapping her teeth together at my friend. Sam gives a little scream and dances backwards away from her. The witch turns to me.

"And you, boy, did you have a question as well?"

I really don't, but I don't want to seem rude, so I dredge back through the previous conversation.

"Uh, ma'am," I start hesitantly. "You said ... earlier ... well, how do you drown a *water* nymph?"

"Not in water, my dear," she cackles. "Not in water."

And with that, she vanishes back behind the door and slams it firmly, leaving us standing open-mouthed.

We retrace our steps hurriedly, looking back every few moments, wondering if we're being followed by something monstrous and hungry. Thankfully, the woods are completely silent as we return, wild beasts and witches leaving us alone with the blue sky, birdsong and fresh air.

I pause just outside the bungalow, uncertain of whether you're supposed to knock when you're entering someone's house from the back door. It seems polite, so I do, Mr Andrews opening the door a moment later.

"Did you get what you needed?" he says, ushering us both inside and closing the door behind us.

Sam nods. "Ugh," she says. "But that old woman was *so* weird. Is she *really* a witch?"

Mr Andrews kisses his teeth. "She is at that, and a mighty fearsome one," he drops to one knee and lowers his voice conspiratorially. "A word to the wise. You'd do well to keep her name to yourself, if you know what's good for you. In fact, it's probably best if you forget everything that you've seen and heard this afternoon. Get back to sunlight and ice cream, you know? Tell you what – if the ice-cream shop in the village is still open, you tell Mr Wilson to put two double scoops with a Flake on my tab, ok? Treat yourselves on me."

"Wow!" we both cry, thanking him profusely.

We hurry down the lane back towards the village, Mr Abbott and more importantly, the ice-cream shop. Halfway down the lane, Sam glances back at the Manor cottage and scoffs, shaking her head.

"I don't care what they both said," she says quietly. "There's no way she was a witch. She didn't do any magic at all."

I stay quiet, still wanting to believe in magic, and a little enchanted by the lush forest and its occupants. But I also don't want to upset Sam, so I hurry down the lane silently.

Mr Abbott is embarrassingly grateful for his medicine, his eyes crinkling and filling with tears as we drop the package into his lap. I think Sam and I are both relieved to be done with the chore and unused to such displays of emotion from an adult, so we flee back into the sunlight as quickly as possible.

Thankfully, the free ice cream seems to erase all traces of witches, monsters and sick adults from Sam's mind. She chats away about how lemon sorbet is so much more of a grown-up flavour than mint choc chip.

I know she's repeating what her mum says, but I don't say so. After all, no-one in their right mind would prefer soggy ice to actual ice cream. But really, I'm just relieved to have a friend on a nice afternoon like this.

We hang out in the playground, swinging on the swings and messing around until we're both tired and thirsty, still giggling about our adventure.

Neither of us sleeps very well that week, and Sam never mentions the strange old woman or the creature in the undergrowth again. I find myself staring down the lane towards the Manor more than once, scared of seeing the witch screeching down the road, dagger-like fingernails outstretched.

If I'm honest though, I'm also scared of never experiencing something that weird and wonderful ever again.

I try to ask Mr Abbott about it a few weeks later, when my parents are taking him dinner, but he hushes me. "Best leave it behind, boy," he says. "That place isn't for the likes of you or me."

My next question dies on my lips and I think he's about to apologise when my parents come back into the room with a cooked meal for him. He just inclines his head, gives me a sad look and doesn't say anything else.

I'd hoped to share my story with him, to tell him about the magical fireplace, the monster in the woods and the horrible old witch who almost made me pee my pants. I can't help but wonder why he'd told me all of those stories when I was younger, why he'd given me books of fairy tales for Christmas if he didn't know something else – and if he knew something else, why didn't he want to talk about it?

I tell mum that I think I've left my music on and without waiting for her to tell me it's ok to go, I trudge out of the house and head back home, feeling angry, sad and alone, sitting in my bedroom staring out of the window at nothing in particular.

~

A year later, as I'm starting secondary school, Mr Abbott dies, something that registers only dimly amidst the excitement of a new class, new lessons and a bus ride to a nearby town. My parents attend the funeral, both sombre in black.

Seven years fly by quickly, a blur of classes, exams, sports, drinking for the first time, kissing a girl for the first time.

My parents separate when I'm eighteen, right before I go to university, sending me into a spiral of drinking and casual sex, briefly flirting with drugs and self-harm. I scrape through my first year, retaking exams over the summer. My dad moves back to London and my mum keeps the house. She gets a new job as an executive assistant to a busy CEO in Bath, rather than being a remote PA, which seems to pay better and momentarily takes less of a toll.

But then the company struggles, a new CEO arrives and she works all hours to juggle his schedule, managing meetings with shareholders, staff, customers, partners, a million and one other people. She misses my graduation, but when I see her next, her tired, drawn face makes my righteous anger vanish before I can utter a single syllable.

Every time I speak to her, she seems more and more worn out.

A year into my new job as a market research analyst in London, the doctors find a small tumour growing in her bowel, and she embarks on a long, tiring traffic jam of appointments, therapies, support groups, surgery, and brief moments of hope.

A course of chemotherapy makes her vomit; the radiotherapy makes her skin red and sensitive. When the tumour is small enough, after being repeatedly blasted with radioactive waves, they remove it with part of her colon, forcing her to acclimatise to the sudden addition of a colostomy bag.

After the surgery, she seems upbeat, hopeful that it's the end of a long and painful year in her life, but a follow-up scan finds smaller tumours growing in other parts of her intestine and liver. Stage four, the doctors say, putting her firmly in a Bath hospital ward for the foreseeable future.

With the pragmatism and diligence that perhaps only a long-suffering executive assistant can muster, my mother prepared herself to die as neatly as possible. I was given a long list of jobs, from informing distant members of the family to selling our home.

Ever since my parents separated, I'd lost my faith in happy endings, but rather than being inspired by my mum's quiet, organised dignity, it seemed to paint a grey wash over my world. I couldn't sleep, I couldn't concentrate. Food lost its appeal, and after a few days of putting the issue off, I decided to go and stay with her, potentially for the very last time.

Chapter 3

The next day I'm walking into my office in London, my timing leaning towards the fringes of 'acceptably' late. I do market research and analysis for a relatively large software company, looking at new markets, product acceptance, that kind of thing. It's a quiet, studious kind of job where as long as I deliver stuff on time and look keen, I can keep my head down, not really talk to that many people and avoid working late. It's not that well-paid, but the lifestyle suits me.

"Jamie," a voice calls from across the foyer. I look over; it's my boss's boss, Maria. I report to the head of research, Angela, but she reports into the COO, Maria, who has always been very decent to me.

I turn to face her; it's rotten luck bumping into someone so senior so early in the morning. Usually, I can be at my desk and spend at least an hour working before I have to have a conversation with anyone.

"Maria, hi,"

"Jamie, I was so sorry to hear your news," she says.

I feel my face crumpling a bit. "Uh, thank you," I manage, desperately wanting to change the subject and simultaneously realising that she's actually the person I really need to speak to. "It's … it's tough."

"I can imagine," she says, her face softening. "If there's anything we can do to help, just let me know."

"Thanks," I say, feeling awkward at repeating myself, but not really knowing what else to say. "Uh, Maria, there is something I needed to talk to you about if you have a moment."

"Of course," she says, sweeping me into an empty conference room down the hall and pouring us each a glass of water. "How can I help?"

I take a drink. "Um, well, mum wants me to sort out the house," I say. "And I think I'd rather get it over and done with. I had a holiday coming up next week, but …"

"Jamie, you take whatever time you need," she says, cutting me off gently. "Hell, go home now if you want. I'll sort everything out with Angela."

"No, no, it's ok," I say, taking another sip of water, more to distract my brain than anything else. "I've got a few loose ends to tie off with a project. I'll get everything tidy today, talk to Angela and come back after my holiday."

Maria smiles at me. "Of course," she says. "No problem."

I manage to dodge most other conversations that day, and Angela is similarly understanding about it, especially when I mention that I've already spoken to Maria.

There's a small project focused on a manufacturing company that I manage to sink myself into, eventually conceding that I *will* need to hand over a few details to Angela, but she doesn't mind. It's not a lot of work. The time flies by, and to be honest, it's all a pleasant distraction from the family stuff.

I do find myself staring into space a couple of times thinking about the weirdest details. I mean, how does this work? Do I just box everything up and call an estate agent? I'm not sure that it's worth a lot, especially compared to house prices in London, but a house is a house. Knowing mum, she's probably written me a list already, but I should be looking after her, not the other way around.

And how can I stay there when every time I walk into a room, I'll remember my mum reading, looking through bills, talking to – or shouting at – dad, all the normal stuff? How long does mum even have left? I should have asked, but how do you say something like that?

I flick my mind back to work and try to switch off for a bit. It sort of works, although I notice Angela looking at me sympathetically a couple of times.

"Jamie," she says, her voice suddenly stirring me from my reverie. "Jamie, it's five thirty."

I start and look at the clock. I'd almost finished the manufacturing report I was working on, but it's at the end of a section, so it's as good a place as any to wrap up.

"Thanks," I say quickly. "Sorry, lost track of time. Uh, the report's almost finished, just the last ..."

"It's fine," she says, interrupting. "We've talked about it. I'll handle it. You go, sort your stuff out and look after yourself."

"Thanks," I say again, packing up my stuff. "Ok, sure, will do."

"No problem. You let me know if you need anything else."

That small act of kindness brings tears to my eyes and I find myself ducking down to get my bag so that I have an excuse not to say anything else and recover for a moment.

Rising up and standing a few seconds later, I give my desk a quick glance before I sling my bag up onto my shoulder and head out of the office.

Outside I pause and look back at the nondescript building; it's not really where I'd envisaged myself after university, but I guess real life takes you where it takes you – and I had no money. A few people nod to me as they leave, some of them slightly baffled, presumably as to why I'm staring at a 1960s brick and glass ... well, some people call it a monstrosity, but I've never really been that fussed. It's warm, has coffee, pays the bills and the job is reasonably interesting.

A few spots of rain land on my head and I quickly check that it's definitely rain and not something worse from a bird. Thankfully, it is rain, but obviously I don't have an umbrella; it's mid-summer. I glance up and see dark clouds drifting this way, so I pull up the collar of my light jacket and hurry for the tube, a sea of umbrellas blooming around me. Clearly, some people are better prepared than I am, however weird the weather is.

Fortunately, the office is close to the tube, and there's not far to go at the other end.

My London 'home' is a three-bed flat in Clapham that I share with two other people, Mark and Emily. I knew Mark at uni, and Emily is one of his friends, but to be honest we're not getting on that well right now.

There was a flurry of making-an-effort, just-moved-to-London drinks and exploring and doing all the immersive cinema, pop-up bar, curry festival, Brick Lane, Shoreditch stuff in the first six months, which was fun. But then Mark got a new job with one of the big law firms, started working much longer hours, doing more coke and often I wouldn't see him for days. When I did see him, he looked pretty grim, and despite earning what I imagine is at least twice what I get paid, most of our interactions were me passing on messages from our landlord that he needed to 'pay the fucking rent or I'll turf you out'.

The landlord's words, of course, not mine. I'd kept my nose clean, in both senses of the phrase, and our landlord is generous enough not to lump us all together in his judgment, but it's still awkward.

You'd think that this would have brought me and Emily closer together – a common enemy and all that –

but she seems to revere Mark in a weird, self-destructive kind of way. I'm pretty sure they've slept together a few times, which seems like a terrible idea for flatmates, and she's become really messy. She was never that fastidious to begin with, but I wrote it off as a 'creative's prerogative'. She works as a fashion designer for a boutique men's brand, which I was slightly awed by when I first met her, but the shine wore off pretty quickly amongst the stacks of dirty plates and crockery in the kitchen.

I'd been hoping for a pay rise in the next round of appraisals so that I could move out. Given that I'm about to take three weeks off, my reputation for industriousness might be about to take a hit, but I guess people will understand.

Also – I don't really know anyone else in London. I could move in with complete strangers, but who's to say that wouldn't be worse?

Anyway, with any luck neither of my flatmates will be in right now, the police won't have raided the place and found drugs, and Emily's hair straighteners won't have ignited one of her notepads, stacks of unwashed underwear or a line of coke, Mission: Impossible-style.

Well, maybe if I can sell our family home, I can eventually afford a deposit on a small place in London by myself, or rent to someone who isn't only nominally house-trained.

I guess that's a pretty poor way to think of your family inheritance, but I'm not in a good place right now.

Enough of this.

Thankfully, the flat is empty.

I hurriedly throw enough clothes for a week or so into a suitcase, keen to be out of here as quickly as possible. It's not too bad a journey to mum's place on the train, and after rush hour has passed, it's not normally too expensive either. I could do without this, but I guess it's my responsibility; mum does have a string of brothers and sisters, with families of their own, but a lot of them live a long way away.

Suddenly annoyed at the circumstances, and ramming a last shirt into the case, I zip it up and glance around the flat. My own room is bare, clean and tidy, but devoid of character. What have I become in the last two years? I feel like I've shrunk, preserving a tiny piece of peace and quiet in the middle of busy old London, but otherwise somehow diminishing myself.

I take a deep breath and then let it out all at once, trying to stop myself spiralling. I hurry downstairs, locking up the flat and awkwardly bashing my suitcase on the narrow stairs as I go. I should really let Mark or Emily know that I'm off, but I can do that from the train.

Paddington station is a lot quieter than when I usually see it at rush hour; there's a few office workers who have had more drinks than they should have and aren't quite sure when their next train is, but otherwise it's fairly empty. I flinch as a pigeon swoops down for some abandoned takeaway, trying to disguise my slightly panicked movements by turning and wandering over to Marks and Spencer for some snacks.

The harsh strip lighting starts to give me a headache, so I hurry through the self-checkout, shoving a sandwich, a drink and some crisps into a bag before heading out and getting a ticket from a nearby machine.

The next train home is in fifteen minutes and remarkably, it's already sitting in the platform. I navigate my bag through the ticket barriers and find the right carriage, settling into a seat in the quiet coach. Tucking my bag underneath the seat, I dig my headphones out of my jacket pocket and put some music on, trying to ignore everyone else.

I barely notice when the train pulls out, but eventually find myself staring out of the window, watching the flats and offices go by before they become larger houses, warehouses and countryside. I feel a bit numb, like there's a big black gap where my feelings should be. Shouldn't I feel grief or at least some kind of relief that I can spend some more time with mum before she goes?

I barely taste my crisps and sandwiches, washing them down with something vaguely fruity and sparkling, although which fruit, I couldn't tell you. I stare at the countryside as it speeds by, realising that I'm half expecting mum to be home when I get there. I've done this journey a fair few times in the last two years since I moved to London; I'll admit, I started coming home at weekends when Mark first got into his drugs. He'd be loud and unpredictable at all hours; I'd never know if he'd be in, how many people there'd be in the flat at any time, whether stuff I'd left out would go missing…

I definitely need to move out.

I take a deep breath. I shouldn't be annoyed at my flatmates; I've had over a year to talk to them or move out – there's nothing stopping me from sharing a flat with someone else. It's my own fault.

Eventually the train pulls in and I heave my suitcase down the aisle before rolling it along the platform. Only two other people get off, and they both scurry down the dark concrete to separate cars waiting for them, headlights dazzling me as I peer at them. They pull away almost simultaneously, as if choreographed, leaving me standing alone.

Not alone.

There's still someone behind the ticket desk, staring at me through the glass as I stand here like a lemon.

"Need a taxi, love?" the woman behind the counter says, her voice distorted by the thick glass partition. "There's some numbers behind you."

Despite living ten minutes away, I still glance over, then look back at her sheepishly.

"No, uh, thank you," I say. "Just … got a headache, that's all."

"Shops are all closed," she offers, kindly. "Petrol station might have something though."

I thank her again and wheel my suitcase out through the door and onto the street, pausing again by a single, orange streetlight. I don't really want to be here, but I don't really want to be in London either. I feel lost; I don't know how to sell a house - what am I supposed to do? Maybe I should have been doing research online instead of staring out of the window on the train.

I start down the road. I'll go and see mum in the morning and talk to her about it. Moping won't help anything, but it seems to come most naturally right now.

I sigh.

Get it together, Jamie.

Chapter 4

"A small earthquake rocked the town of St Austell in Cornwall this morning, the tremors being felt as far away as Truro," the newsreader says. I'm sat watching the news on a small TV in the kitchen, absent-mindedly spooning cereal into my mouth and cursing myself for not picking up any coffee for the house. Mum never keeps any here, saying she doesn't have the patience to make it properly, preferring to pick up a frothy cappuccino or something from a café near her office.

There's traces of her everywhere I look, memories flooding back in every room. I find myself staring at the chipped countertop where she'd banged the door open after dad lost his job when I was a kid. I'd fled to my room and put music on to avoid hearing them argue.

It's a beautiful day but I need to go to the hospital. Mum mentioned that she's already put me on her car insurance and the car's still in the driveway, so there's no excuse really. Nonetheless, I sit and watch the sunbeams shine through the dust by the window, stirred up by my return. The old Formica countertops need a good dusting; I can see which of the condiments mum uses more.

After picking up some milk, cereal and painkillers from the petrol station last night, I'd let myself into the dark old house and poured a drink from mum's scant drinks cabinet. Thankfully, there was still a cheap bottle of whisky hidden at the back, no doubt an abandoned Christmas gift from someone in the village. Despite the booze, I'd not fallen asleep easily, feeling dislocated sleeping in my old childhood bed.

Everything feels simultaneously familiar and alien; I keep having flashbacks to my childhood and teenage years. Serious discussions with my parents about whether I should go to university or do something more vocational, siphoning vodka out of a left-over bottle so that Sam and I could get drunk in the playground … vomiting in the stream afterwards and barely leaving my bed the next day. Eating breakfast at the table, mowing the lawn when dad managed to nag me into it, reading by the window in the lounge. The house is lousy with memories.

I idly wonder where Sam is right now – we'd sort of lost contact during uni. She'd gone to study something serious and sciencey and had stayed on campus through most of the summer breaks, working. We'd seen each other off and on at Christmas, Easter, that kind of thing, but it'd always been a bit odd; I was thrown by my parents separating and her alpha position in our relationship seemed to have softened. She wasn't really the strong – well, brittle – girl I remembered from our childhood, which also confused me. It was good to catch up when we did, but I was also left feeling like something had changed without really knowing what it was.

I shake my head; it's feeling fuzzy even after I've finished my breakfast, so I grab a shopping bag and head out into the village, hoping that the fresh air will clear my head.

Thankfully, being out in the sun and having a fresh breeze on my skin instantly makes me feel better. I breathe deeply, enjoying the crisp cool air in my lungs rather than the polluted stuff I'm becoming used to in London. Everything is green, and aside from the birds singing and a distant lawnmower or tractor, it's quiet.

I find my way down to the local shop, wincing slightly at the prices; I guess we're not in the land of large supermarkets anymore. Maybe I should order a delivery if I'm going to stay for a while.

"Oooh he's a funny-looking one!"

I sigh as I hear two elderly women whispering to each other down the aisle. I still get comments and looks because of my appearance in London, but in a city where difference is the norm, it's much less pronounced than in the countryside. I thank my lucky stars that although my skin steadfastly refuses to tan, I've always been reasonably well-built, otherwise I'd run a serious risk of looking like Draco Malfoy from Harry Potter.

I pick up the most expensive coffee I can find and some other essentials, looking up and greeting the women down the aisle.

"Hello Mrs Fairbrother, Mrs Mitchell," I say, and they peer at me.

"Ooh it's you Jamie," Mrs Mitchell says, the younger of the two. Despite the warm weather – I'm in jeans and a t-shirt – she's in a raincoat and sports a tartan scarf. I wonder if she's starting to lose the plot, although she did just recognise me.

"I wondered if it was you!" she burbles. "You don't see many people with hair your colour in the village … well, apart from us!"

She cackles at her own joke and I smile tolerantly, putting my basket on the countertop as the bored-looking cashier starts to scan each item, thankfully tackling the flowers I'd picked up for mum last, rather than dumping them straight in the bag.

"We were so sorry to hear about your mother," Mrs Fairbrother coos.

"Thank you," I manage, struggling with the words and wishing I'd been able to have some coffee before having to interact with other humans today. "I'm going to see her in a bit."

Their expressions soften with sympathy, but I'm thankfully spared any more conversation by the cashier finishing up with my shopping. I hastily tap my PIN into the card machine, thank the two pensioners for their kind words and hurry out.

I'm desperate for caffeine, but I cudgel my brain into gear on the walk home, trying to make the most of walking along a bright, pretty country lane when I should be stuck behind my desk in the office. Everything smells fresh, like it's just rained, and I stop to watch a robin hop between the branches of a nearby tree.

I get back to the house and drop off the supplies. Then, before I can procrastinate myself out of it, I bag up the few other bits and bobs that mum wanted in hospital, and head out to the beaten-up Fiesta sat in the driveway, fiddling with the key fob until it unlocks. I spend a few moments adjusting the seat and mirrors before I triple check visiting times at the hospital, set up my GPS and head off.

It's about a half hour drive to the hospital, and for the majority of it, I'm concentrating hard on driving safely. I'd learnt as soon as I hit seventeen but fell out of practice when I left home – not many people drive in London, other than taxi drivers. After some nagging from my mum, I'd conceded that it probably would be useful to keep my hand in, and alternated between getting the train down to see her and hiring a car.

Thankfully, the hospital is not only well-signed, but also has a large car park, making life much easier for slightly stressed visitors like myself. I take a moment to gather myself and step out of the car, almost forgetting to lock it behind me.

I don't really like hospitals. It's the layout. I want to arrive somewhere and be directed in a clear fashion, with help on hand if I need it. My experience of hospitals is that it's all too easy to walk past the assistance booths, which are only intermittently staffed, and spend hours going around in circles between the maternity and radiology wards, when you really needed to be in cardiology or A&E.

I feel my shoulders tense as I walk through the sliding doors, and make an effort to breathe, awkwardly catching a woman's eye as I do. She gives me a sympathetic look – I guess there's no shortage of nervous people here. Feeling oddly guilty, I hurry on through the foyer, pulling out my phone and finding my mum's instructions for finding her ward.

The corridors are mercifully colour-coded, and I follow the purple strip until radiology, then switch to a red strip, which deposits me into an empty corridor with numbered rooms on either side. A few more steps take me to room 110, where, thanks to my mum's healthcare plan, she has a private room.

I knock, and hearing her voice, enter.

My first thought is that although she looks ill, she doesn't look like your stereotypical cancer patient. Sure, she looks really tired. Gaunt, almost. But there's a noticeable absence of wires, tubing and other medical apparatus, and she's still got all of her hair.

"Jamie," she says, slowly sitting up in bed and smiling at me. "Thanks for coming."

In spite of myself, I grin back. "Well, since it's you," I offer, putting the flowers next to another bunch on a table. "You're looking well."

She gestures to a chair beside the bed and I sit, offering her the bag of clothes. She takes it, and puts it on the other side of the bed.

"Good days and bad days," she says, curling an errant wisp of silvery blonde hair behind her ear. "They're still trying to reach a surgeon who might be able to deal with my newest little friend, so there's still hope."

I swallow and try to get a grip on myself as a wave of emotion rises up my throat. "Mum, I'm so sorry," I say, hearing my voice falter. She shakes her head and gives a small smile.

"Let's save that until later," she says. "We've got things to sort out."

I take a deep breath and bring up the list of jobs on my phone. "Right," I say. "Yes, of course."

Forty minutes later we've been through most of the jobs on the list, and mum is looking significantly more tired than when I arrived. I reach out to take her hand, which trembles a little.

"I'm sorry, that was a lot," I say. "But I think we're good. Do you want to rest and I'll come back tomorrow or Thursday? Is there anything else you want me to bring?"

She blinks and holds my hands tighter for a moment. "Yes," she says. "That's a good idea. I'm very tired most of the time, but when you're in bed all the time, all you can do is rest. Come back whenever you can or message me when you need help. The Wi-Fi is dear, but the 4G isn't terrible."

"Sure," I say, releasing her hand and getting up. "It was good to see you."

"And you," she says tiredly. "Jamie, if you have a chance next time?"

I pause.

"A caramel macchiato would be fantastic. Although you'd better make it decaf."

I grin. She's always had a sweet tooth, and it's partially her fault that Sam and I spent so long in the ice-cream shop in the village.

"No problem."

Waving, I look at her, trying to fix her in my mind, then turn and retrace my steps through the clinical labyrinth. Naturally, I end up in a completely different ward rather than reception, but manage to find a door to the outside world and walk around the outside of the hospital until I find the car park again.

Once I get back to the car, I call dad and let him know that I've been here. Last week he took a job for a big multinational based in London, but they flew him out to the US for 'orientation' almost straightaway. Him and mum don't speak very much, but I know he's been down once or twice in the last few months. I think it was awkward.

I stop in Bath for some lunch, booking in an appointment with the estate agent before looking through the list of things I need. There's a stationer not far from here, so I head over and pick up more parcel tape and bubble wrap – there's obviously some of my things in the house that I need to move out as well as mum's stuff, which I need to sell or get rid of.

She'd managed to keep up her 'work demeanour' when we were running through the list, discussing her personal matters as if they were meetings to be scheduled, but there were moments when she'd pause, presumably realising that this was her stuff, her life that we were packing up.

This is a lot. I pause for a moment, stepping off to the side of the street and taking out my phone, staring at the lock screen until the moment passes.

I check my list again; I think I've got pretty much everything, although I do pop into a bigger supermarket and pick up some stuff that the village store didn't have.

The drive back passes uneventfully, but it's almost dark when I get home. I put a pizza on and watch a film, updating a few items on my list; I need to sort out cancelling suppliers and getting final bills, and I'd forgotten about the water supplier.

I sink back into the easy chair. This is all just unreal. Suddenly I'm crying into my tea and I don't stop for a long time.

Eventually I'm jarred from my thoughts by the credits rolling on the TV; I should go to bed. It's not that late, but I just about manage to wash up, feeling mentally and physically drained, practically falling into bed and dozing off as soon as my head hits the pillow.

The next day I'm woken by a loud knocking at the front door. Shit – I forgot to set an alarm. I look at the clock blearily; it's ten, and that'll be the estate agent. I fumble with jeans and a clean t-shirt, just making it to the front door as a sharply-dressed woman is about to turn away.

"I'm so sorry," I blurt, feeling sweaty and gross. "I completely overslept."

She looks me up and down, then hands me a pile of post. "No harm done," she says crisply, offering her hand to shake as I put the various envelopes on the side table. "Cynthia Lockwood, Lockwood Estates. We spoke on the phone."

"Yes, of course," I say. "Please, come in."

I usher her inside and start showing her around. Her demeanour does soften a little once I explain that it's my mum's house, but she's still very business-like. I don't get the slippery, untrustworthy vibe from her, which is good. Some of the London estate agents are like that; proper wide boys, wheeler dealers.

Still, every room makes me feel increasingly uncomfortable, and we're almost done before I remember to ask the questions that mum and I had jotted down. Yes, it's helpful to have as much stuff out of the way as possible when they do the photo shoot. Yes, their cut is 2% of the final selling price. Yes, they can organise everything. I try to find something to scribble notes on, eventually taking the top envelope from the pile of post and finding a pen nearby that promptly leaks on my hand. Brilliant.

Cynthia asks me a question and I completely miss it. Sat on top of the pile of post, now that I've removed whatever bill I'm scribbling on, is a thick slab of card, edged in what looks like copper leaf.

And it's got my name on it, but only my name. My first name. In lush, swirly calligraphy.

I'm staring at it open-mouthed when Cynthia says my name again.

"Uh, yes, sorry," I say, looking back at her.

She actually smiles at me. A small, pitying smile, but a smile nonetheless, and her professional demeanour cracks slightly as she follows my gaze and spots the card.

"Calligrapher friend?" she asks, then clamps her mouth closed, as if having a personal conversation might somehow contaminate her with my unwashed, disorganised nature.

"Uh..." I manage. "Something like that?"

"Well," she says crisply. "I think we've covered everything. We'll need proof of identification and the paperwork we've discussed, but once that's out of the way, we can send the photographer round and get this started."

I nod, only half paying attention. "It was pleasant meeting you," she continues briskly. "Please don't worry, I can show myself out."

And she does. Quickly.

As the door shuts behind her, I stare at the pile of post on the side table, almost expecting it to disappear when I blink.

Jeez. I need a shower, coffee, breakfast and a second, post-breakfast coffee. Definitely in that order.

The calligraphy is still staring at me when I round the corner into the hallway half an hour later, coffee number two held tightly for fear of despoiling the creamy white card. Cautiously, as if approaching a stray cat, I take the card between thumb and forefinger and turn it over.

Would like your help
Come soonest
Melusine

And that's all it says. Seven words. Eight, if you include my name on the front.

Chapter 5

I sit down hard, remembering who Melusine is, that day from thirteen years ago coming right back. The ... witch, who lives on the Manor estate. I'd almost completely forgotten about that; the weird fireplace door, the woods, the rickety old hut. It doesn't quite seem real now, and the one time I thought about it when I was at uni, I wondered if it had somehow been exaggerated in my mind, like how things are a little bit brighter and more intense when you're remembering a childhood memory.

And … the thing, the remedy for Mr Abbott. Why didn't I think of this before? Maybe this woman, witch, whatever, can help mum?

I hurriedly glance at the other post underneath the card; something which is undoubtedly a bill from a phone company, a gas bill, something from the council. I need to dig out my passport and send it to Cynthia. I need to pack up more boxes and see what's in the shed.

Suddenly the prospect of a brisk walk over to the Manor seems fairly appealing, however hideous the person at the other end is. She can't have been that bad, I tell myself. She was just old. Everyone over fourteen seems old when you're ten, but she must have been at least seventy. She'd be pretty frail by now, I think, although if my last experience of her is anything to go by, she's probably still got all of her marbles. And if there's the slightest sliver of a chance that she can help mum, I'll take it.

Before I know it, I've laced up my trainers, snagged my jacket off the banister and am pounding through the village, working off some of the weird energy I've got after the odd morning.

It's a lovely day again; blue sky, warm, a hint of a breeze ruffling the leaves. Everything starts to feel a bit more normal as I head past the school, the playground, the church, the local pub.

"Jamie!"

I skid to a halt and spin around at the sound of the authoritarian voice, seeing its equally authoritarian owner, Sergeant Michaelson, strolling down from an adjoining lane. I muster the friendliest grin that I can, waving and waiting for him to catch up. He's impeccably dressed as usual, the logo on his custodian helmet glinting in the sun, vest and utility belt still packed with police paraphernalia. There isn't even any mud on his shoes and we're about as deep into the countryside as you can be.

"I thought it was you, lad," he says. "How's your mother doing?"

He's looking older now, streaks of grey in his hair.

"Not too bad," I say. I feel like a part of my vocabulary is stuck in a loop. "I went to see her yesterday and she seemed to be doing ok."

"Anything I can do to help, let me know."

"Thank you," I say, perhaps more earnestly this time, although I'm not quite sure what local law enforcement will be able to do about me running out of packing tape, or the high commission rates that the local estate agent is charging. "Just clearing my head right now."

"You looked like you were heading somewhere," he says in a deep rumble.

"Yeah," I say, not meeting his eyes. "I was popping over to see ... uh ... Mr Andrews."

The name almost doesn't make it into my head in time, and to this day I'm not quite sure why I didn't say Mel's name.

"Hmmm," he says disapprovingly. "You be careful around that one, Jamie. We had to investigate his house a while back. Trail of shady characters, all drug-related, leading right to his door. Searched it from top to bottom."

He snaps his fingers, making me jump. "Nada. Nothing. Some strange stuff in there, but nothing illegal. Not the smallest trace of weed, not the tiniest pill. You tie up your loose ends and steer well clear."

His tone puts it in no uncertain terms that doing anything other than taking his advice will be Very Much Not Appreciated.

"Ok," I say, slightly weirded out by all this. "Sure, uh, I'll keep my eyes open."

"You do that," he says. "Good seeing you."

And with that, he marches back up towards the school. I watch him until he vanishes around the bend, then set off again. Drug-dealing groundsmen, old calligraphers and snotty estate agents. At least it's more interesting than a day in the office.

On the other hand, I can't help but feel slightly aggrieved that this is yet more life admin on top of the already sizeable job of oh, I don't know, sorting out the estate of my mother.

That leads me down into a spiral of thoughts about how unfair life is, how rubbish my flatmates are, how badly paid my job is, and before I know it, I'm knocking maybe a little too loudly on the door of Mr Andrews' bungalow.

There's a muffled crash that makes me jump, then I hear footsteps. I take a step backwards, but the visage that greets me is a jovial one.

"Welcome!" Mr Andrews booms. "Jamie, isn't it? I was terribly sorry to hear about your mother, but I suppose you must be hearing that a lot these days. News travels fast in a small village like this. Will you come in and have some tea?"

Unlike the good police officer, Mr Andrews – Beckett, I should say – hasn't aged a day. There are no greys in his hair and his face is as unwrinkled as the last time I saw him. He looks like he's in his mid-forties, which, accommodating for childhood memory, is exactly what I would have said if you'd asked me when I was ten.

"Uh, no, thank you," I say, waving the thick card in front of me. "I, uh, got this ... from Mel?"

His good humour evaporates a little. "Ah," he says. "Yes, the troublemaker. Caused me all kinds of headaches these last few years with the local force, that one."

He stares behind me for a moment, making me glance over my shoulder. I don't see anyone, but when I look back at him, he's paying attention again.

"Well, shouldn't keep an elderly woman waiting," he says, ushering me inside and seeming to regain some of his good humour. "Tell the old bag to keep off the silken way or whatever they call it."

I pass down the hallway, all the doors still firmly shut on either side, until I reach the kitchen, inhaling deeply. It's just like it was before, although there seems to be an actual cookpot on the fire, the aroma of a meaty stew filling the room. It smells great, and my mouth waters despite my recent breakfast. There are still a lot of old-looking cooking utensils lying around, although I can see a fairly modern slow cooker and a dishwasher to one side.

Beckett slips past me and stands beside the back door.

"Don't suppose you remember how this works, do you?"

I stare at him mutely.

"Look, I'm not always around," he says. "And if *she* needs you, then you come on through. I'm not her secretary. There's a spare key underneath the flower pot outside, ok? Now, watch closely."

He turns to the back door and pulls the blind down, turning the key twice in the lock, before heading over to the sink and rapping his knuckles smartly on a green tile six times in a rhythmic pattern.

"Blind down. Turn the key twice anti-clockwise. Then one, two, three knocks on the tile. One, two, then three, ok? Say it back now."

I repeat it to him, and he nods, satisfied. "Don't write it down. Ever. Now, you remember which door to go through?"

The memory of the fireplace comes flooding back and I point at the small stylised door at the side. It can't be more than ten inches high.

"Good," he says. "Well, go on then. Like I said, don't keep her waiting."

Not really knowing what else to do, I take one step towards the fireplace, then another. Once again, I get that weird sense of dislocation and vertigo, before the walls of the bungalow stretch upwards like a cathedral. I want to pause and look around, but there's something pulling me forwards.

Three steps later, I'm through the doorway and stepping out onto damp grass, inhaling deeply; the Manor grounds are as lush and fragrant as I remember them being all those years ago.

The grass is a much deeper shade of green than the fields outside, the trees larger and more blossom-filled. I can hear birds in the trees and small things running through the undergrowth.

I actually feel a whole lot better just being here. This place seems separate somehow to the world outside, like I can leave all of the admin, guilt and despair behind for a moment.

I want to take a photo, but there's a part of me that resists; I don't want this to be a post on my social media. I slowly walk down the path and try to take it all in; it's exactly like it was when I was younger. I spy the patch of purple flowers that I saw last time and laugh out loud as I see them trying to grow up a tree. There's a scattering of them in between two large, protruding roots and even one growing from a knot on the trunk.

A little way down the path, bright red and green mushrooms have sprouted, and I stop, going down on one knee to just look at them. There's a ladybird crawling over one, but it flies off when it spots me getting closer. Down here, everything smells like leaf litter, and I can almost feel the woods growing around me. I can't see very far into the undergrowth but I spend a minute trying to peer deeper in; the brambles get thicker and the trees closer together the further in I look, almost like they're drawing nearer to each other to stop me seeing anything.

I shiver and stand abruptly, feeling slightly disconcerted. I glance around hurriedly, then start walking down the track again, the birdsong resuming. Funny, I think, I didn't notice it stop.

The path forks a moment later, and I take the left path, like last time, wondering what's down the right one ... maybe this isn't the best time to go exploring. Everything seems quiet here, more free, natural, but it feels like there are other things ... maybe dangerous things that might also be free. I recall the crashing in the woods the last time I was here and wonder if there's a wolf or a boar or something else that lurks in the undergrowth.

I feel the odd urge to hug myself, but instead try to walk a little faster, relieved when I see Mel's hut up ahead. At least, I hope it's Mel's hut, although when the choices are between seeing a hideous old crone or some ... unknown, then it's not really a choice.

Remind me why I'm here again?

Right. Quality stationery and the time she helped an old guy dying of cancer.

I sigh and walk up to the door, rapping my knuckles on it twice. In stories, witches' huts are always small hovels with cauldrons bubbling away merrily. This one is large enough for an eight-person après ski party at the very least.

The door cracks open and Melusine peers out. She's just as I remember, her hooked warty nose twitching, dark beady eyes staring at me intently, her leathery skin wrinkled. She's not actually wearing her hat this time, but has her jet-black hair tied into a ponytail – although there seem to be a few small sticks, a red object that might be a button, and even a beetle in it. I'm not sure if it's alive, but it's kind of gross.

She grips the door, her long, black nails clacking on the wood, pushing it open enough to step outside and pull it almost closed behind her. Her long, black robe, tied at the waist with a leather belt complete with tarnished silver buckle, flaps in the slight breeze.

I'm distracted from my scrutiny as a fat frog jumps out of the house and starts making its way across the clearing. She notices it and shrugs, then looks back at me.

"Huh," she says, her voice rough and grating, but not unfriendly. "I wasn't sure if you'd come. I suppose thanks are in order."

I'm not quite sure what to say, so I find myself waving the invitation.

"I, uh, well I thought we might be able to help each other," I say, awkwardly at first, then regaining some semblance of normality. "And I'm a sucker for good stationery."

She regards me evenly and narrows her eyes. "Hmm," she says. "You'd better come in for some tea."

Honestly, I'm not really a tea person, but I'm feeling a little uneasy being outside, much as I'm reluctant to set foot inside this woman's house. I nod, and she opens the door again, suddenly whistling loudly, making me flinch.

Nothing happens, and she clears her throat. A moment later, the fat frog hops back out of the undergrowth and slowly lumbers towards the house.

"Fucking familiars," she says shaking her head. "Nine times out of ten they're completely useless, and the one time they do help, you can't understand a bloody word they're saying."

The frog hops between her legs into the house, pauses and distinctly croaks the word 'wanker' at her before continuing inside.

I stare, open-mouthed.

"Well, come on, boy," she says, holding the door for me. "We haven't got all day."

I kind of feel like I have, but I don't disagree as I head in.

Melusine almost walks into me as I freeze two steps into her house. As she swishes past, I can smell herbs, spices and rotting leaves, all at once.

Her house is something else.

The front door opens directly into a large lounge-cum-study-cum-kitchen, which is something like the bastard child of the British Library and the Hunterian Museum crammed into a space the size of Mr Andrews' kitchen. Bookshelves line all four walls, virtually floor to ceiling, packed with all manner of old-looking books, the spines occasionally annotated in black calligraphy. Scrolls stick out, untidily filed on top of each other, beside books in heaps, tied with ribbons, string, or in a couple of cases, what looks like a bramble. Some of the shelves have been removed, and in their place, horizontal, glass-fronted chillers sit, all neatly labelled.

I take a step towards one to try and read the writing, then notice what's actually in the chiller. There's a Tupperware container with something in it, something small. 'Mouse', the label reads. My gaze slides across the others, which promise that they contain lizards, rats and even a snake at the end. There's a white opaque cabinet below them that looks like a freezer. How many dead animals does she have in here?

In the centre of the room is a large, low table, a ceramic pot of some kind sitting on a tripod with a Bunsen burner underneath, an occasional wisp of blue smoke rising from the pot. There's a chunky book open on a bookrest with a pair of spectacles next to it, arcane drawings just about visible on the page.

I do a double take as I notice the sleek silver laptop next to the hefty tome, then start spotting other modern touches; although there's a fireplace burning merrily, a large cauldron on top of it, not to mention the stag's head mounted on the wall, there's a smartphone plugged into the wall on the mantelpiece. The laptop has some kind of speakerphone attached to it, and I wonder who she was talking to before I arrived. There's a very new-looking set of knives on a side table, next to a bowl of herbs and a kettle, which Mel takes into another room beyond.

A row of jars and brightly-coloured bottles sit on one bookshelf, and another is completely obscured by a map of Britain, a few locations ringed in ink, notations scrawled next to them. I take another step into the room, trying to read her writing.

"Seen enough?" Mel says sharply, making me spin around and look at her. "I don't allow many visitors here, so mind your tongue when you're back in the real world."

"I ... uh ... I haven't mentioned it to anyone," I admit, perhaps unwisely. "I told Sergeant Michaelson that I was coming over to see Mr Andrews, ah, Beckett, I mean. He didn't seem very happy about that to be honest."

Mel cackles abruptly, making me jump, her shrill, harsh laughter drowning out the burbling of the kettle. "No," she giggles, showing her uneven teeth, spotted with brown marks. "No, he wouldn't. Poor man can't take a joke."

"He said something about the silk road," I add. "But the Sergeant didn't seem to think it was him. Were ... were you buying drugs online?"

"Buying drugs? No, never," she says, turning back to the kettle, pouring boiling water into a mug and flicking a teabag into the back room. She hands me the mug. "I was selling them. It's amazing what you people will buy online."

I can feel my jaw dropping again, so I clamp it hastily shut and take a sip of the tea. I'm ninety five percent sure that it's Yorkshire Tea, which just heightens my sense of dislocation.

"You know," I say, trying my hardest to retain the power of speech. "This doesn't really look like a meth lab."

She snickers evilly. "Meth? Look around you Jamie. Mushrooms, obviously. Try and keep up."

I wonder if I should give up my attempts at a normal conversation as I find myself nodding silently.

"So, what do you need?" I ask after a long pause. "I'm not some kind of drug mule, if that's what you're after. Is this about … last time?"

Melusine takes a sip of her drink and fixes me with a steely stare. "I need someone who can keep their mouth shut," she says. "And you've done well enough over the years. Gaia's in trouble and I need another pair of hands. There's something wrong with the earth spirit and it's playing merry hell with my work, not to mention getting the rest of the faery all riled up. You've probably heard about the earthquake by now, and all the storms out of season. Poor thing's getting knackered by something and I need to find out why, who's responsible and then mess them up. Badly."

Chapter 6

Brilliant. Just when I thought it was all too much. I sink down onto the wooden chair by the table and look back at her, uncomprehending.

"I'm sorry but what?"

"Gaia," she says slowly. "The earth spirit. She who gives life. Jamie, I get that this is going to be strange for you, and that you've had limited exposure to the wee folk, but I don't have time for any training montage bullshit, ok? I need your help for about two weeks, and I'll pay you five thousand pounds in cash. One now, the rest later. No questions, keep your eyes open and do what I say. Are you in or out?"

My mind reels. This woman is actually claiming to be a witch. A serious, magic-doing, potion-making, elves and goblins witch. And there's a … life spirit?

I try to think quickly. What's the worst that could happen? Even if there's a chance that this woman can help mum, I need to try it. I steel myself and summon as much energy as I can muster.

"Tell you what," I say, only stuttering slightly, trying hard to keep my voice even. "Make it four and a half, and you throw in some of that magic cancer drug from when I was a kid. Four if you've got a cure."

She shrugs. "Four and a half it is, but it'll take a day to get things together. No cure or I'd be the wicked witch of the Cayman Islands rather than dossing here in Somerset."

"Fine," I find myself saying. "But I've never seen magic before, so you'll have to excuse me if I'm a bit disbelieving."

Melusine cocks her head to one side and grins, an ugly, toothy smile, her dark eyes glinting. She looks over at one bookshelf, where a stuffed owl perches, stiff and glassy-eyed. Then it seems to shiver, slowly stretching out one wing, then another and hoots, making me jump. I can feel something change in the room, something surging around, flowing. I can't quite describe it, but there's something in motion in the air.

I stare as the owl flaps its wings and launches itself off the shelf, swooping around the room in a tight arc before returning to the shelf, resuming its original stance. It seems to stiffen, harden, and the life vanishes from its eyes once again.

I look back at Melusine, who raises her eyebrows. "That good enough?"

"Did you … bring it back to life?" I ask tentatively.

"Not at all," she croaks. "Flesh and blood, that's my speciality, but I don't have the power to bring something back from the other side. Now, obviously, you're a smart man, so one thing alone won't suffice. Come with me and I'll give you a quick tour."

I fix the owl with a hard stare, daring it to move. Mel heads over to the door, taking an envelope from a bookshelf and throwing it to me.

"Come on," she says, sounding faintly amused. She moves pretty quickly for an old woman and it's a bit unnerving.

I push my chair back, take another sip of tea and follow her outside, ripping open the envelope and glancing inside. It's full of cash.

I swallow, hard, then slide the envelope into my back pocket for more scrutiny later, but it looks like she wasn't kidding. I'm feeling a bit dazed.

The clearing is thankfully empty of owls, dead or otherwise, and I feel a bit better once I'm in the sunshine; everything seems a bit more normal. It's bright, the sky is blue, the leaves in the trees whisper to each other and I inhale deeply, enjoying the fresh, clean country air.

Then Melusine ruins it all.

"Now don't run off," she says. "I remember the last time you were here and you scared the hell out of the Ypotryll, so I'm going to call for it and see if you can make amends."

I don't understand what that word means. The 'pot rill' one, not 'amends'. Obviously, I know what that means.

Mel puts her fingers into her mouth and whistles loudly, making me flinch again – I do that a lot and it delighted the meaner kids at my school, years ago.

There's a distant roar, then I can hear something coming, heavy steps, almost like a horse, only much bigger if I had to guess. The steps grow closer and I can hear plants and trees being pushed aside as the steps get nearer and nearer.

Bloody hell.

It's a giant boar. I can't see all of it, but there's a large boar with curly tusks getting closer. I can just make out its coarse brown fur, long head and cruel-looking tusks. But it must be five or six feet high because the bushes and undergrowth are hiding the rest of it. It's … huge.

Then the grass and thorn bushes part and it blows my mind.

It doesn't have a boar's body. It's got a camel's body. At first I think it's a horse, because it's got hooves, long legs and a pretty substantial body; think of a sturdy carthorse, not a lean racehorse. But its hair is as coarse as the stuff on its face … muzzle … whatever, and it's got two humps like a camel. And for the final straw, a long, scaled snake's tail curls between its legs.

It makes a soft whickering noise and looks at Melusine with intelligent eyes. Mean eyes, I think, but still, there's something going on there. She smiles and searches around in one of the many pockets in her robe, eventually pulling out something that looks like half a brick, then holds it up and tosses it just to one side of the … thing.

"Ypotryll," she says. "Ee-pot-trill. Half boar, half camel with a snake's tail. No-one really knows anything about their origins. Famous for being ugly, but who really cares about that? They're good for guard duty, easy enough to tame, more or less, and they come when called. Now, what do you say?"

I'm still staring at the grotesque creature in front of me. It kind of smells like a pig or a horse or a cow or something, like a farm. I suppose this is what was crashing around when Sam and I came here the last time. It's slightly terrifying, but kind of amazing at the same time.

"Uh," I manage, feeling supremely self-conscious as it starts tearing at the thing – presumably food – that Mel threw over to it. "Um, I'm sorry if I disturbed you last time."

The hideous beast pauses for a moment and looks over at me, fixing me with one big eye, peering past curly tusks. Then it blinks and returns to the food, or whatever it is, chewing and swallowing noisily.

"Good," Mel says. "All better. Now, come on, I need to introduce you to someone else."

She strides off down the path and I edge nervously around the clearing, keeping my back to the house and a nervous eye on the Ypotryll. I swear it makes another whickering sound as I turn away, almost like a low laugh.

I hurry down the path after Melusine. A few paces down the track we turn down the right-hand path from Mr Andrews' bungalow.

"So how big are the Manor grounds?" I ask, catching up with the bizarrely spry old woman and trying to sound nonchalant.

"Oh, I think they were a hundred acres at one stage," she says, her voice scratchy like a nail on rusty metal. "But they sold some off after the young ones moved away to America and lost touch; investments did badly, Martin died and Margaret eventually moved to an old people's home on the coast. I think it's up for sale now. Why?"

"Well, won't that affect you?"

She pauses, and gives another short, barking laugh. "Oh Jamie," she says. "We're not *in* the Manor grounds. We're connected to the huntsman's house, but other than that, you can't get to the Manor, the village, or really anywhere else from here."

I skid to a halt, and Mel rounds on me, her robes billowing slightly in the breeze.

"W...what do you mean?" I say, gaping at her. "Where are we?"

She sighs loudly. "Did you really think that the drama with the fireplace was normal?"

I ... I guess not. It was all a bit ... Alice in Wonderland. I shake my head. "I didn't really understand it," I admit.

"And that's normal when people first come across the faery folk," she says. "Your mind writes it off as an oddity, best forgotten. But the more you see, the harder it is to forget. Best start accepting it now, or it'll give you a headache."

"So, like, where are we?" I manage. "How big is this place?"

"I've never measured," she says, shrugging expansively. "I imagine that if you kept walking, you might get back to this point, or you might end up somewhere else entirely. It's not the biggest little realm but it's not the smallest either."

"I don't understand," I admit, feeling helpless. "So, if I walked out of the back door of Mr Andrews' place, I'd be in the Manor grounds?"

"That's right," she says, giving me a toothy grin. "But if you follow the steps, the fireplace door activates and you can reach us here. Now obviously, as you've seen, you can use his regular door to go back into the bungalow – the faery world is full of contradictions like that."

"And are all the places like this through fireplaces?"

She laughs, and looks at me like I've asked a really ridiculous question. "No, that'd be completely impractical. But they all have very specific steps to reach them."

My mind reels and I try to stay quiet for a while as we walk along the cool forest track. I wonder how many secret places there are hidden around the world, why people don't spot these things happening and what other weird, horrible and wonderful creatures might be living in them.

And mum. Maybe the weirdness in this place can help mum. If there are earth spirits and monsters and magic, then maybe there's something that could do more than just stave off the inevitable. It sounds like nonsense in my head, but what if? Surely that's worth two weeks of my time and holiday? Especially if I'm getting paid for it. Technically, twice.

Before long, we reach another clearing with a house not unlike Mel's. It's single-storey, but rather than the roof slates that Mel's has, it's thatched. The thatch desperately needs some work; it's loose in parts, thinning in others, and underneath I can see brick and wood.

"Come on," Melusine sighs. "We've got a lot to get done. Do you need to make arrangements with your work?"

I shake my head, following her towards the house. "It's fine," I say. "I'm on leave for a couple of weeks."

She nods, then stalks up to the front door, knocking crisply three times.

Nothing happens and I can almost see Melusine counting in her head. She lets out an exasperated sigh and knocks again.

This time, there's a clicking from inside, then footsteps, and a moment later the door swings open and a very peculiar-looking person opens it.

I can't decide if they're more evocative of *Biggles* or some kind of steampunk comic; they're dressed in a long brown robe that looks almost like leather, splattered with black marks that could be burns. They're about five feet tall but wide, like a well-fed chef or a blacksmith in a Disney film. They've got the hood of their robes pulled up, and a chunky pair of goggles obscures their eyes. I can't for the life of me work out if their features are male or female.

"Melusine!" the figure says happily, pushing the goggles up onto their forehead and flipping the hood of their robes back. An untidy fuzz of brown hair sits on their head, like it's been buzzcut a few weeks ago but not cared for since. Kind brown eyes and an androgynous, happy-looking face regards the witch, before turning to me.

"Jamie, may I introduce Merovech Drake, mechanist extraordinaire," Mel says.

I step forward and extend my hand. "I'm very pleased to meet you," I say, as Merovech grips my hand firmly and shakes. I notice that two of their fingers are made of some kind of coppery metal, cool to the touch.

"It's very exciting to meet you!" Merovech squeaks in a high-pitched voice. "Please, call me V. Everyone does."

"No problem," I say, wondering how to continue the pleasantries, when there's a noise like an old-fashioned steam engine from inside and Merovech whirls around, looking dismayed.

"Oh no!" they say. "Please, step back!"

Melusine and I back away from the house as a large, scorpion-like creature seemingly made of bronze metal and clockwork gears scurries out of the doorway past Merovech.

"V, what is this?" Mel says sternly, but the small inventor has already rushed back inside.

"Controls, where are the controls?" V says distantly, in a sing-song voice. I hear a few bangs and crashes a moment later from inside, but glance back at the scorpion-thing anxiously. It's scuttling around in circles a few metres away from us but doesn't seem to be attacking or dangerous.

"Can't you…" I gesture at it, as if flicking a wand.

Melusine rolls her eyes. "Flesh and blood, I told you earlier," she says. "I could have one of the creatures come and stamp on it, but V will be back soon enough."

"Is V…" I trail off.

"Safe? Unpredictable? Entertaining?" Melusine supplies. "Always burning things down?"

"A guy or a girl?" I finish.

"Humans and your binary categories," she says, sounding disgusted. "Them and us, him and her. There's more than just that, Jamie - why do you think the world falls so neatly into your little boxes?"

I feel a bit deflated, but then the scorpion makes a whistling sound, two of its inner gears popping off in different directions and the whole thing settles down to the ground. The whirring noises trail off and eventually stop, a small column of steam rising from a tiny exhaust port at the back.

Merovech suddenly appears back in the doorway, holding a small metal box, then sees the creature and their shoulders sag abruptly.

"Oh. That's a shame."

They wander over to the broken contraption and peer down at it.

"Looks like the left engine and the main control system didn't get on well together," they say mournfully, looking over at me. "I'll have to strip it down and start again."

"I'm sorry," I say. "It's very pretty."

"Thank you!" they grin broadly. "It is, isn't it? And I suppose I can make all kinds of improvements while I'm repairing it."

"Merovech," Mel says sternly. "What is this thing?"

"Oh," V says, looking over at her. "It's the guard dog we were talking about. I've made five so far. They can have all kinds of things mounted on them: guns, crossbows, food dispensers for your beasties. The possibilities are endless, really."

The little inventor keeps up a steady stream of burbling chatter as they pick up the scorpion, straining slightly, turning as they reach the front door.

"Would you like to come in?"

"Not today," Melusine says. "But we might be back soon."

"Good good," V says. "Well, anytime."

And with that, the door closes behind them.

"Now Jamie," Mel says, fixing me with a firm stare. "You're going to see some weird shit in the next few weeks, so if you're going to get all judgey and narrow-minded about something as ridiculous as gender, then this job definitely isn't for you. I think you should go home and think about this. Come back tomorrow if you're willing to keep an open mind, is that clear?"

I nod, suddenly feeling guilty. I liked the inventor, I really did. I just ...

"I'm sorry," I blurt out. "I didn't mean anything by it."

"Good," Melusine says. "I'm sure you are. Now go home."

Feeling slightly downcast, I wander back down the path towards Mr Andrews' cottage. I do actually have a choice about this, I think. I could simply say no, sort everything out here and spend some time with mum.

But then I think about the Ypotryll and how huge it was. How I kind of loved seeing it, the feeling of wonder – albeit completely terrified wonder – at watching it, and V's weird clockwork scorpion things. Hell, even this forest is quite something on its own.

I reach the bungalow and let myself in.

"Hello?" I call, but there's no reply. I pad down the hallway and open the front door; Beckett must have gone out somewhere. The emptiness makes me think of my flat back home, and that makes me think of my flatmates, my job and dirty old London.

And if there's more to life than that, I want it. Even if it means not knowing what to expect in any given second, even if it means not understanding what's going on. Although ... I feel a small but stubborn twinge of doubt about Melusine's drug dealing. Can't she just magic money up? I guess not, thinking about her reaction to the scorpion.

And then there's mum, and how Mel's drugs might be able to help her.

I shake my head. Maybe she's right. I do need a day to think about this or at least consider what I'm getting myself into.

Feeling strangely furtive about coming out of Beckett's bungalow, I head to the local store again and grab some lunch, before spending the rest of the afternoon packing up more boxes. I take a photo of my passport and send a copy to Cynthia at the estate agent, receiving an email in reply asking if I would be available for the photographer tomorrow morning. Sure, why not, I think. More time to sort stuff out here.

It gives me focus, and I try to shift as many things either out of the way or into boxes and storage as neatly as possible. By dinner I'm dusty and aching, but the house looks vaguely like something you might see in photos on an estate agent's website.

I keep packing late into the evening, eventually stopping after I cut myself on a cardboard box, wincing and sucking my finger. I should stop, I think. How long have I been at this? And I haven't even really thought about Mel's offer, although I know in my heart that I have to take it. If there's any chance of helping mum, then I have to do it.

Instead of finding the next box, I wander back into the kitchen and hunt out the whisky again, pouring myself a generous measure and settling into an armchair, sighing and flicking the TV on. It's another report of the earthquake from yesterday – only a minor tremor, but we don't often get quakes in the UK, so it's getting a lot of airtime.

I glance around the room; I've taken down all of the pictures, packed up most of the books. It's pretty bare, other than the stand with the TV on it, the coffee table and the floral wallpaper that my mum was always on at my dad to change. He never did; I've not done any wallpapering myself, but I imagine it's not that easy, especially without anyone to help you, and mum was always too busy to help him. Never too busy to nag, mind you.

But then she did pay most of the bills, I muse, as I hold the whisky up to the light and look through it. Dad's freelancing was irregular, and although this place wasn't dear, the mortgage, the bills, looking after me, it would have all added up. I remember them arguing when the car broke down. It seemed to go on for days until I tried to give mum my pocket money to help pay for it. Her and dad had exchanged looks, gone into the garden for a talk and I never heard them say another word about it. I'd forgotten about it quickly; Sam had come around with her new bike, so we'd gone out to try it, but there was an air of tension in the house for a while after.

Empty or not, this place still feels like home. I can walk around it in almost complete darkness and not bump into anything. I know exactly how many stairs there are and when to turn to get to my room. What am I swapping it for? A place in London? I'm not sure I want to live in London, long-term. But I can't commute from here.

I sigh. My mind is running in circles again, so I down the whisky and call it a night. This time, I make sure to set an alarm before I doze off.

Chapter 7

Cynthia's photographer is a lot more pleasant than I'd hoped. I was expecting more of the upturned-nose brigade, but instead get a woman not that much older than me, toting a heavy camera and several piercings. Her eyes sparkle and I feel an instant surge of attraction.

"Felicity," she says, sticking her hand out when I answer the door. "Call me Flic."

I'm also a bit more prepared than I was last time, having managed to wash, dress and eat before she turned up. I usher her in and listen as she explains about the process and what she needs – which thankfully, turns out to be pretty minimal. The odd thing moved here or there, nothing major.

I manage to blurt out why I'm selling the house, which I guess isn't really necessary, but she takes it in her stride, offers sympathy and I change the subject quickly, asking whether a piece of furniture needs moving. She shakes her head and then keeps up a steady chatter about other jobs she's done, weird things she's seen, funny stories about other people's houses. Somehow, it's all very reassuring, very down-to-earth.

Towards the end she pauses, turning to face me.

"Is that all alright?" she says. "Everything clear?"

"Yeah, yeah, definitely," I reply. "All good, thank you."

She gives me an even look. "You looked a bit unsteady there," she says. "Are you feeling ok?"

"Fine, thanks," I say. "Just, well, everything, you know?"

"Course," she says lightly. "No worries."

She pushes a strand of hair back behind one ear and bends down to pick up her tripod bag, giving me a grin as she stands back up, feigning a struggle with the long bag.

"Occupational hazard, you know?" she says, laughing. "But it does mean I don't need a gym membership."

I almost ask her out for a drink right there and then. It could be that she's the first decent, normal person with no agenda that I've met since I arrived here, but ... well, she's also pretty, funny and kind.

"You seem to handle it well," I say, returning the smile and holding the door for her. "Hey, Flic, you got a card?"

She digs around in a pocket, eventually offering me a business card.

"Catch you later," she says, eyes sparkling.

It's a terrible time for a crush and I really know it, but I still wave and watch her car pull out of the drive like a sappy teenager, the house feeling quieter and emptier without her in it.

Get a handle on it, Jamie, I think to myself. You've got weird shit to do.

After a hearty lunch – who knows what Melusine eats – I hurry back along the country lanes, knocking on the door of Huntsman's Cottage as a stiff breeze pulls my jacket away from my body.

There's no reply from inside, so I lift up the first flowerpot on the right-hand side, revealing a couple of worms.

Brilliant.

Muttering, I pick up the next – much larger – pot, and to my relief, there's a little-used Yale key underneath.

Taking care to replace it once I'm done, I let myself into Beckett's bungalow. Resisting the temptation to look around, I wander down towards the kitchen.

Only ... the second door is open a crack. I guess a peek wouldn't hurt. Without pushing, hell, without touching or even breathing on the door, I peer into the room beyond. I can only see the wall, but there's definitely a crossbow mounted on it, above a longbow, above a shotgun. In fact, the whole wall is stacked with hunting paraphernalia. There are a couple of saddles, shorter bows with quivers of arrows, some of them blunted, some wickedly pointed – even a few that are barbed. I shudder. I guess Huntsman's Cottage is right, although I'm sure that if he hunted in the village, I would have heard about it from my parents.

Wait. Of course he doesn't hunt in the village.

Revising my opinion of Beckett's bravery, I hurry through the kitchen, which is reasonably empty today. No pots sit cooking, no food half-done. The spit sits idle, and I can smell ashes from the fireplace. There's still a fragrant scent of herbs from the drying plants on the walls and ceiling, but it's faint. I wonder where Beckett is.

Pulling the blind down, turning the key twice, I find the green tile and knock on it six times, remembering the rhythm. Feeling slightly nervous, I take a step towards the fireplace and feel weirdly relieved when the strange Alice in Wonderland sensation kicks in and, hurrying onwards, I pop out into the still, crisp fresh air of ... well, wherever I am.

Melusine isn't surprised to see me, grinning evilly when she opens the door.

"Thought you'd be back," she croaks. "Your father always had a bit of a taste for the unknown and wasn't afraid of admitting when he was wrong either."

I enter her house, puzzled.

"You know, both you and Beckett have mentioned dad now," I muse. "I can understand that Beckett knew him from when he worked at the pub, but I've never seen you around the village. How do you know him?"

Mel cackles shrilly. "Would you believe me if I said he ran errands for me too?"

"No," I say evenly. I can't reconcile the mental image of my book-loving, accountant father with this world at all. It's more likely that she knows him from the village pub or something. Maybe he cut the grass in the Manor once or twice.

"Then you'd be wise," she grins, gesturing at a seat. "Sit."

I suddenly notice the large flipchart on a stand that has appeared in the room since my last visit. Despite all the other modern touches in the room, regular office furniture seems even more out of place than the sleek laptop still purring on the table.

Wait, no. There's an actual cat next to the flipchart – that's what's purring. Of course, it's the regulation black variety, and as I stare, it opens one eye, regards me sleepily and then closes it again.

I sit down at the table and Mel perches on a high stool next to the chart, flipping over the first page. It's got three columns on it, labelled 'permission', 'access' and 'support'.

"I'll recap," she grates, her voice going right through me. "Gaia, the earth spirit, is sick, which is causing weather irregularities of ever-increasing severity. In time, plants may stop growing, magic will work less efficiently and the doors connecting the faery world to yours may even begin to decay. Now, unfortunately, even in the faery world, protocol is protocol and we can't just march up to where Gaia resides."

She pauses and takes a drink from a mug of greenish liquid that steams gently.

"Uh, Melusine," I say hesitantly. "If Gaia is the earth spirit, why do we need to go somewhere specific? Isn't it, like, everywhere?"

She regards me with an intense stare, and I notice a wart on her nose looking red and angry today.

"Not bad," she says after a moment. "Not an entirely ridiculous question. Gaia's influence is all across all the world, but there are a few sites where her spirit is strong. Not many, but some. Of course, I suspect that Gaia herself is still safe; if someone had breached the inner sanctum, we wouldn't be having this conversation, it'd be war. Only representatives granted access by both the Seelie and Unseelie court can access the site, or those using an artefact blessed by both. There's precious few of the latter knocking around, so we'll need the former, even if my errand boy in 1920 claimed there was one not far from here. Too clever for his own good, he was. You listen to me when I say that Gaia's chamber is not a place for just anyone to waltz into."

The cat stretches out, extending its claws and trying to hook onto one of the legs of the flipchart. Failing to find purchase, it curls up into a small croissant shape and goes back to sleep.

"What we need to find out is what's going on, and to do that we need permission, support and access. You can't find a murderer without searching the scene. We need permission from both the Seelie and Unseelie Courts. We need their support – if something is messing with Gaia

I don't want to go there alone and I'm not too proud to admit it – and we need access. According to Google Maps, there's a small scientific site right where we want to be. I've got a plan for how we handle that. And to make sure you survive the trips to the Courts – don't worry, I'll be coming too – unfortunately for me, you're going to need training."

"Training?" I blurt out. "Wait, scratch that. Another question. If Gaia is the earth spirit, who's on your suspect list? Is that why we're going to see this Unseelie Court? They're the bad fairies, right?"

Melusine sighs. "So nearly an intelligent question, Jamie," she says. "But not bad for someone whose prior experience probably stems from the Grimm brothers."

I'm trying to work out whether that's a compliment or not and eventually give up – I'd actually learned about the 'good fairies' in the Seelie Court from Dungeons and Dragons as a teenager, but it's probably best not to admit that right now. I don't need praise from a strange old woman, I just need the money and an indication of whether this stuff has the potential to help my mum.

"And no," she says. "To answer your question, both the Seelie and the Unseelie draw power from Gaia, and Gaia makes our existence possible. It's anathema to any faery creature to pollute her, so it must be something that you humans are doing. But none of them should be able to get anywhere near the site without faery assistance. There's something backwards going on and no mistake."

So, I'm helping a witch track down a non-faery, non-human creature that's messing with the earth spirit. I should have asked for more than four and a half grand.

"Right," I say, wondering if I should have asked for some tea as well. "So, training."

"Training," she says, regarding me evenly. "Now, it's been a few hundred years since I had an apprentice, so I may be a little rusty. Back in the sixteen hundreds, it was considered perfectly acceptable to beat your apprentice if they didn't behave, but apparently not today. Ah, the screams that Evelyn made when I pulled her fingernails out after she blew up her third cauldron! That was almost worth the cost of replacing it. We'll both just have to try our best."

I'm starting to feel a little sick, but I put on my best unfazed expression, nod and smile a little. It's a strained smile.

"Good," she grates, flicking through a book next to her. "Now, my speciality is flesh and blood, but unfortunately your aptitude may lie elsewhere, so we'll have to do a broad set of tests."

"Magic is generally about change," she says, leaning forwards and interlacing her long bony fingers, hands discoloured with liver spots. "Making something grow, making fire come from the air, changing a person into a toad, that kind of thing. This needs energy and you'll find that energy easier to access in a place like this than the outside world. The means of reaching that energy varies from spell to spell, but it will always require you to understand and feel it, and that does need some innate skill."

"So, let's try something very simple. I want you to hold in your head the feeling – the overall impression – of what it's like being in the outside world, and then contrast that with what it's like being here."

At first, I'm not quite sure where to start, but Melusine simply sits back and starts reading something on her laptop, so I don't think we're in a rush. Home, the village, always feels ... normal, regular, comprehensible. Here, it feels more ... lush, more vivid, richer somehow. I try to compare the two in my head and I'm left with a feeling of this place somehow being *more* than the other, growing more, being denser with life.

"Ok," I say.

"Good," she says, placing a stick in a small vase on the table. "Now, I want you to ignite this. The incantation is *ignicio*, and it's almost like cracking a whip. Plenty of flexibility, and you need to take hold of the difference that you've created in your head and channel it towards the stick. Imagine it changing, the molecules heating up and burning."

Feeling pretty ignorant, I look hard at the stick and imagine the rich, thick air being condensed and try to force it towards the stick.

"*Ignicio*," I spit out, forcing the words towards the twig.

Nothing happens.

"*Ignicio*," I try again, undaunted. The stick wobbles a little – or maybe that was just my breath.

I look at Melusine. "Don't I need a wand or something?"

She smirks at me. "Of course," she says. "But you could set the whole house on fire that way. It's much simpler to test your aptitude like this. Keep going. Be firm, but don't force it too much. Like this."

Mel cocks her head to one side and looks at the twig. "*Ignicio*," she says firmly, almost as if she's commanding an errant child. The top of the twig smoulders for a second, then bursts into flame, burning merrily like a candle. Quickly, she leans forward and blows it out, clamping her fingers over it to stop it smoking.

"Now you," she says, turning back to her laptop.

After what feels like fifty attempts, I haven't even got the twig to smoulder. Sometimes I can sense something in my head that feels faintly like power flowing, but surely there's more to it than this? A word and a feeling?

I must have let out a sigh, because Melusine snorts and looks over at me.

"Well," she says. "Fire magic is fairly basic, but it's not everything. Let's try something else."

Standing up, she opens one of the small fridge drawers on the nearest bookshelf and takes a plastic bag out, shaking a tiny, dead mouse onto the table in front of us. I'm not particularly squeamish, but it's still odd to see someone handling a dead animal so indifferently.

"Now, necromancy is the easiest, laziest kind of magic there is," she continues, bones cracking as she sits back down. "It's been misrepresented in popular culture for being evil, but there is quite often a lot of life essence left in the recently deceased. I don't know why we don't make more use of it. Of course, there's more skill in manipulating flesh and blood beyond simply re-animating it, but this should prove a sufficiently simple test for an apprentice. The word you are looking for here is *revivio*."

As she says it, the mouse twitches, making me jump, but as I look back at it, it's quite motionless. Damn. If I didn't know better, I'd think it was sleeping, but there's a rigidity to its pose that says it's quite dead. And, not to mention that no mouse would be sleeping on a table with two people staring at it and a cat on the floor.

"When you utter the power word," she continues. "You'll have to try and send a bit of your energy to the mouse first to kick-start it. The spell doesn't last forever, but you also don't want to overwhelm the poor thing with your life force; you've got so much and the mouse is very small, so send the smallest possible piece of vitality you can. Think of it like a spark to start a car engine."

"I don't understand," I say helplessly, spreading my hands out in exasperation. "Keeping a feeling in my head was ok, but sending my vitality to a mouse? I don't even know where to start with that."

Then it's Melusine's turn to sigh. "Useless man," she grunts. "You know how on some days you feel fundamentally more alive, more active, and on others it's like you just want to hibernate?"

I nod.

"That's your life spirit feeling the earth's seasons. In winter your body is telling you to curl up, retreat, dig in. In spring, you're feeling the desire to awaken, make the most of the new warmth and light. Imagine those feelings and try to hold them in your mind, pushing them towards the mouse, channelled through the word."

And I try. I really try. But all that happens is that the mouse seems to relax a little – presumably as it gets warmer – and after another twenty minutes, Melusine grabs it from the table and re-wraps it with considerably less care and more frustration than before.

"Well," she says. "Perhaps we should have started with the theory first. I spent a year with Evelyn before I let her try that one. But maybe you'll have more luck with potions and herbs. Third time's the charm."

She cackles at her own joke and disappears off into the back room. I hear her tramping around loudly, sorting through things, before re-appearing with two Bunsen burners, a couple of stands and glass beakers.

"It's a shame," she says, laying out the chemistry equipment in front of us. "If you'd managed the fire spell, we could have done cantrips and hexes. It's always fun making Beckett's toenails grow at fifty times the normal speed."

I'm suddenly quite glad that I couldn't master the fire spell.

"Now, anyone can mix ingredients together and heat them," she continues, lighting both Bunsen burners with the twig from the vase. "And some poisons do occur naturally. But to make them truly potent, or to mix an antidote, we need magic as part of the process."

She retrieves a few sachets of herbs from around the room and lays them down in front of us.

"We're going to mix a poison, and while it infuses, we're going to mix the antidote. You'll drink one, then the other, so you'd best pay attention," she says with a wicked grin.

My heart sinks a little.

Chapter 8

I can imagine the headlines now, "*Troubled son vanishes after two days in dying mother's home*". Who would start looking for me first? Would mum call the police? Would my flatmates? This could go horribly, horribly wrong – do I trust this woman to use her antidote on me if this all goes wrong? I ... well, she needs me, right?

Either way, my hands are shaking as I try to follow Melusine's instructions exactly. The herbs have to be sliced very precisely with a scalpel. The rat's claws have to be stirred into the beaker anticlockwise. The intonation of the phrase we say as we stir the poison has to be varied in a very exact way. To my surprise, as I'm stirring, trying to say '*felicium nostrum imperculous*' whatever that means, I do start to feel a tendril of ... something else, almost transferring from me to the beaker. At first I try to concentrate on it, but it begins to fade, so instead I focus on the words and just let it happen.

And as I do, the stream of ... something ... between me and the beaker returns and the concoction slowly starts turning green.

"Well finally," Mel grates. "That's looking well. Unfortunately, it's no good on its own – well, this time anyway. Put it to one side, on the mat, and we'll move onto the antidote."

Oddly, mixing the antidote is even simpler; I'm reminded of making a Thai curry that I had a few weeks ago; chopping things, mixing steadily, boiling and simmering. Obviously, curries don't tend to glow and turn white as you come close to finishing them, or leave you feeling drained as you finally turn off the cooker, but it's similar.

"Good," Mel says, taking a small, shot-sized glass from the counter and filling it with my poison. "Now, once you've drunk this, it'll make you fall asleep in the next five minutes, unless you've mixed the antidote correctly. You seem to have a fairly natural aptitude for this, which is a shame, because it's one of the least useful applications of magic for what we're about to be doing."

Oh.

"So why did we...?" I ask.

She cocks her head to one side again and looks at me. "Well, you never know."

Then she pushes the shot glass across the table at me and fills another one with the antidote. I'm really hoping that she's telling the truth about it being a sleeping poison, rather than throwing my guts up or something worse. In for a penny – I guess she hasn't hurt me so far, and if she's right, well, making potions on my own could be relatively handy in a couple of situations that I can think of.

I down the poison, almost retching as I do. It tastes like bad eggs, rotten seaweed and silage, all mixed together. I have no idea how you could get someone to drink it and not notice, because it's possibly the most strongly-flavoured and nauseating thing that I've ever drunk. I swallow hard, and Mel slides the antidote over to me.

Quickly, I swallow the white liquid as well, which tastes a lot like milk. My stomach rumbles and I feel really sick and uncomfortable for about thirty seconds, then it fades. A minute later, it's like it never was.

"Well?" Mel says archly. "How do you feel?"

I take stock. "Not bad. Actually, ok. I mean, the first one tasted awful, but I feel more or less normal right now."

"Hmm," she says. "Well, stay there. If you're asleep when I come back, I'll administer the antidote. I've got another idea, but I need to talk to Merovech for a moment. If you're feeling really keen, you can read the potion book."

She hands me a slim black leather-bound book with 'Potions' written in gold script on the front, then hurries out of the door. The cat looks over at me sleepily, and a moment later, the large toad hops into the room.

"Prick," it croaks at me, then awkwardly turns and hops back out again. I look over at the cat, which lazily closes its eyes and starts breathing heavily.

I look around; it's almost homely in here, with the warmth from the Bunsen burners and the fire, the smell of books, the herbs littered around the room. If it wasn't for the fridges and freezers full of dead things, it'd be cosy. Well, maybe it needs an armchair or two, but you know, near enough.

I sigh and turn to the potions book, opening it up. It starts with a fairly long preamble about how potion-making is one of the most skilful branches of magic, requiring expertise with both plants and animals, as well as a grasp of magic and a precision that most witches and wizards don't have.

Judging by Melusine's reaction a moment ago, I'd guess that not everyone agrees with that. And also – I hadn't really thought about this – but if there are witches, then there must be the other kind too. Maybe it's a rogue witch or wizard doing bad things to the earth spirit?

Once again, I feel woefully ill-equipped to be doing this.

I've reached the 'principles of goode potion-brewing' which include tidiness, sharp knives and fresh ingredients unless otherwise specified, when the door bangs open and Melusine walks in.

"Right, we're done for the day," she says, tossing me a small plastic baggie with some greenish-white powder in it. "Here's the mixture for your mother. It's a concentrated dose, so just stir it into any drink – it'll dissolve better in hot water, obviously – and it should help to inhibit tumour growth. The efficacy decreases substantially with each dose, so it's more or less a one-time thing, ok?"

I nod, realising exactly how I'm going to administer this.

"You'll come back tomorrow and spend some of it with the mechanist. If you see Beckett on the way out, ask him if he can teach you to shoot tomorrow, ok?"

She swooshes past me, robes flowing behind her, and disappears into the back again, leaving me alone in the room.

"Can I take this with me?" I ask, holding up the potions book, but there's no reply.

Maybe best not to, I think. Leave the magic world to itself.

It's starting to get dark as I wander down the path back towards Beckett's bungalow, and my stomach rumbles again – I'm hungry. Maybe I should bring snacks next time?

As I near the house, I see lights on inside, and Beckett waves as he spots me from the kitchen – and that kind of blows my mind. Which 'outside' does his bungalow look out onto? I'm still mulling that over as I turn the door handle and enter.

"Jamie, hi," he greets me warmly, his bass voice somehow reassuring after the constant scratchiness of Mel's. "The old hag pressed you into service then?"

"Yeah," I admit. "But I'm not going to be a wizard anytime soon, apparently."

"Well, it's not for everyone," he says. "Thankfully so."

"Definitely," I agree. "Actually, she asked if you'd teach me to shoot tomorrow, if you have time?"

"Hmmm," he says, glancing down the hall at a couple of large packages. "I'm supposed to be re-thatching Merovech's roof, and getting started on the windows here, but I can probably spare an hour or so."

"Thanks," I say. "I'm terrible at everything apart from potions, so it'd be good to take it out on something."

He snorts and looks away. "Lord, I know how that feels."

I start to walk across the kitchen, inhaling deeply as I do, savouring the rich smell of stewing bacon and potatoes, half hoping for a dinner invitation, but Beckett is already busying himself with something else at the counter. I stop halfway across, looking back through the windows. There's a small but ornate garden there, complete with a fountain. Low bushes are arranged on either side of a path leading towards a set of rose bushes laid out in symmetrical patterns. I'm confused.

"Beckett, how did you see me when I was coming back?"

He smiles kindly, turning back to face me. "It's something you pick up after a while, lad. Anyone will see the Manor grounds when they look through, unless they're really looking. And that takes some skill."

"Huh," I manage. "This place."

"Yes," he agrees softly, turning back to the stove. "You're not wrong."

It's not a long walk back to the house, but it's well after visiting hours at the hospital, so I tuck the small baggie into a jacket pocket and wonder what to do with myself.

I mull over calling Flic, the photographer from the estate agent, but decide against it. Partially because it might look too keen, but I'm also guessing that someone will have to get back in touch with me once the photos are up on the Lockwood website. Obviously, I'm hoping that it's Flic rather than Cynthia.

I end up just killing time boxing up a few bits and pieces, emailing people that mum wanted me to contact and tracking down suppliers before turning in for the night.

The next morning, I head back to the hospital, parking a few roads away from the main building. I make my way to a local Starbucks where I pick up mum's favourite – caramel macchiato – and have them put it into an insulated cup. I pause outside, glancing around furtively before adding the powder and stirring it in, hoping that it still looks and smells the same. All I can smell is sugar and caramel, so I think it'll be fine.

I thread my way through the corridors, feeling a modest surge of pride as I navigate successfully back to mum's room, knocking quietly on the door. There's no reply, so I peer in through the window and see her looking over at me and beckoning me in.

I push the door open and I'm shocked at how different she looks. It's like she's not slept, like she's just had really bad news, like … like she's a different person.

"Mum," I say, setting the coffee down on the table. "What's happened?"

She takes her time in sitting up; she's dressed and looks neat, but her eyes are red and she's definitely been crying – and that's not like her at all. She's not really a crier.

"You brought me coffee!" she says, cracking a weak smile. With trembling hands, she takes it from the table and inhales, her smile widening as she does. She instantly looks a little better for it, and tentatively takes a sip.

"Lovely," she says warmly. "Thank you, Jamie."

"Mum…" I say, my voice rising slightly.

She pauses, setting the cup down on the table again. "Yes," she says, suddenly a bit more business-like. "Well, I had a scan yesterday, and it seems that my little friends have spread more than the doctors thought they had."

Before I know it, I'm hugging her, trying to be careful and trying to hold her as tightly as I can at the same time. We're both crying a little by the time I pull away.

"I'm so sorry," I say, feeling the terrible inadequacy of the words as soon as they're out of my mouth. She looks at me and tries to smile again.

"We knew this kind of thing would happen, I suppose," she says. I can't seem to find any way to reply to that, so I hug her again.

Summoning her customary briskness, she eventually diverts my attention to more practical matters; her online passwords for the utilities, which items can go to a charity shop and which ones might still be worth money. I take notes on my phone, having forgotten once again to bring any kind of notepad with me – which is stupid, because I've got loads of them back home.

"You know Jamie," she says, as I eventually turn to leave. "You don't have to sell the house."

I pause at the door and shake my head. "It's a long way from London," I admit. "And it's, well, it's got a lot of memories in it."

I realise that I've kind of blurted that out and try to correct what I've said. "You know, I mean, that's not always a bad thing, but, just…" I trail off.

Mum nods and looks sad. "I know," she says. "I know. Take care, Jamie."

I try to smile at her and close the door behind me, retracing my steps back to the car. The drive home is a bit of a blur as my mind whirs. Will the mixture from Mel work? How long does it take? How much longer will it give mum? What if she doesn't finish the coffee?

I'm distracted for the whole drive, almost missing my turn at a roundabout and causing an Audi driver to honk their horn at me. I flash my lights to apologise, and tear my mind back to driving safely for the rest of the trip home.

Chapter 9

Once I've parked the car and walked back through the village, I let myself into the Huntsman's lodge again, hurrying through the fireplace door. It's still a strange feeling, but it's gradually starting to feel oddly normal and reassuring to me after the disquieting morning. I pause to enjoy the rich syrupy air as I emerge, taking it deep into my lungs, suddenly having a flashback to when Sam and I came here the first time. It's a shame we didn't stop and enjoy it a bit more, but I guess that when you're young, you're always running around everywhere.

Only there's something different. Something not quite right. It sounds strange, but I can almost hear the leaves on the trees whispering to each other anxiously. There's a slight breeze blowing, enough that I can feel it on my skin, but the leaves are rustling more than I'd expect.

I catch myself. That's silly. How much would you expect leaves to rustle in a breeze? I shake my head, trying to dislodge whatever gremlins have taken up residence, and hurry along the path.

The sensation doesn't so much disappear as fade slowly as I walk down the path towards Melusine's hut. To my surprise, she's already outside, organising a planter bed. Rather than her usual flappy flowing robes, she's in a fairly plain pair of black corduroy trousers and a matching roll-neck jumper, making her look more like a pensioner doing gardening than an old witch who reanimates dead owls for pleasure.

"Morning," I call out, and she slowly pushes herself to her feet, turning to look at me.

"Good morning," she replies. "Took your sweet time in getting here, didn't you?"

I look at my watch; it's barely eleven thirty.

"I was at the hospital," I manage, feeling a flash of guilt. "Sorry. We didn't agree a time."

She shakes her head and mutters to herself. "Apprentices used to be up at sunrise to train with their teacher. Well, no harm done. Come on, we're going straight to the mechanist. No more potions or spells for you."

I try not to look too relieved, but I don't think I entirely succeed.

"I'm resigned to the fact that you're completely unskilled at magic," she says bluntly. "If something comes up, it comes up, but I don't have time to waste."

For about half a second, I wonder about suggesting management training and then realise that I should just shut up and do whatever she says before she turns me into another foul-mouthed toad.

Wait – is that what happened to Evelyn? Surely toads don't live for hundreds of years?

"Sure," I say diplomatically. "Whatever you think is best."

"Good," she says, scrutinising me. "Go on, spit it out."

"Uh," I manage, feeling incredibly self-conscious. "Do your pets have names?"

"I can't imagine why that's the foremost question in your head," she says. "But as a matter of fact, they do. The cat is Copernicus, and the toad is Brian."

"Brian?" I laugh. "Seriously?"

"He's troublesome," she says. "And rarely worth the trouble."

Thankfully, any further small talk or attempts to find out if the witch's familiars are in fact previous apprentices are interrupted by our arrival at the mechanist's hut.

I spy Beckett soon enough; he's currently pulling bundles of thatch off the roof and has neat rolls of fresh-looking stuff stashed off to another side, propped up against a few trees. Something glints underneath the roll, but I'm surprised to see that it's mostly brick and wooden beams underneath, rather than some ornate coppery contraption.

Merovech is sat outside at a picnic table, fiddling with one of their odd scorpion-creations, parts of it strewn everywhere. Melusine stoops down and picks up a spring from the grass, putting it in front of the inventor.

"Oh! Thank you!" Merovech says, looking up. They're wearing the same style of brown robe that they wore the last time, although this one looks a little less stained. Large goggles still obscure most of their face, and I have no idea how they manage to handle the small clockwork components wearing such a well-worn pair of thick leather gloves. "I've almost got the self-navigation components working! It's going to be very exciting when we're done!"

"V, I need some help with my new apprentice here," Melusine says, turning to me. "Jamie has proven singularly ungifted with magic, so I was hoping we could try out the guns you developed for our vegan friends a while ago."

Merovech cocks their head to one side and looks thoughtful. "Oh yes," they gush enthusiastically. "We'll need to do some reconfiguring for a non-faery, but I'm almost certain we can make the stealth component and caching work happily together for you. Wait here and I'll go fetch a pair."

Almost tripping over the seat of the picnic table, the little inventor dashes back into the house, nearly colliding with Beckett. Beckett manages to step aside at the last minute and sets the bundle of thatch down on its end, leaning on it and breathing heavily.

"Don't suppose either of you want to give me a hand, do you?" he says, wiping sweat from his brow.

"With these old bones?" Mel cackles. "I couldn't lift something half that size, and Jamie is about to be much too busy."

"Maybe once we're done?" I offer, not wanting to seem unsympathetic.

"We're done when I say we're done," Mel says curtly. "Time is not something we have a lot of, young man."

I try to look apologetic, but I'm sort of relieved to be missing the manual labour. "Sorry," I call over to Beckett.

"Don't worry about it," he says kindly. "Give me a shout when you want help with the shooting."

He hefts the thatch onto his shoulder easily, and I notice that his arms are all scratched from it. He doesn't seem that bothered, although he does occasionally grunt with frustration when a section of the wire cage springs out of the way.

Just then, Merovech charges out of the house again, door banging behind them. They set a wicker box down on the table and hurriedly sweep the scorpion-thing onto a metal tray. I notice a small cog caught in between two sections of the table and pop it onto the tray as well, earning me a wide grin from the mechanist.

"Thank you!" V says. "Very kind. And observant. A rational mind – it's no wonder you don't do magic."

"Huh," Melusine says. "That's one way of putting it."

"Now," Merovech continues, pulling vaguely gun-like components out of the box. There seem to be far too many of them, including some oddly-shaped panels, almost like sleeves. "I assume that you'll be doing the concealment spell?"

"Concealment spell?" I ask.

"Yes," Melusine says slowly. "Did you expect that you could walk down the street in Britain with a pair of guns?"

Ok, I had that coming. That does actually make sense.

"Uh, ok," I stammer, feeling quite uneasy about the whole thing. "Look, what exactly am I going to be shooting?"

"If I knew that," Mel says. "We wouldn't be arming you. Don't worry – those daisy-loving Seelie Court-dwellers make a nice variety of non-lethal bullets as well as the regular kind. You won't be gunning down innocents, that's for sure."

That doesn't particularly make me feel better.

"V, if you would handle the assembly," Mel croaks, clearing her throat of phlegm noisily before leaning to the side and spitting a gobbet into the forest beyond. I feel queasy. "I'll prepare the incantation. Jamie, this may feel a little painful, but we'll keep the incisions and markings small."

Incisions? Markings? Jesus. It takes all of my self-control not to leap up and run back down the path to the safety of home, cute photographers and snotty estate agents.

"Stretch your hands out and keep them still. If you move, I'll have to strap them down."

I do so, and Mel grabs my left hand, pinning it to the table firmly. I'm momentarily distracted from her vice-like grip by seeing Merovech assembling gun parts faster than I would have thought possible. Although that said, they really aren't quite like any guns I've ever seen. Well, the gun-like parts are, but they're also bigger, and more organic-looking than the pistols I've seen on TV. They've got cases on them that look like...

Ah, I get it.

It's a wrist-mount, only all-encompassing. It looks like they'll sit in my hand, but there's also a hand-protector that sweeps up from a little past the rear of the gun to the tip, and at the same time, there's a sleeve over the side panel, concealing the trigger. It sort of looks like a weird gun-puppet that you put your hand into, although in theory I can kind of imagine some of the force being dampened by the wrist stabiliser. It also seems to be decorated in light brownish-pink camouflage for some reason.

I stare at it; how do you put it away? Maybe V is going to make me some magical holsters or something.

"Ow!" I blurt, feeling a sharp slice across the top of my hand, just by the bony part at the very base of my thumb. It's hot and painful for a moment, but thanks to Mel's grip, I can't move, even if my instinctive reaction is to jerk it away. I glance back, seeing that Mel has marked my hand with a tiny tattoo from a – well, it's part scalpel, part syringe, by the looks of things. There's now a small purplish-red circle on my hand with an 'x' in the middle, the lines of the 'x' extending for half a centimetre or so outside the circle. It's probably not what I would have chosen for my first tattoo.

"Don't touch that," she warns. "We won't be able to

do it again today if you mess it up. Give me your other hand."

Her grip eases, and I cautiously let my left arm hang down by my side, feeling blood slowly drip down onto the grass.

I try to distract myself by watching Beckett, who is now spreading the thatch over the roof of the house. It doesn't look that easy, but once again, he's slinging the bundles around like they don't weigh anything.

I wince as the cut comes again, giving Mel a chance to finish up before looking at it; an identical tattoo now adorns my right hand.

"Will that, like, fade or anything?"

Mel looks at me and wrinkles her already-wrinkled face. "If it ever fades, it won't work, so you better hope it doesn't. Lucky for you, I'm the best blood witch for five hundred miles."

"My lucky day," I mutter, and she cackles merrily.

"Hey Merovech," I say, trying to distract myself from the bleeding, and hoping it stops fairly soon. "You make these amazing things – why isn't your house all copper and bronze or whatever it is?"

The mechanist finishes assembling the second gun, leaving absolutely no components on the table this time, only two finished, vaguely organic-looking weapons. Merovech pauses and blinks at me through the outsized goggles.

"Oh that's very simple," they babble. "Most of us are worried about our own inventions being turned against us. So I don't have any metal in the walls of my house, only the inventions and the inner lab. It's like Melusine. She doesn't have any blood. I mean, she wouldn't have any flesh if she could help it, but I've offered to make her a new body and she said no."

"V," Mel grates. "You're giving away trade secrets."

I think my mouth is pretty much wide open, and I'm trying to think of something to say, but my mind is still reeling from all that.

"Oh," Merovech burbles. "I'm sorry. We don't have company very often."

"You ... you don't have any blood?" I manage.

"Correct," Melusine says. "And if you mention this to anyone else, I'll turn you *and* your mother into toads."

"Christ," I breathe, wondering if Mel's magic could really do that.

"Let's finish this up," Melusine grates impatiently. "Put your hands back on the table. Stretch them out like you're about to grip something."

I do so, rivulets of drying blood running down to my thumbnails. Melusine scowls and mutters something under her breath, and slowly the blood starts to vanish. Or rather, no, it's somehow gathering by the tattoos and sinking back inside me. A moment later, my hands are unblemished, except for the ink. I mean, I suspect that the ink is partially blood as well, but essentially I don't look like I've just been involved in some kind of eldritch scarification ritual anymore.

"V?" she says pointedly, and Merovech slides the guns towards me, one at a time. Somewhat surprisingly, considering that there wasn't any measuring involved, they both fit very snugly in my grip.

"They feel like, well, like they were made for me," I say haltingly.

"And they were!" Merovech gushes happily, a broad grin splitting their face. "I knew they'd fit right when I made them. I loaded them with silenced rounds for now, but you can swap them so easily. There's a tiny little button to the left of the inner grip."

I feel around and do notice an indentation, pressing it on the right-hand gun and making a small magazine pop up. I press it back down using the back of the other glove-gun.

"So, how am I supposed to change magazines when I've got a gun in each hand?" I ask, looking at Merovech. "Is there a holster to go with each one or something?"

V looks at Melusine, who grins evilly, and mutters an incantation softly. Slowly at first, then faster and faster, the guns shrink, growing smaller and smaller, somehow balancing on the very base of my thumbs.

"Woah!" I manage as they get really tiny, then seem to vanish into the tattoos. "Where did they go?"

"The question really," Melusine asks archly. "Is where are you right now? Are you inside the fireplace, in Beckett's lodge?"

My mind reels. "They're ... inside me?" I stammer.

"No," she says, shaking her head and sighing with frustration. "They're inside faery magic, in what is best described as a small place. A place between places. If you want to re-summon them, I've made the incantations simple but keyed to you. Practice it with me now."

It turns out that saying *gun sinister* causes the weird, organic-looking gun to emerge or vanish from my left hand, and *gun dexter* does the same for the right-hand one. It doesn't seem to require any magic, which Melusine takes great delight in reminding me, only my voice or hers.

"Now, if you go with Beckett, he'll teach you to shoot as Merovech and I spend our valuable time making more ammunition for you. Take these."

She nods to V, who slides a few more magazines over to me, which I cautiously put in my pockets.

I have no idea if it's ok to put live ammunition in your pocket, but I don't really have any alternative.

"Beckett," Mel shrieks across at the huntsman on the roof. "Are you done yet?"

He deliberately ignores her for a moment, taking the time to lay down his thatch bundle and spread it around neatly, before affixing it with some kind of wire. Only then does he steady himself and starts to climb back down.

"Infuriating man," she curses. "Damn shame he's so useful."

"Come on lad," the big man says once he's meandered over. "Let's go down the ways a little and get you warmed up."

I follow him around to the other side of the house and down a smaller track through the woods. It's sunny and there's a light cooling breeze. Everything is green and smells fresh and clean, with the occasional hint of bracken. The trees here look old, some of them warped and bent into strange shapes, intertwined with each other. Birdsong breaks the quiet from time to time.

A moment later we round a bend in the track to reach a long clearing, almost like a firebreak in the woods. It's grassy, but otherwise pretty bare, and stretches for some way in either direction.

"Melusine and I talked the trees into falling back a little," Beckett says. "Just in case, you know. Most of them would get out of the way of fire if there was a serious one, but you never know, especially in winter when they're sleepier."

"Right," I say. "Trees moving around. Course."

He grins at me. "Just take it all in, ok? At some point this will all seem normal, but until then, it's best not to make such a scene. It'll annoy Mel and upset V."

I take a deep breath. "Ok," I say, exhaling. "So, what are we shooting at?"

He nods down to the left where I can see a large, lumpy-looking boulder. "Come on," he says, heading towards it, pausing to bend and pick up a few pinecones from the edge of the woods on the way.

"You ever shot before?" Beckett asks.

"BB guns at Centre Parcs a couple of times," I admit, feeling embarrassed. "A crossbow too, once."

He has the decency not to laugh.

"How's your co-ordination generally?"

"Not bad," I say, trying not to sound conceited. I'm not really the sporting type, but I used to play squash at university and got pretty good.

"That's the main thing," he says. "With handguns, you've just got to think about it as pointing rather than aiming, ok? The rest is muscle memory and practice."

He sets up the pinecones on the rock; it's got odd indentations like a face, complete with a ghoulish mouth, elongated eyes and a sunken nose. I try not to think about it. The pinecones look awfully small.

"Here we go," he says, walking back away from it. "Now, bring up one gun and I'll show you how to stand properly."

Any thoughts of standing there and firing my guns like a gangster vanish as Beckett talks me through various elements of how to stand – leaning slightly forwards – and where to put my feet. I'm surprised to learn that unlike most of the films I've seen, guns shouldn't kick back if you've correctly compensated for them. In fact, the only thing that should move, apparently, is the trigger. It's ok to grip tightly, it's ok if you feel the recoil of the gun, but the best way to shoot – situation permitting, of course – is to squeeze the trigger slowly and firmly.

After what seems like an age of theory and standing still, Beckett gestures at the pinecones. "Go on," he says. "See if you can get one of them."

"*Gun dexter*," I say, and the organic-looking gun suddenly snaps into existence around my right hand, my fingers wrapping almost instinctively around the trigger and grip.

Glancing back at Beckett, who gives me a minute nod, I try to adjust my stance back into something vaguely resembling what we just talked about. I raise my arm, pointing the gun at the topmost pinecone and as slowly as I can – with a death-grip on the gun – squeeze the trigger.

For about half a second, nothing happens and I wonder if this is all some kind of hazing joke, almost relaxing my grip, but then there's a *phhhut* from the gun, then a loud *crack* as a chunk of rock to the right of the pinecone flies off towards the forest.

"Not bad," Beckett says. "Try again."

I try to focus and aim down the sight on top of the gun, bracing myself and squeezing again. This time, there's the satisfying sight of the pinecone exploding, bits flying everywhere.

"Nice work, lad," Beckett says. "Keep going until you hit all of them, then switch to the other gun. I'm going to head back and keep thatching. You think you can find your own way back?"

I nod, and he turns away down the path.

A quarter of an hour later, I'm sore and my hands feel like they're vibrating. The recoil from the guns is far less than what I was expecting, but both my hands and wrists are aching from it. I settle down onto the grass, tearing into a sandwich and stare at the rock. It stares back.

"Your posture slipped towards the end," a low, sonorous voice says, making me jump and drop my sandwich. I glance around, pivoting and looking over in the direction of the voice.

It takes me a moment to pick anything out of the undergrowth, but suddenly it snaps into view. A broad, green, bare head, twice as wide as a regular person's. A vast torso, brownish green and covered by a rough-looking vest. Two large, dark eyes staring at me, and a hand easily three times the size of mine, chunky and gripping a nearby tree.

"Holy shit," I breathe.

"You must be Jamie," the thing says. "Enutef mentioned that she'd seen you with V yesterday."

I stand up and just stare. It's at least seven-feet tall and ... well, sort of man-shaped, but much bigger. It kind of reminds me of the Incredible Hulk.

"Are you ... are you a troll?" I ask, realising what it looks like.

"Oh, yes," it says slowly, stepping through the undergrowth towards me. It's got legs like tree trunks, and I have no idea how it found trousers to fit, although they look very home-made. "I'm Kopek."

"Pleased to meet you," I stammer.

There's a rustling in the bushes and the troll slowly looks over at them. "Oh, here's Enutef. Is this the human that you saw yesterday?"

I take a step back as something from my nightmares steps out of the foliage. I feel bile rising in my throat and swallow hard, staring at it. It's got a stag's head and antlers, but it stands on two legs and has a mostly humanoid body, albeit a tall, emaciated one. Somehow, its ribcage is horribly exposed – I can see bare bones, raw flesh and pulsing organs inside. Two long arms ending in clawed hands brush the forest floor and its legs end in cloven hooves. I'm pretty sure I can see blood on its muzzle.

"Yes," she grates, sounding like a horse with a forty cigarette-a-day habit. "Hello there. I'm Enutef."

"Jamie," I manage, swallowing again. "Hi."

There's an awkward moment of silence where the two beings stare at me. Are they going to pounce, I wonder, and tear me limb from limb, leaving parts of me from here to Beckett's bungalow?

"You should try a different stance," Enutef says. "With one foot at ninety degrees to the other."

"Mmmmm," Kopek says. "Good stability."

I gape for a moment longer, then decide to get on with it. At least shooting will mean I don't have to stare at them anymore.

It's actually good advice, and I feel a bit more stable than with my feet spread out. I'm not sure that it makes a difference to my aim, but it does help.

"You're getting pretty good," Kopek says. "Try a few from further back."

I'm on my last magazine, but the troll might have a point. I take a few paces back, the two monstrous beings stepping through the undergrowth lightly to keep up with me. I wonder what they eat.

It's definitely harder from further away. I'd become used to the range, and now I'm shooting a bit low. I try to compensate, with Enutef offering surprisingly constructive advice.

"Ah, ok," I say, when my right-hand gun clicks empty. "I'm out – time for me to head back. It was … nice to meet you both."

"And you," Kopek grunts. "See you around."

Enutef raises one horrifically-clawed hand and waves. "Later," she says.

I hope neither of them realise that I still have half a clip in my left-hand gun; I don't want to offend either of them, but I don't want to be careless either. Although, given that Enutef's bones were exposed, I've no idea whether shooting would actually have had any effect, or whether I would have needed silver bullets or something. I make a mental note to ask Melusine whether I'll need any special ammunition for where we're going.

I manage to find my way back to her hut, latterly guided by the sound of Beckett's voice as he hefts the thatch piles. Mel and V are still sat at the table, a basket of magazines next to them, but they seem to have finished. Melusine is examining what seems to be the inside of a dead frog, while Merovech is tinkering with their scorpions again.

"Kopek said you were pretty good for a beginner," Mel says without turning around. She seems to have supernatural hearing, although given that she re-animates dead creatures without breaking a sweat, I suppose that's not too big an achievement.

"Thanks," I say, sitting down beside her and wondering how a seven-foot troll managed to beat me here, have a casual conversation and then vanish into the undergrowth. "Thanks for all the ammunition."

"Hmm," Mel grates. "Well, you might as well have it and not need it than need it and not have it. Now, pay attention. The green casings are silenced non-lethals. They'll put almost anything under for a few hours, but you might need to shoot larger things more than once. The white casings are standard ammunition, the gold casings are armour-piercing, the black casings are explosive rounds and the silvers are hollow points. Know the difference?"

I actually don't know what a hollow-point is, but I'm too embarrassed to say so, nodding mutely instead. I'll look it up online later.

"Ridiculous male ego," she scoffs, reading me like a book. "I don't know why you're embarrassed given the gun laws in this country. Hollow points expand after hitting a target, so you get maximum damage and less chance of the round penetrating through and into another person or object. Now I know we're arming you well, but stealth and guile are always your best friends. Think first, shoot second."

"Ok," I say, feeling a little embarrassed. "Thanks."

"Now," she says again. "Since you're not a complete disaster with the guns and you weren't too terrified of our friends earlier, tomorrow we'll go to the Seelie Court. Time's a-wasting."

Was the whole thing a test then, I wonder? I guess I must have passed the 'having a casual conversation with a troll and partly-dead man-horse' exam well enough, but the thought of going to an actual court of, well, elves I guess, makes me feel a bit sick.

"Do I need to learn any etiquette or anything?" I ask, having seen a few fantasy films. Elves are always snooty and overly polite in them, when they're not stabbing each other in the back or scheming.

"Not if you let me do all the talking," she says. "And if you must speak, be polite, consider your questions and don't stare. You have a car?"

"Yes," I say. "Yes, of course."

"Good," she says. "Meet me outside Beckett's at eight tomorrow morning with the car. We're driving to the Forest of Dean."

"Uh, sure," I manage, feeling like I'm being dismissed, standing up and stretching.

"Jamie?" she says, and I turn to look at her.

"Yeah?"

"Good work today."

Merovech looks up from their tinkering and waves happily. I raise one hand in a wave back and head home.

Chapter 10

I hurry through the village, torn between calling my mum and not wanting to phone before the magic coffee has time to do its thing. I decide not to, and just as I'm walking through the door, my phone bleeps and an email from Flic appears, letting me know that the photos are done.

I click through to the password protected website; she's done a great job of making this place look a lot tidier and generally more saleable – but I guess that's what she does.

I email her back and thank her, telling her that everything looks great. My finger hovers over the 'send' button, and I add another line, asking if she wants to go for a drink sometime. I hesitate, but then my finger jabs down, almost of its own accord and the mail sends. Was that inappropriate? I mean, she was working, and doing a job, but I guess people meet in all kinds of ways, right?

I pause, wondering if I'm taking on too much. After all, sorting out all everything here at home is one thing, let alone whatever Mel needs me to do. Is it stupid to try and date at the same time?

Maybe you can't straddle two worlds. Maybe you have to choose one or the other.

My mind flits back to my last relationship; Jen, a girl I'd met in my final year at university. We met in a bookshop, got talking and before I knew it, we'd lost the entire afternoon. After a few dates we realised that we actually did really like each other and it had become fairly serious, fairly quickly. Despite the tumult of my first year at uni, I'd settled down in my final year, and was pretty content when I was with Jen.

It hasn't lasted. We graduated and she fell weirdly silent that summer, eventually telling me that she'd had some revelation about the direction her life needed to take, which was immediately followed by a big 'girl's holiday' in Ibiza where she drunkenly ended the relationship. I'd been pretty gutted for a while, but then forgot all about it with the big change of moving my life to London after getting the research job.

I had always assumed as a kid that Sam and I would get together. I'd flitted between that and being scared of her, so I guess it was a weird kind of friendship, but we'd had a lot of shared life experiences together.

Jamie, this isn't helping, I tell myself. Don't curse your future dates with the ghosts of past ones.

I sit back in the chair, suddenly craving a cup of tea or better yet, a beer. Maybe I should go to the pub.

My mind flits back to Melusine. I can't help but entertain a fairly substantial sliver of doubt about her good intentions. I mean, she's definitely a witch, even if I haven't seen her do anything actively evil yet and I didn't get a sense that she was lying when she told me about Gaia and the effect that this was all having on the world around us.

Turning back to a news website, I look around for any other weather irregularities; sure enough, there's been a fairly vigorous hailstorm off the coast of southern France, in midsummer. Apparently if it had been a few miles further north, we might have had a wine shortage in a particular variety this year. Well, either Mel is telling the truth or it's the apocalypse. Or just weird.

My train of thought is interrupted by another email from Flic. I feel slightly sick as I open it, but then I read it.

"Thanks," it says briefly. "A drink would be nice. Let me know when you're free – you've got my number."

I sit back, feeling relieved and slightly smug. Well, now I've just got to survive the elves and I can start dating.

Snorting and laughing at myself, I look around and realise that I've got a lot more packing to do – I'd best get on with it.

The next morning, I carefully back the car out of the drive and park outside Beckett's house. As I get out, Mel and Beckett emerge. While he looks relatively normal, she's essentially dressed as the Halloween edition of Gardener's World; a dark tweed jacket with elbow patches over a black blouse, grubby jeans of the deepest indigo, stained with mud and a few marks that I'm pretty sure are dried blood. We might get a few funny looks, but I guess her outfit is more or less normal enough.

"Enjoy your break," Beckett says, waving as she heads towards me. "Must be nice to walk away from all this once in a while."

Mel mutters something under her breath that sounds obscene and I shrug at him. He gives a brief grin back before wandering back inside.

"Come on, come on," she says. "Let's get this over with."

"No problem," I say, attaching my phone to the dashboard mount. "Where are we heading?"

"Mallard's Pike," she says. "There should be a car park there."

I plug the name into the maps app and sure enough, there is. It's a couple of hours with traffic but doesn't look too tough a drive.

"What did Beckett mean," I ask, once we're clear of the small roads and on the motorway. "About it being nice to have a holiday? It sounded pointed."

Melusine looks up from browsing what I assume is a spell book. I wonder if she's got a broom as well? I can't really see her on one – much too undignified.

She sighs then looks at me. "Another secret," she says, her voice rasping and dry. "I must be feeling generous. Most of us are tied to our place."

She clears her throat and then swallows. "There's an exact measure for it, but in your terms, we can't travel more than ten miles from our homes without the express permission of both Seelie and Unseelie Courts, for more than two weeks at a time. If we do, we grow sick and eventually die."

"Die?" I manage, perplexed by her sudden earnestness. "Seriously?"

"Jamie, this trend towards confirming everything I say may be fashionable on television, but it's really very wearing. It's also not a problem – I have television, the internet, my books, potions, spells to create and improve – why would I want to move?"

"But haven't you been there for a really long time?"

"Yes," she says simply.

We both fall quiet for a while, although I try to break the silence by offering to stop at the services, which she refuses. It almost makes me laugh out loud when I try to imagine her queuing up for the toilets with all the other tourists and travellers, but I push the image from my head.

"So, is there anything I should know about the Seelie Court?" I ask. "I mean, what's the difference between the Seelie and the Unseelie Courts?"

"The Unseelie form their magics widdershins," she says. "There was a time when there was just one Court, but they were cast out for practicing pursuits that the Seelie found unwholesome."

"Unwholesome?" I say, raising one eyebrow at her as I navigate a roundabout. "Making you Unseelie?"

"I am above such divides."

"That's a yes?"

"I *will* turn you into a frog one day," she says, glaring at me. "I think it would be instructional."

"When you're not busy dealing drugs?"

"I do not deal drugs," Melusine says frostily. "I make high grade herbal and pharmaceutical products that others have found a ridiculous use for. That use just happens to be highly lucrative for me."

"Right," I manage. "And you also happen to be untraceable because you live on the other side of a magical fireplace?"

"Well, it does have its fringe benefits," she says. "Jamie, what do you want from this conversation?"

Honestly, I'm not entirely sure.

"Just trying to get my head around everything," I admit after a moment.

"I don't often take a human apprentice," she says, long, warty nose twitching. "And even less often do I take one who is as ungifted as you."

I'm not sure where she's going with this either. If it's flattery, it's not working, but maybe she's needling me in return.

"So be patient," she finishes. "It often takes humans years to understand the faery worlds."

"Fair enough," I say evenly, changing lanes and overtaking. "But there is one thing that I was thinking about. What does this Gaia do again?"

She fixes me with a long stare and answers slowly.

"The Earth Spirit is at the heart of everything that grows and lives. This planet exists in a delicate balance, and Gaia works to protect life, regulating pollution, the weather systems, the natural world. You think it's odd that trees still grow by the side of this motorway when a hundred cars belching toxic fumes go by every minute? That's Gaia. Erratic weather, crops not growing – something is wrong and I mean to find out what."

"And why's this on you?" I wonder out loud. "Why is it the job of some witch from the countryside?"

She cackles, startling me. The car wobbles in its lane and I hurriedly turn my attention back to driving safely.

"Oh Jamie," she says. "I've killed people for less. But I'm not just a witch from the countryside, I promise you that."

"Sorry," I apologise hastily. "I just meant … well, you know I don't understand all of this."

"Hmm."

There's an uncomfortable pause.

"And uh … this Gaia," I add eventually. "Could it, you know, heal people?"

There's another pause and Mel sighs. "It's complicated, Jamie," she says slowly, her malice gone. "Gaia is a force for growth, for life and death. I've been inside the main Gaia chamber once, and it's chaotic. Life, death, birth, growth, all at the same time, everywhere. You might be able to bottle it, but don't forget that cancer is alive too. There's an equal chance that even if you did get into the main chamber, whatever you took from there – assuming she allowed you to take anything – would prompt other forms of growth in an untrained body."

"Untrained?"

"It's not something I specialise in," she says, shaking her head. "There are witches and wizards who spend decades learning to commune with Gaia, and even they don't regard her as some kind of medical lucky dip."

"But there are people who know?" I say, seizing at the sliver of hope. "Can we talk to one of them?"

Another sigh. "Yes," she says, her voice creaking. "Unfortunately. But you won't find it helpful. Jamie, believe me, if I could do anything to help your mother, I would tell you. The more powerful magic is, the more dangerous it becomes, not simply because of its effects, but because of its ability to unbalance the very fabric of nature itself. Of course, Gaia is the essence of nature herself, but in a highly concentrated form."

She seems unwilling to say any more, and neither of us speak for a long time after that, even after I pull into a service station, grab sandwiches and go for a wee.

Well, that's another option for helping mum out of the equation then. Maybe one of the Courts will know something that this witch doesn't? After all, if the elves could help Frodo in *Lord of the Rings*...

I really shouldn't base anything on Tolkien. I've not met any dwarves yet, but the troll I met seemed pretty relaxed, so J.R.R was clearly way off the mark.

Maybe I'm clutching at straws. I should just take my money and do whatever she says. Perhaps I should take my one grand and go back to my normal life right now. Forget the elves, forget the beasts, forget the cute photographer and go back to London, get some decent flatmates and buy a small house once mum's place goes through.

Only...

Only there's a part of me that doesn't want to. A part that wants to see how far this all goes, however terrifying and strange it is. A part of me that wants to understand what Enutef is, and how there are trolls and witches living in a secret place in the countryside. A part of me that wants to spend all my time in that richly vivid park in the Manor grounds that isn't really in the Manor grounds.

"Jamie?" Melusine croaks. "A penny for your thoughts."

I glance at her wrinkled face, raggedy teeth and dark, beady eyes. "Sorry," I say. "I'm dealing with it."

She nods slowly. "Sure," she says evenly. "It'll come."

Half an hour later, we're pulling into a car park in the Forest of Dean, tall trees flanking us and darkening the sky. Birds sing, and I can see the occasional squirrel scurrying away as we drive slowly towards a parking spot at the end.

Melusine gets out of the car and looks around for a moment.

"This way," she says, gesturing.

I follow her down a trail heavy with pine needles, softening the sound of our footsteps. It smells great here, lush and brimming with life.

"When was the last time you were here?" I ask.

"About fifty years ago," she says. "I needed some ingredients for a spell and they were very specific. I bargained and left a goodwill gift."

"You're on good terms?"

"Not exactly."

The trail starts to wind up a hill, the surface changing from pine needles to a sort of half-gravelled track. It's quite steep for a moment, but Melusine doesn't seem to struggle at all. Magic, maybe?

She curses softly ahead of me and I look around. We're heading down a smaller track, but it's also signed 'Sculpture Trail'.

"Last thing we want," she says. "Attention. Keep your eyes and ears open."

A runner passes us in the other direction, not stopping, but definitely giving Melusine an odd look. The witch glares at him but we keep going, and thankfully don't see anyone else for a while. The sculpture is either a bit abstract and boring, or spectacular – at one point, there's an entire stained-glass window hung from two trees. It's across the path, so the sun shines through it, casting red and green patches onto the path. It's really quite beautiful, and even Melusine pauses to admire it for a moment.

"Alright," she says, a bit further down, spotting a set of wind chimes hung from a tree. They're wooden and make eerie tonal noises that I've been hearing for a while now. "Stand next to me and don't move."

We're exactly parallel with the wind chimes, with two trees bent over the path in front of us. They almost look like they form some kind of gate, which I suppose is highly likely, given that Melusine has stopped and is scrutinising them intently. The chimes are maybe ten feet further down to the left. We're both still on the path, and I hurriedly glance behind us, earning a scowl from Melusine.

"Stay still," she hisses, and gestures at the wind chimes, making them clank and whistle seemingly at random, then in a steadily ascending tone.

"Now, keep walking," she says, taking a step forward. I mirror her step, and suddenly feel that sense of dislocation as the world around me grows larger and larger, blades of grass towering over me vertiginously for a moment. Then it all snaps back, and although I can see the wind chimes, the trees are all different; sparsely growing instead of densely packed, oaks and silver birches instead of pines.

But that's not what really gives it away. It feels different. Older, somehow. There's something in the air, something almost crackling. I wonder if it's magic.

"Melusine," a deep voice says from behind us. "This is an unexpected surprise."

We both spin around – well, I spin, Melusine turns slowly – to see what I imagine is an elf, although it's only vaguely like the elf I'd expected.

Slender build – check. Pointy ears – check. Light blue, ageless eyes – check. But this guy, and I think it's a guy, although there's also a graceful femininity about him, is in black jeans and a leather jacket, open, with a roll-neck jumper underneath. He looks elegant, but I'd expected … well, something a bit more courtly and less modern day.

"Alariel," Melusine says, sounding unsurprised. "We need to see her."

"Charming as ever," Alariel says musically. "It must be almost twenty years since we last saw each other."

"Al, we don't really have time for courtly manners right now," she says, making the elf wince at the abbreviation. "It's important."

"Yes, I imagine it is," Alariel purrs, recovering quickly. "The witch of flesh and blood so rarely leaves her post, important post that it is. Unfortunately, there are a few matters that demand Lisilya's attention and she is unable to entertain guests, however eminent."

"I'm not posturing," she growls. "And I don't invoke this lightly. We need to talk about Gaia. Now."

Something changes in the elf's posture. "Hmm," he says swiftly. "Our interests may align. Come. And bring your apprentice."

The last word is full of something that I think is distain, but I'm too distracted by his walk to say anything. It's like he flows past us, moving like a ballet dancer. I could never be that graceful, not if I trained for years. Melusine looks at me, shrugs and hurries after him, down the wooded path.

Silver birch trees climb around us on either side, small leaves dropping in the light breeze. I've never seen a variety this big; they're usually slight and willowy, but these are large and chunky, like the oaks by the gate-portal thing.

I feel uneasy, like we're being watched, but I can't see anyone other than our impromptu guide. I stay silent and try to convince myself that there's no-one around.

Although, given that this is a magic wood, the chances are good that we're being watched by all kinds of things.

And then we arrive. It takes me a moment to register, because the forest doesn't so much stop as starts to feature houses. Well, not really houses like I'm used to, but beautiful, flowing structures of wood and some other unidentifiable material, built into and around the trees. I'd kind of expected a Robin Hood-type set up with tree houses or something, and although the houses do seem to mesh with the trees, a lot of them start at ground level.

I get the impression that it's been done with the utmost respect for nature, without moving a single plant. The houses aren't a uniform shape, some stretching between multiple trees, some simply growing up where the ground is rocky, or flowing up a hill where the gradient changes.

"Come on," Melusine scowls at me. "Plenty of time for gawping later."

I'd stopped to stare, but hurry to catch up with her, threading my way through the dwellings. All around me, there's motion; elves hurrying gracefully around the buildings, and although there's an overwhelming sense of peacefulness and nature here, it's got an edge. I start to get a feeling like the anticipation before an exam. Not an unprepared, sick feeling, but one like when you've studied a lot, but you're still half an hour away from starting.

Most of the elves seem to be armed, a couple of them checking magazines and inspecting guns that look quite similar to mine. They seem calm and unhurried, but there's a definite tension in the air.

As we get further in, the silver birches turn to gold, and I earn another dirty look from Melusine when I pause the first time I notice.

It's not just elves here either; I distantly see a horse which turns out to have a human torso – not a bare one like the centaurs you see in Dungeons and Dragons, but instead wearing a light jacket. If I'd been able to get closer, I swear I could have confirmed whether or not it had the Helly Hansen logo on it.

"Don't get all glamoured on me, Jamie," Mel says. "You wander off and I'll never see you again. And the elves sure as shit won't bring you back."

I try to focus on the witch rather than the beauty all around me, which is easier said than done. Thankfully, a short way ahead, Alariel points to a staircase winding around a tree, flanked by two slightly sturdier elves in suits, both carrying rifles. I thought my guns were elegant, but these – well, the wooden stocks, each covered in flowing symbols, wind around their arms, the grain of the wood gleaming, two large magazines curling out of each one.

"Gentlefolk," Melusine says as she nears them. "You know who I am."

I don't know anything about elvish expressions, but I swear I see a flicker of something like fear run across the faces of these two suited heavies. One of them nods, and they take a small step back from the entrance.

"She's expecting you," one of them grunts. I wonder how she – whoever 'she' is – can be expecting us when we've literally just arrived. Melusine starts up the stairs and I briefly glance up; it's a long way to the large, circular platform at the top, but whatever it is, it's where the leader of the Seelie lives.

I steel myself and start the climb.

Chapter
11

All the way up, I have that same odd sensation of being watched; there's a faint chittering noise and I can almost feel the eyes on my skin. We climb up and up the spiral staircase until my thighs and lungs burn. I swallow hard, flirting with vertigo; there's only a slender handrail between me and an incredible view of the forest, but it's a hell of a long way down.

I almost walk into Melusine as we reach the top. Just in time, she takes an extra step past two guards even burlier than the ones downstairs, and I move to stand beside her. We're in a small antechamber, golden doors in front of us carved with ornate woodland scenes, stags and unicorns rearing, elves reclining, that kind of thing. Everything here is graceful and tasteful, swirls of silver and gold birch bark seemingly woven into the walls.

There's one other slim elf in the room with us, up ahead by the doors and if there's anyone I'm more afraid of than the guys with the guns, it's her. Electric blue tattoos run up her arms, and despite her everyday appearance in tight-fitting jeans and a vest top, she radiates power. I swear I see a crackle of electricity running over her knuckles when I arrive in the room, and she quickly fixes Melusine with an icy stare.

"Alariel told you we were busy," she says with a voice like frostbite; cold and killing. "And yet, here you are."

"Hello Silvai," Melusine says, seemingly not out of breath at all. "Alariel also seemed to think that our problems may be aligned."

"Even if that were true," the elf says, pacing in front of the doors. "We would not ask *you* for help."

"I don't recall hearing anyone *ask* for help," Melusine hisses. "But before you start a war, I would speak to Lisilya."

Silvai glares at her, then stands to one side.

"Fine," she spits. "But be prepared to be barred from the Sylvan realm forever if you're wasting our time."

"I waste many things," the witch says curtly. "Human money. Small and medium-sized rodents. Internet bandwidth. But never time."

The deadly-looking elf waves at the door dismissively, but Melusine seems entirely oblivious to the snub. She sweeps past and pushes both doors open, revealing a long corridor ending in another set of double doors. I hurry to catch up with her, trying not to look at Silvai as I pass.

"I didn't realise you were such a big dick around here," I whisper, my nervous humour sounding weak even to me. Mel scowls at me, then lets out a cackling laugh.

"Ah Jamie," she says. "You're quite refreshing sometimes, particularly around these prissy fuckers."

Mel pushes through the next set of doors and the view takes my breath away.

The room is roughly spherical and is set around the trunk of the tree, defying my previous understanding of its proportions and size. Maybe we've passed into yet another realm, but the amphitheatre curves upwards with ornately carved wooden pews all around, laced with gold thread of some kind. The seats are about half full of magical beings armed to the teeth and checking their weapons. Most of them are elves, slim and deadly-looking. They're either inspecting magazines and taking guns apart then reassembling them, or consulting large tomes and making obscure gestures that give me the fleeting impression of pressure, like when an aeroplane changes altitude.

The others are a mixture of short, squat creatures – some slim, some larger – a few more centaurs, some men and women who seem to have the legs of … well, goats or horses, I think, and beings who look like the genie from Aladdin. The non-elves have markedly different weapons, from chunkier rifles with clockwork innards that I'm sure Merovech would love to get their hands on, to larger machine guns – mostly in the hands of the centaurs. Everyone looks intent on preparation and

I wonder how close they are to doing whatever they're about to do.

Mel strides across the floor, which is inlaid with mosaic tiles. I can't quite work out what the pattern is; it's abstract, but seems to be mostly green and presumably nature-related. I'm also a bit puzzled by our heading: we seem to be walking towards an empty throne in front of the giant trunk of the tree, flanked by yet more rifle-toting elves.

One of the guards raises an eyebrow as we approach, but they're otherwise impassive.

"Lisilya," Melusine calls, and for once her voice is clear, absent of its usual croaking or rasping. "We need to talk before you start a small war."

There's a creaking sound like a tree bending in the wind, which gets louder and louder. The bark on the tree in front of us starts to change, slowly resolving into a face. I see a huge nose, a mouth, eyes that briefly fix on Melusine and flit to me, before something starts emerging from it. They're like dust particles, like something's detaching from the tree itself, flowing out in front of the throne.

There's a faint popping sound and suddenly a large, tall woman appears in front of us. She's at least seven feet high, twice as broad as Silvai, clad in a flowing green robe, has skin the colour of grass, and to top it all off, she's got antlers – or maybe it's a crown. I'm not sure.

She doesn't seem to have pointy ears, but given that she just coalesced from a tree, I suspect that she might be a kind of tree spirit rather than an elf.

Mel doesn't seem fazed at all.

"Melusine," Lisilya says in a voice that's both casual and razor-sharp. She sits down on her throne. "What's it been, fifty years?"

"About that," Mel says evenly. "I know I'm hardly welcome here, but it seemed like an appropriate time, given what I suspect you're about to do."

"And what is that?" Lisilya asks silkily.

"Declare some kind of war on the humans," Mel says. "Reveal yourselves. Violate the oldest pact known to the faery."

There's a low hissing from around the room, and about a third of the assembled host falls silent, cocking guns ominously. Melusine ignores it and I wonder if I should have had my guns out by now. Then again, every single one of these soldiers looks like they could rip me in half and set me on fire with their magic before I even pointed a gun anywhere, so maybe it's better to keep a low profile.

"The humans have violated Gaia," Lisilya hisses, her green features contorting with rage. "Our magics fizzle and fail. One of our realms re-integrated with the outside world; a community of fauns suddenly in the human domain, only escaping notice because Alariel happened to be visiting. This is serious, Melusine, or have you lost all respect for the secrecy of the pact?"

"The humans are incapable of finding the Gaia site," Melusine says quickly. "Or have you forgotten the charms that surround it? Your first response should not be an all-out war."

"Do not counsel me, witch," Lisilya spits, pacing angrily towards us. "What do you suggest our first response should be? An aging hag and her human apprentice?"

"There was a time when you heard my counsel well," Melusine replies. "And yes, although I would ask for your blessing, support … and that of the Unseelie."

If Lisilya's guards look outraged at the idea, Lisilya herself looks fit to explode. She glares at Melusine and shakes with anger, fragments of bark scattering across the floor before she regains control and resumes her icy stare.

"You have a talent for offering the most offensive solutions possible," she says in a low voice.

"You know I'm right," Melusine says. "A problem with Gaia needs both courts. I don't want access. I want to make sure we're acting on the truth, not centuries of mutual suspicion. Their magics will be having the same problems as yours."

"Our magics are *nothing* like theirs," Lisilya growls.

"I know," Melusine sighs. "I've heard all it before. Rage all you like, but give me one week and a small delegation. We'll go in by stealth with a team of the Unseelie and if a war is merited, you'll get your war."

"Pfft," the giant woman looks to one side. I wonder whether it hurts more to be killed by magic or bullets.

I dimly register the doors behind us opening and Alariel walks up to stand beside the assembled guards.

"You grace," he says. "Our plans are still in progress. We can wait a week but no more. If anything, it will give us time to prepare our magics, if they are weakening or unpredictable. A decisive battle is … preferable."

Lisilya looks at him, obviously pissed off. "Fine," she says curtly. "But in eight days, we re-take Gaia's mount and leave no survivors. And I want two things: first, you and Alariel restore the fauns' realm. Second, that necromantic bitch Kiriel is making an army for Balthamel. In the event that we do have to take Gaia's mount by force and the Unseelie decide that it would be a good time to try our strength, I want a counter-weapon to her skeletons. You'll make me one."

Melusine glares at Lisilya, scrutinising her.

"One," she says. "Or the other. Not both."

The two elves nearest to Lisilya take a step back at the same time. Her very frame seems to tremble in the air and I can see her fighting for self-control, breathing quickly and clamping her mouth shut.

"The fauns," she says quietly through gritted teeth. "And if you are successful, you'll take both Alariel and Silvai to Gaia's site, as well as a contingent of my best."

"Thank you," Melusine says, obviously biting back a retort. "Have the delegation at the mount in two days. And keep it quiet."

"Fuck off back to your grove, witch," Lisilya hisses. "If we're lucky, it'll be your blood spilt and our paths will never cross again."

"It's unlikely," Melusine says, turning away and heading back towards the door. "But you never know."

The room seems to let out a collectively-held breath as we pass down the corridor, Alariel still flanking us.

"Melusine, must you aggravate her so?" he asks musically, a grin cracking his otherwise solemn demeanour. "I thought she was about to start puréeing bodyguards."

"Why the support, Alariel?" she replies, ignoring the question. "There's no love lost between us, especially after Stonehenge."

We pass the second set of doors, the guards watching us like hawks as Melusine starts down the stairs, Alariel close behind.

"I can't say I support your methods, or the filth you keep as company," he says pleasantly, as if discussing the weather. "But unlike many of my compatriots, I'm not too proud to recognise when you're right. Not to mention that an all-out war with the humans won't end well for anyone."

"Mellowing in your old age?" Melusine cackles. "Or did you read a few books without pictures in the last twenty years?"

"That was almost witty, grandmother," he says evenly, making her sigh heavily.

"I wish you wouldn't call me that," she says. "It was a necessary deception."

He doesn't reply, and there's silence until we reach the bottom of the stairs. The slender elf scoops up a backpack as we start to walk through the settlement, attracting stares as we go.

"So," she says. "Do you have any other intelligence on the Gaia site? Because you've obviously had spies there."

He sighs, and I wonder whether he's about to share information that Lisilya was holding back.

"The humans have established a scientific site on the edge of the hill," he says slowly. "They've dug in and it's relatively well secured, but the host would have no problem in retaking it. It'd be a bloodbath though. They seem to know where to dig and are making slow but steady progress towards Gaia's chamber. Our plan was to overwhelm the site as quickly as possible, cut off all communications and render it forgotten as soon as possible."

"You know I love blood," Mel says. "But even that seems rash for the Seelie."

"Lisilya has been directly affected by this," he says quietly. "We've all seen it. It needs to be solved quickly. A week may be too long."

I guess that if the earth is being harmed by the interference with Gaia, and Lisilya is somehow linked to a tree, then it's only logical that she'd be feeling the effects. I muse on that until we leave the houses of the settlement behind and start down the path towards the gate.

"And where exactly are these fauns camped out?" Melusine asks Alariel. "I'd rather waste as little time as possible wiping the arses of the hoofed hippies if I can avoid it."

"Standish Wood," Alariel says. "Not far from Stroud."

"Figures," Mel says acidly. "Dense enough woodland to go unseen, close enough to a town to restock when they need to."

"Our cousins are in need of help," he says innocently. "How can we deny them that?"

"You're up to something," she says, fixing him with a narrow stare. "Every time I come here, it's like wading hip-deep through your political shit."

"Unlike the Unseelie Court," Alariel replies mildly. "Where they actually *live* in their own shit."

"Racist."

"You know they're not really a different race, don't you? Just uglier, dirtier and more inbred."

Melusine sighs noisily and the elf looks smug.

"Human," he says, suddenly turning to me. "How did your people find the Gaia site?"

"I have no idea," I admit, after a pause. "Our science isn't like your magic. It's logical, rational. It's social networks and nano-technology, 3D printing and the internet. It's not earth spirits and unicorns."

"Hmm," Alariel says, flashing Melusine another smug grin. "This one does have a touch of the fey about him after all."

She scoffs and gestures at the wind chimes as we reach the gateway back to the human world.

"Coming with us?" she says. "Might as well get this done now, assuming that you've got the necessary goods."

He gestures to his pack and she nods, rolling her eyes.

"Guess we're going for a family road trip then," she says. "Hope you don't mind the back seat. I get travel sick."

I know she's lying, and if Alariel does too, then he doesn't say anything. A moment later, we're back in the human realm.

Chapter 12

Back in the regular forest, Alariel pulls a black Hugo Boss beanie down over his head, covering the pointy tops of his ears. It's enough to pass a cursory glance, but there's still something otherworldly about him and the way he walks. It's too graceful, too lithe for a regular person.

We get a strange look from a family walking the other way, but otherwise make it back to the car park without incident, although Alariel stops and sniggers when he sees the car.

"Hundreds of years of investment, all your dealings and this is what you decide to drive?" the elf asks Melusine archly.

"Hey," I protest. "This is my mum's car!"

"I wasn't addressing you, human," he says curtly.

"There's nothing wrong with travelling under the radar from time to time," Melusine says, clearly enjoying his discomfort as we get in. She even pushes her seat all the way back, forcing him to shift over to sit behind me rather than bunch his legs up.

"So, Alariel," Melusine says, as we pass Gloucester. "If your brain can comprehend the meaning of straight talk, what's the scheme this time?"

The elf doesn't reply, and I glance back at him in the rear-view mirror. He's staring – somewhat sullenly – out of the window.

"Perhaps we could simply be cordial," he says after a long silence. "You might not be concerned with your standing at court, but that was a substantial snub for me. I happen to believe that you're right, so a little more credit would be fitting."

Melusine's expression softens. "Of course," she says more gently. "Although if I can ask, what were you doing with the fauns in the first place? If I remember rightly, there's no love lost between you, and if Lisilya has sent you to repair their realm, then she clearly disapproves of your association with them."

Alariel sighs and doesn't reply for a moment. "Let's just get on with this, shall we?"

She sniggers.

Ignoring their bickering, I find myself thinking about mum and hoping that she's ok; I should have checked in with her after I gave her the coffee. I completely forgot to ask Mel if the drugs had any side effects, or how long they'd take to kick in. I get the impression that I shouldn't ask with Alariel in the car, so I try to make a mental note to bring it up with Mel later.

Fifteen minutes later, I almost miss the entrance to the car park, because it's essentially a gap in a drystone wall with a National Trust sign on it. There's a confusing moment where I'm not quite sure whether we've come to the right place – it's also marked on a sign as Shortwood car park, which was the last village we drove through. It looked quite idyllic, although the pub sounded uncharacteristically noisy for a place in the countryside.

I navigate a variety of potholes in the mud and gravel to the far side of the car park. There are woods on three sides, with a spectacular view of what I think are the Brecon Beacons on the far side. The land drops away down the side of the hill and you can see for miles before the sharp rise of the Beacons. It's impressive.

It's made less impressive by the raggedy group of men and women standing by a couple of park benches, smoking and drinking. I stop a reasonable distance away and look at them cautiously; the guys look a bit, well, retro. They're all bearded and have a kind of sixties look about them, and their clothes don't quite fit properly, like their proportions are wrong. Come to think of it, they're standing kind of funnily as well.

Huh. I guess these are the fauns.

Then I notice Alariel looking at me through the window. I didn't even hear him get out.

"Are you coming?" he says cordially, but there's a bite beneath the words. I can see why Melusine doesn't like the Seelie elves.

I turn the engine off and get out, looking at the group uneasily. They look a bit shifty. There's only one other car in the car park, so at least we can do this without too much attention from the outside world.

"You're new at this, aren't you?" Alariel notes, and it's not really a question.

Melusine sighs. "Don't answer him, Jamie," she says. "We've got work to do."

One of the guys in the group waves and starts singing a Paul Simon song drunkenly, although I laugh when I recognise it. Alariel rolls his eyes, muttering something about 'the indignity', before striding over to meet the group and talking with them in hushed tones. Or rather, he talks in hushed tones amidst their raucous laughter, loud, slurred voices and the occasional verse of song.

I grin, but seeing Melusine's serious expression, it evaporates quickly.

"Should we say hi?" I ask.

"No," she says curtly. "They know who I am, and unless they've been at this all day, they'll know what we're here to try and do."

The wind changes direction and blows a waft of marijuana smoke towards me. Maybe Mel's right – this isn't the time to expand my knowledge of faery folk in the modern world.

A hush falls over the group and one of them stubs out their joint, all of them looking intently at Alariel. Their concentration is almost comically painful, like watching a group of drunks trying to work out the bill at the end of the night.

I glance at one of the women, and there's definitely something wrong with how her legs bend, although if I remember my fantasy literature right, fauns should have goat's legs, so it's no wonder their jeans look odd. I try to see if I can pick out any horns or remnants of horns, but they're all either wearing flat caps, beanies or again, weirdly retro headbands that make them look like they're from the nineteen sixties.

A dog walker appears from the side of the woods, her German Shepherd growling at the assembled group. The dog's Barbour-clad owner glares at them – or more likely, their smell – and hurries over to the other car, giving me a look as she pulls off her wellington boots.

Two of the female fauns look like they're about to do something, but Alariel holds up his hands and makes hushing gestures until the muddy Golf has done a three-point turn in the car park and pulled out onto the narrow country lane. There's a burst of laughter and the women start dancing with each other, holding hands and spinning around in a circle. There's a flash of blue light, and Melusine winces a little.

"Careless spell," she says. "Best keep your eyes open."

Alariel comes back over a moment later. "The woods are empty," he says tiredly, pulling a roll of police tape from his bag. "We can begin now."

"Good," Melusine says. "Jamie, go with Alariel and one of the fauns and get to taping off the realm. I'll start the work with the others, if they can manage it."

Alariel gestures to one of the fauns, who skips over to us, looking excited. He's fully bearded, but has quite a youthful face, curly dark brown hair, and is wearing a pair of bright green trousers and a yellow button-up shirt.

"Are you making us a home now?" he says.

"If it'll take," Melusine says. "Alariel?"

He nods and attaches one end of the police tape to a tree nearby. "Come on, both of you," he says.

"Hey," the faun says, looking over to me. "I'm Brach. Great to meet you!"

"Jamie," I say warily. "How are you?"

"Pretty good," he burbles. "The human realm is great, isn't it? I mean, so many things to drink, smoke, eat. How do you keep track of it all?"

"Brach," Alariel interrupts. "Let us know if there are any particular features or places you'd like included in the realm."

Brach grins and nods at him, looking at me expectantly.

"Ah," I say, unsure of how literal to be. "It depends what you like, but most people eat out from time to time and try a couple of new things every so often."

Alariel sighs and starts to lead the way around the edge of the woods, occasionally looping a spool of tape around a tree. I wonder if we're going to have to unwind it once Melusine is done with the spell.

We reach the edge of the hill and start working our way along it. It's slightly tougher going because the ground is quite uneven; I'm constantly having to watch where I'm stepping. Small rocks litter the grass, poking through the soil, which is interspersed with trees, bushes and plants. We're not really following any kind of footpath.

"Wonderful!" Brach says. "And the same for drinking? How about smoking? Do you smoke?"

"No," I reply, quickly tiring of this.

"Oh, you should," he says quickly. "It's wonderful. I was hoping that you smoked and that you had a vaping thing and I could try it. I'd really like to try it. Do you know if you can put weed in it?"

"Brach," Alariel interjects. "We're working here."

"Oh, yes, of course," he apologises. "Sorry. Alariel, do you smoke? I can see you as more of a cigar kind of guy."

Alariel rolls his eyes and sighs.

"Alariel, who's this Kiriel that Lisilya mentioned?" I ask, trying to fill in the space so that Brach doesn't start talking again.

Brach gives me an injured look. "You're a real downer, do you know that?"

Alariel snorts. "Jamie, you should know that the best way to offend a faun is to begin a serious conversation, but since you asked, let's continue, if Brach can deal with a levity-free moment."

The faun shrugs airily. "As you wish," he says, but I can tell that he's offended.

Alariel laughs quietly, then glances back at me. "Kiriel is one of the Unseelie Court's necromancers," he says. "This isn't unusual; they deal with all kinds of vile magic on a regular basis. But Kiriel has found a way to make her undead creations more durable than we're used to. Our scouts came across one and although they were able to return it to the grave eventually, it was a lot more sturdy than previous creations. Lisilya quickly became concerned that this represented something of an escalation in the arms race between the two Courts and started looking for weaknesses."

"And how do you make a skeleton or zombie more hard-wearing?" I ask, not really grasping what we're dealing with.

"Skeleton," the elf says curtly. "And we're not sure. Most undead have some kind of animus in them, a life-spark imparted by the necromancer themselves. But these creations were treated with some kind of resin, as well as having a stronger animus so that they could travel further from the source of their unnatural life."

"Seriously guys," Brach says. "We've just met – do we have to talk about this? Does anyone want a drink?"

The faun proffers a small bottle of what looks like brandy.

"No thanks," I say. "I'm driving."

"Not right now you're not," he says pointedly. "I can see."

I roll my eyes again. "No, thank you," I say, trying to be cordial. Honestly, I don't know why Alariel would have been spending a moment longer than he had to with these annoying creatures.

"Al?" Brach offers the bottle, but Alariel shakes his head.

"No," he says patiently.

Thankfully, the faun doesn't make any more overtures, and falls into what I assume is a dejected silence as we tramp around the hillside, trying to tape off the edge of the woods. Somehow, the roll of police tape doesn't get any smaller, although Alariel does occasionally mark individual trees with symbols of some kind.

After an hour of walking, Alariel turns, heading up the hillside and following the treeline. I'm starting to need the bathroom and get a bit hungry. Should I have brought something to eat or drink with me? There are snacks in the car, but, well, I didn't think this would be a long excursion.

"We've never liked this part of the woods," Brach says suddenly. "We can cut back along the path if you want."

Alariel raises his eyebrows at the faun, then shrugs, turning inwards with his everlasting reel of tape. The air is starting to cool, especially in the shade, but I try to enjoy the woodland smells and sounds. There's something soothing about walking through forests, and Standish Wood has acres of beech trees, their small waxy leaves rustling in the breeze.

Brach seems slightly uncomfortable with walking this far, and his hopping gait becomes more of a limp.

"You ok?" I ask, after a few minutes of wondering whether to re-open the conversational floodgates.

"It's a little sore," he admits. "When we're in human territory, we have to clip attachments onto our feet so that we can wear your shoes. We'd normally go barefoot – we're hooved, don't you know?"

"Ah," I say, admittedly intrigued and trying not to stare at the faun's feet. "I'm sorry, that sounds painful."

"Only over long distances," he says. "Normally it's ok, but we don't usually go for countryside walks in the human world. Unless we're stocking up on food, drink, smokes, drugs, you know, the essentials. Hey, have you had kombucha? Why do humans drink that? It's nasty."

I have to admit that I haven't, but I do explain to him about how it's supposed to be healthy, although he seems unimpressed. Perhaps fauns have a different metabolism to humans?

Alariel comes to a sudden stop, holding up one hand, palm forwards. I spot it and also stop hurriedly, but Brach only comes to a halt once he's alongside the tall elf.

"There's something moving up ahead," Alariel says. "Something human-sized."

Brach peers into the undergrowth and sniffs. "Smells like one of us," he offers. "Oh! I wondered where Dion had gone."

"I thought you said the woods were empty," Alariel says through gritted teeth.

"Well, they were empty of humans," Brach says

cheerfully. "That was the question. Why would a faun matter?"

Alariel starts to answer, but the faun up ahead rises from the grass, spots us and lets out a piercing shriek, bounding away on its long, springy legs.

"Jamie, get after it," Alariel sighs. "Shoot it if you have to – non-lethal, of course. Brach, go with him."

Glancing around for memorable landmarks, I hare off into the forest after the faun, pounding through bushes, between trees, jumping over babbling streams and clambering over mossy boulders. The faun is much faster than I thought it'd be, but I suppose this is its native environment after all.

"Hey!" I shout after it. "Stop! We're friendly!"

That doesn't work, so the next time I skid around onto something vaguely resembling a forest path, I summon my right-hand gun. Wasting valuable seconds checking that it's got a non-lethal magazine in it, I draw a bead on the rapidly receding faun and fire off a volley.

It goes down with a thud that makes me wince, quickly eroding my elation at actually hitting it, and I hurry to make sure that it's ok.

It's weird seeing one up close. This one – Dion, I should say – is wearing a faded black t-shirt, but no trousers, and has legs as hairy as a highland cow. I don't know how the others managed to conceal them in standard jeans; maybe they shave them? That said, it's even stranger seeing the two chunky goat's hooves where regular feet should be.

I'm a bit shaken, but I grit my teeth and roll him over to make sure that he's breathing. He doesn't seem to have hit anything hard on the way down, which is lucky – I'd rather not cause an inter-species incident on my first week on the job.

"You got him!" Brach cheers, limping up the path behind me. He's also discarded his shoes somewhere along the way and seems a bit more comfortable now.

"Uh, yeah," I reply. "Um, sorry for shooting your friend. He should wake up in a few hours."

"It's ok," Brach says happily. "It's no worse than what he's done to himself in the past. Here, let me take him."

Dion looks like a fairly heavy faun, but Brach scoops him up with little effort, lifting him onto one shoulder. "Come on, let's get back to the car park. I hope we'll have a new home soon. I do love the human world, but you people aren't very durable, if you know what I mean."

I'm not sure I do, and I'm not sure that I want to explore that concept any further, so I follow the bounding faun as he saunters along the forest path, babbling about his favourite tipples.

We arrive back in the clearing just as Alariel does, two of the fauns peeling off from the main group to come and help Brach with Dion. A little way up the path, where Alariel has tied off the police tape, Melusine is standing in a large silver pentacle, which seems to have been sprayed on the ground. The fauns are standing at the other five points of the star, and there's a low chanting going on, with an occasional flash of blue light.

"They're nearly done," Alariel says, and as if to prove him right, I feel, rather than hear something in the air coming to a crescendo, then closing off, as if a knot is being tied and tightened. There's a flash of silver light as a spark starts racing down the police tape, vanishing from view a second later. There's a pregnant pause where nobody moves, lengthening into a full minute before the spark races back towards us and disappears with another flash as it reaches the end.

I blink, and suddenly the police tape is gone. The feeling of expectancy in the air has completely dissipated, something in the air lightening, pressure lifting. Melusine looks around and nods approvingly.

"Well," she says. "That's done. Come on Jamie, let's go home."

"We could show you around?" Brach offers, the other fauns nodding. "This calls for a celebration!"

"No," Mel says firmly. "I've been to one of your celebrations before, thank you very much. And I don't remember much of 1896 for that exact reason."

Brach chitters with laughter, an unexpectedly high laugh for such a stocky, bearded creature.

"That was a good one," he says, lighting up a cigarette and tapping his fingers on a nearby tree trunk. "Although I never could stand the taste of vermouth after what Semele did with that poor human."

He takes two steps forward and vanishes, followed quickly by the other fauns, laughing gaily.

Alariel turns to face us. "I'll settle them in," he says. "Someone should."

Melusine nods knowingly. "Sure," she says. "See you in a few days, Al."

Wincing, he disappears into the new faery realm and we turn back to the car.

Chapter 13

I take a while trying to order my questions on the way back, finally tackling them as we navigate around Bath.

"What do you think he's up to?" I ask, and watch a slow smile spread across Melusine's face.

"You tell me," she says. "Spell it out."

"Well," I say, marshalling my ideas and hoping that I don't sound like a complete numpty. "He said that he agrees with you about Gaia, so he's backing you. He's clearly confident in his own court, so I'd imagine that he's fairly sure that whatever is causing the problems will get sorted out. So that leaves either an Unseelie problem or something closer to home. He seemed pretty dismissive of the Unseelie Court, so I'd say that he's worried about Lisilya. Maybe he's making a bolt hole in case she goes ballistic?"

"Very good," Melusine says, her withered face creasing in a broad smile. "Next."

"How do you create a faery realm?"

She laughs. "A fair question. The spell copies a portion of the human world and sends it into faery space, passing it through a gate – like the fireplace, or the space between the trees in the case of the Seelie Court."

"So, what we were doing with the police tape," I say hesitantly. "Was fencing off the part to be copied?"

"Exactly," Mel says. "You know, you might be getting a feel for this after all. What else is buzzing around in your head? I'm feeling generous."

"How do you think scientists found the Gaia site?" I ask, making her snort.

"No idea," she says briskly. "That's exactly why we're going. We're going to investigate and stop the Seelie Court from slaughtering the humans. Sooner or later, you people will realise that there's more to the world than what you can see, and it'll be sooner if there's fifty or so families who never see their loved ones again."

"Is Lisilya always so angry?"

Melusine shakes her head. "The Seelie Court are a prissy, constipated bunch," she says. "Entitled at the best of times. But she used to be a fair ruler – she's deteriorated quickly in the last hundred years. She needs to step down and let someone else take charge."

"But not Silvai?"

"She's even more bloodthirsty than Lisilya," Melusine sighs. "If she'd had her way, they'd have charged into the site at the first sign of trouble. And that might not have been a bad idea: humans shouldn't even have been able to get close. Charging in would have shed blood, but it might have uncovered something."

"But shed blood," I offer.

"Hmmm, yes."

"Then it's good that Alariel calmed things down," I say. "We can help, and we can avoid killing."

"He's got his own agenda," Melusine says distractedly. "And his agendas have their own agendas."

I think I'm out of questions, until something else occurs to me.

"What did you mean about Stonehenge, by the way?" I ask. "Have you and Alariel worked together before?"

She looks at me and rolls her eyes, then sighs again. "I suppose if I don't tell you, he probably will, and he'll do it to gain leverage," she says. "Yes. It was New Year's Eve in December 1999 and there were all kinds of faery hunters and doom-mongers gathering at sites like Glastonbury and Stonehenge. Alariel and I were there, keeping watch on the stones, because one set opens up into an elf realm, Lithiel, and although it's deserted, there was a small chance that someone would accidentally trigger the invocation. We were posing as relatives; he was my grandson, discovering alternative religions for the first time. Everyone was drunk and security was poor, so we were in the crowd posing as these … pagans."

I try to imagine her and the suave elf in a packed field of revellers. I fail.

"There was a man, a human man, with a bomb strapped to his chest, about to set it off a moment before midnight, and that would have meant re-setting and finding Lithiel again, months' worth of work and quite impossible in a tourist site like that. I had Alariel to bump into him, give him a tiny cut so that I could work magic, but I still needed a distraction. I charmed the two humans next to me to think that Alariel was some kind of celebrity, someone from Star Trek, they eventually believed, hence the pointy ears."

"An elf as a Vulcan?" I almost laugh.

"That was it," she says. "They called him Spork. Suddenly everyone was frenzied, asking for autographs, hoisting him on their shoulders and making him drink. I hurried and liquified the bomber before he could trip the explosives. It looked like someone had dropped a vest covered in milkshake. I took it and left Alariel to his adoring fans."

"Ugh," I manage, feeling a surge of sickness in my throat. In the same breath, this woman has just admitted to a horrific murder and saving the lives of a load of people. "What *are* you?"

She fixes me with a stare. "Complicated," she says, clacking her teeth together. "Now pay attention to the road."

I swear again and turn my attention back to the motorway, my brain trying – and failing – to make sense of what she's told me.

Twenty minutes later, we pull up outside Beckett's place, and I feel something like relief as Melusine gets out. She says something that I don't hear, so I turn off the engine and climb out, seeing Beckett open the door and greet her.

"Jamie," she says, looking impatient. "I need some time to prepare for the Unseelie Court. Take the morning off tomorrow, then meet me at my house after lunch."

"Ok," I say, feeling wrung out. "Sure."

"Still with me?" she asks acerbically.

"I'm just here for the money?" I manage, trying to sound glib and probably failing miserably.

"That's my boy."

She turns, waving dismissively and heads inside.

"Rough day?" Beckett says, and I notice the bags under his eyes.

"Not what I expected," I admit. "You ok?"

"Tired," he says, gesturing expansively. "Think I need a day off tomorrow as well."

"Take them when you can get 'em," I offer half-heartedly, and he nods.

I give him a wave and get back into the car, turning around carefully and heading for home.

That evening, I sit for a long time nursing the last of the whisky. I'd tried to distract myself with packing up the dining room, but I kept seeing that huge room at the top of the tree, the amphitheatre throne, the giant nature spirit.

So instead, once I've cleared up, I sit, mulling everything over. And it keeps coming back to one thing. Despite the intensity of the day, despite the cool reception in the Seelie Court, I'm annoyed at myself for not finding a way to ask if their magic could cure mum's cancer. But maybe if we can pull this off, I'll win their gratitude and be able to ask … what's it called? A boon? A favour? Although knowing what I know about the elves, I'm sure it wouldn't be that straightforward.

I sigh and put my whisky glass down on the table a little too firmly, because I'm not sure if I want to be part of the magic world either. It's grimy and unpleasant and just as bad as this one. It turns out that elves and fauns can be more annoying and difficult than even my flatmates back home.

Although … well, I don't know. They were hideous, but the troll and the stag thing in the woods the other day seemed pretty genuine. And Merovech … well, Merovech is clumsy and hilarious and kind, and suddenly I'm laughing just thinking about them.

I shake my head at how complicated things have become. Elves and goblins and witches are supposed to be straightforward. Good and bad, light and dark. Not this diplomatic messing around.

At least I'll be pretty well-off after this, what with Mel's money and the money from the house. Not that it really helps with finding any broader meaning in my life.

I stare at the whisky, feeling myself spiralling a little. Enough. Time for bed.

Of course, I dream that night and they're not good dreams. Isn't that weird? That I can meet a troll and a visceral stag-creature and it doesn't register – but a trip to elf land and I'm shaken. In my dreams, I'm being zapped by blue electricity coming from the fingers of an evil-looking elf woman. In another, I'm being smothered by a giant tree, grabbed by steely branches and dragged into the trunk. That one has me sat up in bed in a cold sweat.

When I wake up the next morning, birds singing in the trees and not a cloud in the sky, I feel like my head is full of cotton wool. I stumble into the shower, hurrying through my breakfast and making the strongest batch of coffee that I can.

It clears my head a little, but I'm glad that I'm not heading over to the Manor until lunchtime. I wander around the house listlessly, tossing the odd ornament into a box and looking at bare shelves. Thankfully, my phone rings, distracting me – it's the estate agent.

"Jamie," a crisp, business-like voice says at the other end of the line. "Cynthia Lockwood, Lockwood Estates."

I roll my eyes and manage a polite greeting.

"We have several viewing requests for this afternoon. Can you accommodate them?"

Shit. Not really.

"I've got an errand to run," I manage after a moment of mentally flailing around for an excuse. "Can I leave a key here, or drop one at your office?"

"Of course," she says. "I'll be driving the first set down from the office, so leave it with us whenever you can."

"Uh, thanks," I say. "Oh, Cynthia?"

"Yes?"

"Do I need to get rid of the furniture or anything here?"

"It's best to wait until you've got an offer," she says briskly. "Some first-time buyers will ask for the white goods, so it's down to individual negotiation. It's best not to remove any fitted wardrobes or bookshelves, but I would recommend disposing of small desks, individual chairs, that kind of thing."

"Ok, great," I say, thanking her and hanging up. I should sort that out. And I should probably make the bed as well.

I speed around the house in a frenzy of tidying, before hurrying out to the car and driving to the hospital in Bath. Mum's awake and seems to be doing much better than she was the other day. I can't tell if it's the medicine from Mel or if she's just having a good day, but I'll take what I can get. We talk, avoiding 'business' too much – she tells me about hospital life and her doctors, and I talk about my job.

I eventually drive back home, parking the car and dropping the house keys off with Cynthia's assistant, grabbing a sandwich from the local shop once I'm done.

"Jamie?" I look up from my ham and cheese sandwich and see a silver-haired woman walking down the lane towards me. It takes me a moment to place her.

"Mrs Jones!" I say, finally recognising the kindly woman who owns the antique store. "How are you?"

Brushing crumbs from my front and wondering where I can stash the other half of my sandwich, I give her a smile. She was always kind to me when I was a kid, even if I never really understood the appeal of antiques.

"Very well, thank you," she says. "I wasn't sure if it was you, but – well, you must have heard this a lot – I was so very sorry to hear about your mother. Can I ask … how is she?"

"Thank you," I say. I think I'm getting better at this. Acknowledging it doesn't bring tears to my eyes anymore, even if it also doesn't make it any easier. "I saw her this morning. She's, well, she's doing as well as can be expected."

"Please, send her my best if you can," she says. "She's a dear woman. Headstrong, but dear. And how are you? It can't be easy."

"It's been tough," I admit. "I've got to pack everything up, sell the house, a hundred and one things."

"You're selling the house?"

"Yeah, I think so," I admit. "I mean, I like the village a lot, but it's a heck of a commute. I'm not sure I could pay the rent in London and the bills down here, so I'm a bit stuck, you know?"

"Oh, that's sad," she offers. "We'll miss you and your family. I have such fond memories of seeing you and that Samantha girl running around. You always seemed like such happy children."

"Thanks," I say, honestly touched by the sentiment. "How's business?"

"Slow," she laughs. "But that's normal when you own an antique shop. Although mind you, I did have a few very strange emails the other day enquiring about certain items."

"Strange?" I ask, wondering if our definitions of strange are even vaguely similar. "How so?"

"Well, there were three of them, and I think they were from the same buyer. Interested in larger items, they were; an old statue, an antique mace and a rocking horse, although I don't know why they bothered – when I told them the prices, they never replied. What with the police trouble the other week, I don't know what's going on in this place."

"Police trouble?"

"Oh Sergeant Michaelson likes to keep everything under wraps," she says, leaning in conspiratorially. "I wouldn't know about it if I hadn't heard him on the phone, but it sounded like something had been smuggled here and the police had lost track of it entirely. Horses, I reckon."

"Horses?"

"Mmmm, fetch a lot of money a stallion does," she burbles. "Especially if it's a good breed; put it out to stud and it'll pay its own way. You only need to cut a fence and coax a few out and you've made thousands of pounds."

"Wow," I say. "I had no idea."

"No, well, I could be wrong," she says. "But it'll be the talk of the pub for weeks. Nice seeing you, Jamie."

I give her a wave as she totters off down the road, before fishing the remains of my sandwich from my pocket and peering at it. I think it's more or less ok, so I set off down the lane the other way while I'm eating.

A slightly ragged-looking Beckett lets me into his bungalow after a bit of a wait. He's covered in thatch, so I figure he's just finished V's house.

"No more thatch?" I ask, raising my eyebrows at him.

"Not for another forty years," he says, sounding relieved. "Uh, if you'll excuse me Jamie, I have thatch everywhere ... and I really mean everywhere. There's a bath with my name on it."

"Go, go," I wave him away down the hall laughing, and pass into the kitchen, letting myself through the fireplace into the forest.

I get the strange feeling of unease again as I walk down the main track. There's not a cloud in the sky, and it's perfectly still, but I can hear the leaves in the trees rustling. I must be hearing things, because it even *sounds* nervous to me, and that's not really something I've ever connected to forests before.

I pause and look around. It's the same woody vista, oak trees stretching out their low, leafy branches, a myriad of green shoots and plants poking up through the soil. Even the rotting leaf litter smells great. It could stretch forever for all I know – and given that Mel said you could keep walking and get back to the same spot, maybe it kind of does.

Tentatively, I take a step off the path and lay my hand on the nearest trunk, whipping it away quickly as I swear I hear a low vibration in my head. Dammit, that was weird. My heart hammers in my chest and I look around, wondering if it's a trap of some kind, if the tree is about to crash down and scoop me into its trunk, like in my dream.

Nothing happens.

I'm being ridiculous. Cautiously, I put my hand back against the trunk and hear the low sound again, like a car engine softly revving. Strange. Again, nothing happens, so I take my hand away and head down the track towards Mel's place.

I arrive to find her at her table, bent over the Bunsen burner, which is heating a glass container that then drips into another attached container. An alembic, that's it.

"Good," she says, looking up at me. "There are a few things you need to know before we go to the Unseelie Court tomorrow."

I sit on the stool at the table and try to look attentive. Melusine raises a crooked eyebrow at me, but then continues.

"First – we can't go directly there. Since they were cast out, the Unseelie have become excessively paranoid, so we have to go through a limbo realm. The Unseelie are more numerous and violent than the Seelie – and they respect strength, so don't be afraid to shoot anything. But above all, do not stare. They may seem hideous to you, but we need their help."

"Got it," I say. "Limbo realm. Shoot first, don't stare. Hey, what's a limbo realm?"

"Imagine a tunnel between underground stations," she says patiently. Well, I think there's some barely concealed irritation there, but for her, that's patience. "If your world is one station and theirs is the next. Only bigger and more labyrinthine."

"Right," I say. "Sure. Anything I should know about the limbo realm? And also how do I know if I'm shooting something or someone important?"

"Just follow my lead," Mel says, sounding a bit tired. "And unless you're shooting Balthamel himself, you'll be fine. Before you ask, he's a giant."

"No problem," I say, a host of questions multiplying like rabbits in my head, but – perhaps thankfully for Melusine – there's a knock at the door.

"Melusine, Jamie," Merovech's voice calls through the wood. "Can you help me with something?"

Melusine flicks her head at me and I open the door for the little inventor, who has a large sack slung over their shoulder.

"Hey," I say. "How you doing?"

"Oh, I'm great, thank you!" Merovech laughs. "I've finally finished my inventions and they even recognise friends from foes!"

"The ... scorpions?" I manage, still not entirely sure

how the bumbling mechanic has been creating killing machines.

"Yes! They're wonderful! They're quiet, and can take all kinds of armaments, and the clockwork almost never runs down! They should be great at stopping Ypotryll from ruining the roof again, although I'm sure it didn't know better."

Melusine stares. "So how can we help?"

"Well," Merovech says hesitantly. "I was hoping you'd be able to destroy one for me. You know, I've given Beckett a control key but you always say never build something you can't unbuild, and they seem quite resistant to magic and weapons so far. I built them to be sturdy, you see!"

"Sturdy, silent killing machines?" I say.

"Well, deterrents," Merovech says. "Although they could kill things. You know, like Lisilya? I don't like her at all."

"You know, buddy, I'm starting to agree with you."

Melusine rolls her eyes. "Jamie, why don't you take this one? Try a few of each round – I doubt that the hollow points will do anything, but start with the standard rounds, the APs and then the explosives. Then you and Merovech can find out what it'd take to dismantle them."

"Oh, would you? Thank you!" Merovech giggles with glee. "Come on, come on!"

We head outside and they set down their bag close to the edge of the forest, taking a scorpion out of it and placing the large contraption on the grass.

"Now, I've deactivated it, and the switch is underneath the belly, so it's not easy to turn off that way. Try shooting it?"

"Uh, V?" I ask. "Why didn't you build in an override or something if you're worried about these things going rogue?"

"Oh, it's very unlikely," V says with a broad grin. "And that's what the control switch does. But Melusine made me promise that I'd never make anything indestructible, so I always make an extra model that we can test together. And having you around will make that so much easier! Did I already say thank you?"

"Seriously, don't worry about it," I say, muttering *gun dexter* and trying not to be disconcerted as the firearm grows organically out of my hand.

"Oh, they work so well!" Merovech laughs again. "Do you like them? Should we have painted them a nice colour? Like bronze or copper?"

"They're fine, thank you," I say, swapping the magazine and aiming at the scorpion thing. "Are you one hundred percent sure about this? I feel kind of bad shooting at something you invented, you know."

"It's ok," V says, laying one hand on my arm sympathetically. "It's sad. But Melusine has our best interests at heart. Also, it's much better if you shoot them with a gun than if I use a crossbow, or Melusine disembowels a rabbit and uses its blood to make a hundred tiny needles that travel really fast."

"That's ... horrible," I say, swallowing hard.

"I know!" Merovech says. "The crossbow is so heavy and hard to draw, even if I use the boot strap to pull it back. Sometimes it hurts my foot!"

"Uh, sorry?" I say. "Look, never mind, let's just test this, ok?"

Not wanting to get drawn into any more conversation, I aim at the scorpion and try to persuade myself that it's just like the pinecone the other day. Slowly, I squeeze the trigger and there's a loud bang that makes me jump, then a clang and a whine as the bullet ricochets off into the trees. The scorpion is faintly marked, but otherwise seems unharmed.

"Never mind!" Merovech says. "Try the armour-piercing rounds, I like them!"

I unload the magazine and slot in a gold-coloured one, taking aim again and firing. There's another loud bang, and the gun jerks more in my hand – I need to lean forwards a bit. I peer at the scorpion, but despite some charring and a slight dent, it seems quite intact.

"V, what makes an armour-piercing round armour-piercing?" I ask, feeling a bit less awkward asking the bubbly inventor than Mel.

"Oh, they're wonderful!" Merovech chunters happily. "These ones are depleted uranium! Alizon found some deep underwater once – it was poisoning the sea, you see – and she was going to give it back to the humans, but Mel thought of a much better use for it. It's so dense, it's amazing – and sometimes it bursts into flame in mid-air, can you believe that?"

I shake my head, not really wanting to ask about how that had played out.

"Ok, third time lucky," I say, ejecting the magazine and laying it on the ground back by the house. I'm not entirely sure I want anything made of uranium, depleted or otherwise, in my pocket. I slot in the black explosive rounds, even more uncertain about these.

"And, uh, just how explosive are these rounds?"

"Hmmm," V says, rubbing their chin thoughtfully. "Less than a wad of C4, but probably about the same as a breach kit. Still, try aiming between the cogs?"

I don't think I want to know when Melusine and Merovech were playing with C4 and ... whatever a breach kit is.

But still, I find myself aiming more carefully at the metal beastie, trying to lean forwards a little and then squeezing the trigger slowly and steadily.

The first bang is less pronounced – or maybe I've deafened myself a little – but the next, a fraction of a second later, is incredibly loud, making me jump, and is accompanied by a crashing, jangling noise as a large part of the scorpion's chassis tears itself apart and flies off. Part of it embeds itself in a nearby tree. There's a lot of smoke and an acrid smell in the air.

Merovech laughs, claps and does a little dance on the spot. "Oh, wonderful!" they exclaim as I cough and realise that we probably should have put the scorpion a bit further away from us. "That's marvellous. A few of those would definitely stop one. Thank you Jamie, that's brilliant!"

They canter over to their creation and briefly touch it, jerking their finger away suddenly.

"Oh! Hot!" V exclaims, sucking on the burnt finger. "I think I'll leave this here for a bit to cool and let Melusine know."

Just then, the door opens behind us and Mel pokes her head around it.

"Are you quite finished?" she says acerbically.

"Yes, thank you so much!" Merovech babbles. "The explosive rounds were perfect."

"Great," she says. "Come in, I need to talk to you. Jamie, meet me at the station at eight AM sharp tomorrow. Don't be late. We're going to the Unseelie Court."

Chapter 14

The next morning, Melusine is waiting for me at the station, still looking vaguely annoyed and still – as far as I can tell – in the same clothes that she wore yesterday.

I greet her with a nod and a grunt, and she hands me a pair of tickets for the next train to London. I hurry over to the small newsagent and buy a bottle of water and a chocolate bar, tucking them into the small rucksack I've brought with me.

"Come on," she says. "It's almost time."

It's early and we're travelling first class, so the carriage is relatively empty – and it's just as well, because Melusine gets a couple of stares from kids as we pass through the train. She scowls at them, parents instinctively drawing their children closer as she walks past.

We find a set of four seats with a table in the middle, and Melusine pulls a huge leather-bound tome from her bag, dust flying everywhere as she drops it on the table. I sneeze, but try not to say anything as she reads, muttering under her breath.

I half expect an incident as she gives death stares to both the ticket inspector and the man pushing the tea trolley. I try to apologise on her behalf, but they're both halfway down the carriage before I can get a word out. I've never seen a drinks trolley move that fast and honestly, I was kind of hoping for a coffee.

"Freaky white-haired kid and his creepy fucking grandma," I hear the refreshments guy say as he retreats.

Suddenly I don't fancy that coffee after all.

Thankfully, Mel is too absorbed in her book to notice, and stays that way for the rest of the journey.

I almost lose her in the crowd at Paddington, a train arriving alongside ours and disgorging a barrage of tourists that threatens to separate us. Thankfully, although she's not tall, her hair – still complete with small sticks, bone charms and things that might be hairpins or small daggers at a push – provides a handy reference point.

She pauses after the ticket barriers, glancing around before heading in the direction of the underground, before surging forwards and zipping through the gate line with remarkable alacrity. I thank my lucky stars that some of the Bakerloo line trains start at this station, and, more to the point, that there's one in the platform as we arrive.

Mel takes an end seat, and I wedge myself next to her, trying to form some kind of protective bubble for the other people getting on the train. She does scowl at a few of the other occupants of the carriage, but then seems to lose herself in her huge spell book or whatever it is. There's also what seems to be a stag party at the other end of the train, which is proving to be a useful distraction to the rest of the tube.

I never thought that I'd be grateful for a crowd of obnoxious, slightly drunken lads on a train, but there you go.

I hope they don't come down here.

I hope I don't *know* any of them.

I feel slightly sick with relief as we get off at Waterloo, Mel hurrying through the corridors with a speed that speaks of long familiarity. Shit, she knows this place better than I do, and I practically *live* here.

I don't really understand why she's in such a hurry but I scamper to keep up with her as she trips down the stairs not far from the London Eye, taking a right down Leake St, the dingy underpass street full of graffiti.

"Come on," she hisses, looking back at me and making a few spray paint artists jump at the sight of her. "Hurry up."

I catch up with her and she glances around, darting over towards a locked gate that looks like it leads into an underground car park. She pushes against it and it creaks open, the lock and chain unspooling noisily.

I join her on the other side and she closes it behind us, hurrying on. I glance back and the chain … well, it's definitely wrapped around both parts of the gate, firmly locked. I make a mental note to ask Mel about this kind of magic on the way back, assuming that she's in a better mood by then and that we're still alive.

The road curves downwards, and I wonder how far we're going to go. But a short way down, Mel pauses at what looks like a fire door and taps it twice, then rummages in her bag, emerging with a small phial of what looks like blood. Splashing some on the door, she runs one long fingernail around it, the scraping noise making me shudder. She briefly shapes a symbol with it, the rest of the blood dripping down onto the concrete.

The symbol glows briefly, and something clicks.

"Through here," Melusine says, pushing the door open. I strain my eyes trying to make anything out in the darkness beyond, but it's pitch black. Mel vanishes through, and rather than risk being stranded on the wrong side of a locked gate, I swallow, steel myself and hurry after her.

I don't feel quite the same sense of dislocation that I get from Beckett's fireplace, but I definitely feel something as I pass through the door. A change in the air maybe.

Wherever we are, it's dustier and smells old, like the antique shop in the village. As the door closes behind me, my eyes start to adjust and I peer into the gloom, making out a few details here and there.

My first impression of the limbo realm is that it's huge. It's like the entrance hall in the Natural History Museum, that vast, high, brown and grey brick hall with the impressive arches, but it's been crossed with the long underground passage that you walk through from South Kensington station on the way, but much, much bigger. Faded brickwork and rusty metal girders are mashed together with once-elegant murals, too faint to make out, all combined in a sprawling jumbled hall.

The space is interspersed with curling spiral staircases and balconies around the sides of the room. Light shines down from small skylights, illuminating dust trails in the air. Mis-matched stained-glass windows seem to be illuminated by sunlight, but I swear that we're underground. It's mostly empty, dusty space, the floor littered with rubble; rocks, sand, pipes, things that might be old chests of drawers, even the top of what looks like a car. It feels like things have fallen through the cracks and just started rotting here. It's kind of incredible, and the sort of thing that I could never do justice to, even with the best camera in the world.

I wonder if I could bring Flic here?

"When London was built," Melusine says, quietly interrupting my train of thought, but actually letting me look around for once. "They often built on top of other structures. Sometimes those structures sunk and fell through into limbo; basements and ground floors coming to rest somewhere else. This is where they ended up."

There are faint scurrying sounds coming from all around us, a quiet but restless, ceaseless noise. Shadows move in the distance, but I can't make them out.

"Come on," she says. "We're not there yet. *Illuminae*."

On her last word, a bright, football-sized ball of light appears, pulsing in the darkness. A will-o-the-wisp, I guess.

"This way," she says. "And Jamie – best be armed. We haven't technically been invited."

Turning up to the home of the bad faeries unannounced? Doesn't sound like the best idea to me, but I take a deep breath and focus on following her through the gloom.

I whisper the incantations summoning my faery guns, momentarily feeling reassured by their weight and heft, trying not to think about how I've only really shot pinecones and a drunk goat-man up until now.

I realise that I'm missing something, so as inconspicuously as I can I eject the explosive rounds from both guns and replace them with the regular silenced ones; I'm guessing we don't want to announce our presence here if we don't have to. Thankfully, Melusine seems too intent on the path ahead to notice, or more likely, doesn't think it merits a scathing remark.

We pad up a dusty set of stairs that wouldn't disgrace a mansion, before Melusine leads us down along a balcony to another set of steps, smaller this time. Halfway up, there's a gap, and I glance down at the floor maybe fifteen feet below. It looks like a boulder fell from somewhere further up and took a chunk of the stairs with it. Melusine frowns at it and I look around, noticing a dusty old tapestry hung on the wall, so obscured by dirt and grime that I can't make out what's on it. The light floating alongside us doesn't help either, and Melusine makes a gesture, sending it up to the gap in the stone steps.

"We'll have to find another way around," she says.

"Or I could fix it for you?" a deep voice says, and a burly minotaur somehow pulls back the tapestry and steps out from behind it. It's huge.

It's got faded blue jeans on, although its torso is bare and rippling with muscle. But obviously, it's the huge bull's head – horns and all – that really makes this thing terrifying. Not to mention the ease with which it surprised us, although I have somehow managed to pivot and am currently pointing both my guns at it.

Melusine sees it and sighs.

"Hello Drogon," she says. "Is this your doing? I can't imagine that Balthamel would be best pleased to find a route from his domain to the human realm impassable."

And then the minotaur actually flinches. It's a little over six feet high, not counting the horns, incredibly solid and muscular, but it definitely flinches when Mel mentions Balthamel.

"Balthamel has other things on his mind," Drogon says, his voice deep and rumbling. "He's more interested in securing the realm than in one entrance to the limbo."

"Securing?" Melusine says archly. "What information do you have for me? Spit it out."

The minotaur stares at her, implacable.

"Oh fine," she says, rummaging in her bag and bringing out a small velvet pouch that jangles. "Gold?"

Drogon nods minutely and she tosses it to him. He peers into it, then steps over to her and leans against the balustrade.

"Jamie," Melusine says. "Keep your eyes open. Shoot anything that moves."

Drogon lets out a huff of laughter and then bends over to the witch, talking quietly. I catch the occasional hiss of an 's', but otherwise it's amazing how quietly such a huge creature can speak.

I pace back along the balcony, letting my eyes wander around the hall; shadows are still moving around on the far side, but there's nothing coming this way, as far as I can tell. I head back to the steps and use one gun to lift up the tapestry that Drogon seemed to emerge from. It's blank brick behind it, no joins, no hinges, nothing. I'm going to guard fuck all if the Unseelie can walk through walls like this, assuming that the minotaur counts as Unseelie.

Melusine and Drogon are still whispering to each other, so I turn back and look down the balcony, just in time to see one long, jointed leg stretching around the corner of the balcony at the bottom of the stairs. It's about two feet long, and looks a lot like a spider's leg, a suspicion which is confirmed when another leg creeps into view, and another, before a large black body slides around the corner.

It's about the size of a 'stop' sign, an analogy that comes to mind because it's also got a bright red stripe across its body. Multi-faceted violet compound eyes stare at me, daring me to move, and a fanged mouth drips some kind of grey slime onto the floor, which steams slightly as it lands.

Trembling, I raise my hands and send six silenced rounds into its body, dropping it to the floor, legs twitching, blood leaking onto the dusty stone. I'm breathing hard, my heart pounding, and I glance back at Melusine, who has stopped talking to Drogon and is regarding me with something vaguely resembling amusement.

"Ready?" she says, and I nod, lowering my shaking hands. My mouth is suddenly dry and I wish I'd brought some water.

"Well, thank you Drogon," she says. "You've been unexpectedly useful."

"My pleasure," he rumbles. "One moment more, if you would."

The big creature steps back behind the tapestry for a few seconds and reappears with a hammer and a large plank, which he lays across the gap in the stairs, before bashing a nail through it – seemingly into the stone below. He repeats this process on the other side, completely unfazed by walking across such a tiny, unsecured bridge.

Stepping back and straightening up, he admires his handiwork, then gestures expansively for us to cross. Melusine sniggers and hops onto the plank, also unconcerned by the drop and the makeshift nature of the bridge. She crosses easily, and I follow hesitantly, but the plank seems pretty sturdy. It doesn't even creak when I step on it, although I'm glad to reach the safety of the stone beyond.

I turn and nod to the minotaur, who inclines his head slightly in return. "Safe trip," he grunts, leaning back against the stonework and staring at the corpse of the huge spider further down the balcony.

I hurriedly follow Melusine up the next set of stairs, almost losing her as she takes a small, claustrophobic passageway left and turns right at a T-junction; if I hadn't heard her shuffling footsteps ahead, I might have been wandering around this place for days.

The passageways are dry and dusty, and smell like an old, abandoned building site. Thankfully, the passageway turns again and reaches a broad tunnel with a channel running down the middle. The roof is a high arch, pipes running alongside each wall. It looks like a large sewer, although I've never been in an actual sewer before. The water smells a bit faecal and I really hope we don't have to stay here too long – it's kind of making me want to gag.

Melusine pauses a way down to the right, stretching and looking around, her bones cracking. She mumbles something that sounds like a moan about being old, but I don't quite catch it.

"You know, for someone who doesn't get out very much, you do seem to know everyone in faeryland," I say, and she snorts at me.

"Comes of being old," she says croakily. "People come by for herbs or a spell. You visit them for a component or two. A few trips a year add up after a couple of centuries."

She looks around and heads down the sewer a little, then pauses. I stay put in case she comes back again – she doesn't really seem to know where she is.

I hear another crack and look at Melusine, but she hasn't moved. In fact, I don't think it was coming from that way. I spin around and look down the sewer to the left. There's something moving. I stare and try to make it out; I think it's more of those spidery things. I can just about see red stripes and segmented legs.

"Melusine," I say, readying my guns, and I hear her coming back towards me slowly. Three spiders scuttle out of the darkness, then three more behind them. I aim and squeeze the trigger, hitting the first one with a volley, and it collapses down in a heap, making the other two pause. One of them leans in towards its bleeding carcass, almost as if it's sniffing. Do spiders have noses? I have no idea.

As I aim at the second one, I see another pair of eyes – yellow this time – getting closer in the darkness. They're higher up; something taller? I try to ignore it, firing at the second spider, then the third, taking them both down, but the second trio is not too far away now.

Then I hear Melusine murmuring next to me as I'm squinting at the next set of arachnids. Their large, red-striped bodies flex as they move faster towards us, making me shudder. They've got some kind of fur or hair on them, and it ripples, the stripes almost pulsating. Melusine's murmuring becomes a chant, and before I can open fire on them, all three burst open like over-ripe melons, spraying blood everywhere, chunks of flesh hitting the walls with a sickening series of splats.

"Shit!" I blurt out, staring at the carnage.

A large figure steps out from the darkness behind what's left of the spiders. At first, I think it's Drogon again; it's got almost human-like feet and legs dressed roughly in torn jeans, but has a bare chest that's much hairier … furrier, really. However, it's the wolf's head, with gleaming yellow eyes, long muzzle and fangs that make it truly alien. It doesn't look armed, but then I notice long claws on its human hands.

"Werewolf," I breathe.

Melusine hasn't stopped chanting, and somehow the blood from the spiders is moving, slowly at first, then gathering in runnels, streams forming into long lines of red fluid.

The blood rises up, the werewolf freezing in place and staring at the three red rods, which suddenly dart forwards with tremendous speed and impale it right through the chest, almost tearing it in half. It falls backwards into the water without a sound, the blood spears dissolving almost instantly, the corpse slowly starting to wash away down the stream.

"Christ," I swear softly, unable to tear my eyes away.

"Come on," Melusine says. "Werewolves usually hunt alone with their spiders, but the noise might attract some attention. The Unseelie Court isn't far."

"That was…"

"Flesh and blood," she says. "I told you."

And with that, she turns the other way down the sewer and starts shuffling away from the corpses. Giving the shattered and bleeding bodies one more look, I scurry after her, shivering and definitely feeling like I'm going to throw up. Probably not a great first impression to make on royalty, right?

I clamp my mouth shut and hurry on.

The small corridors we follow from the sewer feel somehow restrictive, and I can't help but keep checking over my shoulder every few moments in case there's another giant spider or werewolf following us.

After another short trip down an almost identical-looking sewer, we arrive in what seems to be an old boiler room, a tangle of pipes, gauges and a large pressure door in one corner. I can't see a boiler, but it looks like a lot of water – or some other fluid – arrives or leaves here. There's only one flickering electric light on the wall, and it's not very bright, further adding to my feeling of unease.

"So, in here?" I say, gesturing to Melusine, who has stopped in the middle of the room. She looks irritable and shakes her head in annoyance.

"Only if you want to visit the spider queen," she says. "Be my guest."

I shiver, glancing back down the corridor towards the sewer, feeling even more enclosed in this room. Melusine finally seems to make up her mind and draws a long dagger from somewhere in her bag, dragging it up the brick wall. It makes a hideous scraping noise, mortar and brick dust cascading around her, but she repeats the process about two feet to the right, then makes a horizontal line at just above head height.

"Not easy to hack into the Unseelie Court," she says. "Even if this is technically an entrance. Well, an old one."

She presses a bundle of twigs and feathers against the brick. Something trembles and the brick itself seems to ripple, then the entire section of wall slides left on top of itself, leaving an open, inky-black space in front of us.

"Come on," she says. "Reload those guns and let's go."

Embarrassed, I eject the magazines and swap in fresh silenced rounds. I'm feeling much more uneasy about this than the Seelie Court.

Melusine doesn't leave me any time to think about it, vanishing through the wall into the darkness beyond. Reluctant though I am to go on, I'm even less enthusiastic about staying here on my own, and despite the rising sick feeling in my throat, I follow her.

The darkness is almost absolute for a moment. I have a swift moment of intense vertigo, as if I've run through the fireplace in Beckett's hut rather than walked, like a hook attached to my chest is pulling me down and through something. Then it reverses, and I feel like everything is growing rather than shrinking, and I almost bump into Melusine from behind.

I don't quite know what I was expecting from the Unseelie realm; dark elves, goblins, maybe an orc? Certainly not a creepy-looking girl in a hooded cloak, holding a skeleton's hand.

But that's what we get.

Chapter 15

"Melusine," the little girl says in a high-pitched voice. "You're not welcome here."

Despite having shot a bunch of giant spiders and seen a werewolf getting explosively disembowelled – not to mention getting some genuine boy scout-style assistance from a minotaur, this is hands down the creepiest thing I've seen today. I can make out a pair of red lips, a nose and a chin underneath the folds of the deep blue hood, but otherwise the cloak hides almost everything.

Neither of them have moved yet, so I'm not quite sure whether the skeleton is real – it looks like it could be a doctor's model. It's certainly clean enough; no flesh hanging off the bones, but every bone completely visible. Although now that I look, its head is slightly to one side, giving it a slightly jaunty look.

Great. Just what I need. The jaunty undead.

I glance around nervously; we're in a similar-sized

room to the last one. There isn't a lot here at all; four bare brick walls, an old filament bulb dimly lighting the room, a pile of bricks in the corner and a lot of dust on the concrete floor. There's a doorway in the wall behind the creepy duo.

Melusine sighs.

"I need to speak with him," she croaks, the dust in the corner of the room swirling around in a breeze that doesn't reach anywhere else. "Immediately."

"I think the naughty witch needs to be taught a lesson," the girl says in her singsong voice. Knowing that it probably won't do any good, I still raise my guns and point them at the girl.

"You heard her," I say, trying to sound imposing. "We're not here to cause trouble."

Melusine looks at me, amused.

"Jamie West," the girl says, still not moving. "Son of David and Tanya. Resident of Clapham, London. Recent addition to the faery world."

"What?" I manage, my arms dropping to my sides. How does she know that?

Then I hear footsteps from outside and an elf walks into the room, pausing next to the skeleton and looking at us. The black leather of its trousers and jacket makes its ashen-white skin even starker, the dim light of the bare bulb shiny on its bald head. A long, jagged sword in its hand completes the picture.

I'm going to assume this is a dark elf, although the moniker hardly seems fitting. I make another mental note to ask Mel, although remembering how she feels about categorisation, I file it under 'things to ask on a good day'.

"Kiriel," he sighs in a deep, weary voice. "Stop playing with the visitors. I know they broke in, but you obviously know who this is, so unless you want your flesh decorating Mr Chops' bones, let's take them where they want to go."

The little girl stamps her foot and glares at the new visitor.

"Dakyid," Melusine purrs. "How good to make your acquaintance again."

"Melusine," he says, nodding to her. "As much as I often find myself actually enjoying your company, your presence usually implies impending disaster, so I'm sure you'll excuse me if I'm not chatty."

Melusine inclines her head.

"Are we good here?" I ask, a little more hesitantly this time.

"We were good *before* you arrived," Kiriel says, glaring at me. "And I doubt that *you* are."

Dakyid looks at the creepy necromancer tiredly. "Seriously?"

She scoffs and looks up at her skeleton. "Come on, Mr Chops. Let's go."

And with a final caustic look at Melusine, she vanishes back down the corridor, the skeleton following her jerkily, its bones clattering together in a hollow fashion. Feeling a little safer, I banish my guns and stick my hands in my pockets instead, feeling a bit awkward.

"You could have just knocked," the pale-skinned elf says, looking over at Melusine. "And avoided Kiriel's domain. She's becoming more tiresome every decade, I'm certain of it."

"Balthamel made it abundantly clear that the doors to the Unseelie Court would remain barred for at least another hundred years," Melusine says. "And he can be very literal sometimes."

Dakyid sighs again, sheathing his sword in an ornate black scabbard lined with gold patterns. "Right now, Balthamel would have a threesome with a gorgon and a skinwalker if it'd add arms to his defence effort. He's about 24 hours away from permanently locking the direct gate from the Unseelie to the human world and moving everyone to a triple lock."

Melusine nods, straightening her spine, which makes a creaking sound. "It's worse than I thought, but not by a lot. And that's what we're here to help with."

"Then we'd best be on our way," he says. "And mind yourself. Kiriel usually leaves at least one or two traps around. Watch your feet and stay away from the walls."

We both follow as the bald, leather-clad elf turns on his heel and starts walking out of the room, down a small corridor and then into a large, brick chamber with four glass tanks on either side, each bubbling with some kind of clear fluid. Every tank is a little larger than man-sized and has a different kind of skeleton inside, each more bizarre than the next. The first almost looks like there could be a human skeleton inside, except for the horned cow's head that sits atop it, whereas the second seems to be a gorilla skeleton with a sabre-toothed tiger's head on top, fangs coming down to almost the bottom of its rib cage.

"Mind that," Dakyid says mildly, pointing at the floor and interrupting my scrutiny of these monstrosities. I freeze, seeing a rusted steel mantrap sitting there on the floor a way ahead of us, jaws and fragile-looking pressure plate ready to do some serious damage. What kind of a lab is this?

The third and fourth tanks on the right-hand side are both humanoid, except that one has exceptionally long arms, finger bones brushing the floor, and the last has stubs of wings on its back and the head of a large cat-like creature. Each tank is tended by a tall figure in long robes similar to Kiriel's, except that they're adult-sized. They seem to be singing softly to the tanks as they adjust gauges on the side, new fluid occasionally dripping in through a pipe at the top.

I sidestep the mantrap and decide to focus purely on watching my feet so I can try to keep all of my limbs intact. The magical cancer drug for mum had better be worth it. Then again, she's probably not the one that has to worry about keeping safe right now.

Dakyid leads us out of the chamber into a broader hallway with tapestries at intervals.

"I assume that little experiment is Kiriel's domain?" Melusine says archly.

"Mmm," Dakyid says. "Can't say I'm a fan of the undead, but you'd know more about that than me."

"Flesh and blood," Melusine hisses. "Not bone."

It's not often that I've seen her riled, and I deliberately slow my pace to stay a little further behind.

"My apologies," Dakyid replies contritely, although I sense a little wry humour in his words. "I so rarely pay attention to such details."

"Of course," she says smoothly recovering. "Jamie, mind the walls."

I jump, stupidly getting closer to the right-hand wall rather than staying dead centre, which would have been the sensible thing to do. Pushing their way out of the brickwork between the tapestries are a host of arms, seemingly fashioned from some bone-white material, hands grasping for us. I shudder and take a step back towards the middle of the corridor.

"Kiriel has become most inventive," Dakyid says, sighing again. "Balthamel allows her more and more latitude every day, raising this army of hers."

"Hmmm," Melusine mutters. "Paranoia?"

Dakyid skids to a halt and peers at her. "Only the brave would say it to his face, but yes, something like that."

"A dark elf advising caution?" Melusine cackles. "This day was worth the trouble after all."

"I'd advise *more* caution if you want to leave here in one piece," he says amicably.

"Ha!" she crows. "I'd been through a hundred wars,

dismembered worse than those pretties in Kiriel's vanity lab before you were even sucking on your mother's titties."

Dakyid falls silent, and gestures for us to turn down another broad corridor, set with large alcoves. It's loud with chattering and noise, and as we walk, I spy soldiers of all shapes and sizes inside the alcoves. They're loading guns, honing ugly-looking swords, checking the buckles on suits of armour and leafing through spell books.

The residents of the alcoves are closer to what I expected; more ashen-skinned elves like Dakyid and sturdy-looking orcs with stubby teeth reaching up from the corners of their mouths. There are smaller orcs with wicked-looking daggers – goblins, I guess – as well as a few more fiendish-looking creatures; almost skeletally-thin humanoids with teeth like needles and glowing red eyes. There's a half-horse creature that really gives me the willies; it's got the torso and upper legs of a human, but the hooves and head of a horse. Its human hands end with claws that look freshly bloodied, and its wild, staring eyes put it firmly on my list of things to avoid spending time with in the future.

But for some reason, it's the occupant of the final alcove before an impressive set of steel-inlaid doors that scares me the most. At first, I think it's just a woman in flowing white robes and wonder if it's another elf. I can't quite place what's odd about her, but I feel terribly uneasy being nearby. She looks up, her eyes pure white orbs and I really, really want to be somewhere else.

Before either of us can speak, I look back at Melusine, wondering – not for the first time – if I'm going to get out of this alive. Then the doors swing open and I find myself staring at the throne room of the Unseelie Court.

It's set out like a huge feasting hall, concrete pillars reaching up towards the ceiling, all carved with ornate symbols. In the centre of the room is a long table, a host of creatures sat on either side, eating, drinking and arming themselves. It's noisy, hot and smells of meat and damp air.

I'm half expecting it to fall silent as we enter, but no-one even looks around. A pair of Unseelie elf guards flank us as Dakyid leads us along the length of the table and at first, I wonder if my eyes are going a bit, because things seem to be a bit out of proportion. Then, no, I realise, there really is a giant sitting at the top of the table.

Oddly – because I've only really imagined giants as messy, ugly creatures in loincloths – Balthamel is immaculately dressed. He almost manages to look dapper, in a suit and long trench coat that could have come from a store on Regent Street if human tailors made clothes for people nine feet tall. He's got a kindly-looking face, brown hair swept back into a tidy ponytail, and seems to be deep in conversation with another one of those creepy-looking women with the pure white eyes.

Dakyid coughs politely as we arrive at the head of the table. This earns a glare from the dark elf on the other side, who is in the middle of breaking down and cleaning some kind of assault rifle, if assault rifles also had tens of copper cogs and strange chunks of black rock in them.

The giant falls silent and slowly looks over at Dakyid, seeing us.

"Melusine," he rumbles, fixing us both with a thoughtful look. "Kiriel said that you'd arrived. I thought I told you to stay away for a hundred years."

She returns his gaze evenly. "My apologies, Balthamel," she says calmly. "I thought the prevention of a war between the Seelie and Unseelie merited a short trip."

Then the hall does fall completely silent, every wickedly armed elf, orc and creature staring up the table at the two of us. There's a terrifying silence where I wonder which one is going to tear me limb from limb first, but then it's broken by the sound of an infant crying. I look around as a female dark elf in a long cloak hurries across the room carrying a small bundle in her arms, which squirms and cries. She rocks it back and forth and mouths an apology, dropping a brief curtsy as she darts from the room looking embarrassed.

"Speak," Balthamel says deeply. "And remember that we know truth when we hear it. The Seelie are readying for battle, we know this for a fact. What else demands arming themselves on such a scale other than crushing those they have despised for generations?"

Melusine sighs. "Gaia," she says. "Not the Unseelie. There is something wrong with the earth spirit and I mean to find out what. The Seelie were all set to storm the nearest Gaia site, which is teeming with humans, apparently."

"Humans?" Balthamel muses. "Hmmm. That seems ... unlikely. Are you sure Lisilya wasn't toying with you? You can be so stubborn when you get set on an idea."

"Gaia is sick," Melusine says tiredly. "You might not notice it, this far underground, but the earth withers. Magic weakens and the boundaries between realms shimmer and fade. It's no apocalypse, but we need to do something. The Seelie have lent me their support and will wait before launching an attack. Can you do the same?"

The white-eyed woman leans over to the giant and whispers something. He nods thoughtfully and looks back at us.

"Human," he says, looking at me. "What's your place in this? Kiriel tells us that a fortnight ago, you were still working in an office with no knowledge of the faery. That seems very convenient. Is this a trick, little mortal? Perhaps we should gut you here and read the future in your large intestine."

I swallow, hard, ready to reply, but Melusine interjects before I can say anything.

"He's with me," she says. "My apprentice and nothing more. If you doubt him, you doubt me."

"I hardly think you're one to try and harm Gaia," he responds slowly. "But we've all been wrong before."

Melusine seems to bite back a retort. "Will you sanction our visit?" she says. "Or not?"

Balthamel looks back at the creepy woman, then over at the dark elf with the gun. Both of them eventually nod, and he looks back at us.

"Very well," he says. "But if anyone thinks this means our borders will be weaker, then they are welcome to test them. You'll have your support. Tssirai will meet you with her squad wherever you need them."

The white-haired, white-eyed woman looks over at us and grins evilly. "Try and double cross me," she hisses in a low voice. "And all the blood in the world won't save you."

Melusine looks unimpressed. "Just be there, dearie," she says. "Come on Jamie, let's go somewhere that gets a bit of sunlight."

I turn and manage to trip over my own feet, and there's a ripple of guttural laughter from some of the orcs. Melusine rolls her eyes and flows out of the room, Dakyid hurrying after her. I give a comedic shrug and follow a moment later, the laughter growing. They might be ugly as hell, but the Unseelie Court feels a lot more honest than the Seelie.

Two corridors later, it's clear that we're not going out the way we came in.

"Uh, Melusine," I say. "You know where we're going, right?"

She fixes me with a steely look. "Well, since we no longer need to sneak," she says. "I thought we might take the easy way out. But if you'd rather go back through Kiriel's chambers and hunt werewolves in the limbo sewers again, I'm sure Dakyid will take you there."

"No need," I say quickly, raising my hands in a peaceful gesture. "Just checking."

"Dakyid, can we trust Tssirai?" she asks, turning to the dark elf. "I remember her having a rather bad track record when it comes to the Seelie."

"She does," Dakyid says. "There's at least one unicorn in the ground because of the banshee sisters, but if she says she'll behave herself, she will."

I didn't actually hear her say anything about behaving, but I don't interject. We're nearly out. Surely, we're nearly out?

"Hmmm," Melusine muses. "Well she can't be any worse than that shit Silvai, I suppose."

Dakyid snorts. "*Silvai's* going to be there? You do like to live dangerously."

"Needs must, young man, needs must."

"I'm no kind of man at all," he says amicably as we arrive at a crumbling stone archway set into the middle of a large room, empty aside from four serious-looking orcs holding automatic weapons. Dakyid gestures, and one of them moves a couple of bricks up and to the left somehow – the way out, I presume.

"Now, don't take offence, but I hope I don't see you for at least another hundred years," he says evenly.

"None taken," Melusine says. "Although you're a lot less objectionable than I remember you being in our last encounter."

He looks around guiltily, a slight blush suffusing his white skin. "Melusine, that was a hundred and fifty years ago. I was a hot-headed young thing then. I thought that my tributes would have more than made up for it."

The orcs do a really good impression of not listening, but I see something resembling amusement ripple across their faces.

Mel shrugs. "More or less," she says evenly. "Well, so long."

She walks through the arch and I follow a moment later.

Chapter 16

There's the disconcerting Alice in Wonderland sensation of dislocation for a moment, making me feel a bit sick; I wonder if it's ok for us to keep doing this. It feels like travel sickness, but as I steady myself against a wall, it starts to pass. I blink and look around, my pulse suddenly racing; there's a huge spiderweb strung across the room, the walls completely covered by webbing and large white egg-like structures.

"Uh, Melusine?" I say tentatively, looking around for the witch.

She pauses, already halfway across the room. "Oh, don't worry," she calls, looking back. "Little mother isn't around at the moment."

Little mother? I don't ask, instead focusing on not disturbing any of the strands of web that criss-cross the room, each of which is as thick as a chunky bootlace. I try to follow Melusine's route, but she's much more graceful and co-ordinated than I am. We're almost out of this, I tell myself.

"You should try yoga," she says from the other side of the room, where I can see a doorway. "You look a little stiff."

I shoot her a dirty look as I duck under the last strand, watching my feet. I try not to step on any of the eggs, each of which looks like it has more eggs inside it. Ugh. Egg sacs.

"Come on," she says impatiently. "Or did you want little mother to come back and find out who killed her children in the sewers?"

Oh.

I hurry after her, finding myself in what seems to be a tunnel carved directly out of rock; it's roughly hewn, and I can see other tunnels leading off from occasional junctions. Melusine carries on until she reaches a T-junction at the end. The right-hand one seems to lead upwards; I can feel a distant draft and it looks like the rock turns into earth a way on, whereas the left-hand one goes back down, a set of ornate lanterns illuminating it as far as I can see. I can hear footsteps distantly, and the sound of bones clacking together, making me wonder if some of Kiriel's creations are tracking us.

"Ah, here it is," Mel says, straightening. I look at what she's been doing; in what I'd initially dismissed as a pile of old junk on the floor is an old wooden doll's house, missing its front door. It's lying amongst various discarded bricks, rags and what looks like an old car tyre. Quite what this is all doing down the hall from a giant spider's web, I have no idea, but I guess Melusine must have been telling the truth: stuff does literally fall down here.

She taps the roof twice, then the right-hand side, looking at me meaningfully. "You got that?"

I nod, and she walks through the front doorway, shrinking until she's doll-sized before vanishing a second later. Feeling oddly exposed, I start walking towards it, quickly feeling travel sick. The world grows up around me and for a brief moment, I'm walking through the doll's house, seeing the furniture as regular-sized.

Then I'm out the other side, next to the wall of a London alleyway, standing in what I strongly suspect is some drunk's urine from last night. The rank smell fills my nostrils and for a moment my head spins and I think that I might gag. I swallow hard, take a few steps down the alley and look around – Melusine is a short way away and I think I know more or less where we are. We're not far from Cannon Street station, basically between Blackfriars and Cannon St. My mind starts thinking about the best way to get back to Paddington; the Circle line would take an age, so it might be best to walk over to Southwark and get the Jubilee line, then change.

"Back to the station?" I ask.

Melusine looks around and sniffs, then spits something disgusting towards the wall. I shudder and turn away.

"No," she says. "Jamie, it's time for you to see the other reason why we're doing this."

She turns down the passageway towards the river, leading us to the Thames path. It's funny; the river is an integral part of London's identity, but I think a lot of Londoners forget that it's there. There's a catamaran branded with a bank's logo stopped nearby, but otherwise it's quiet.

After our time in limbo and the Unseelie Court, it should be reassuring to see the familiar landmarks on the south side of the river; the Shard, the Tate Modern and, distantly, the London Eye. But everything suddenly seems unreal, as if the elves and monsters I've just been hanging out with are somehow more vivid than the capital city and its busy nine to five.

We wander down the river, Melusine peering over the rail at intervals, seemingly distracted.

"Uh, Melusine?" I ask. "I've been wondering about … well, about magic."

She glances back at me and looks behind us; there's no-one around. I'd already checked.

"Go on, spit it out then," she says. "Quickly now."

"Well, I've seen you do some impressive stuff," I manage, haltingly. "That thing with the owl, the thing with the … werewolf. How does it work? Is there a limit to what it can do?"

"Jamie," she croaks. "There's no such thing as absolute power. Most witches, wizards, elves, warlocks, banshees and so on can do a basic set of things; unlocking doors, making things move, simple elemental manipulations. Beyond that, we tend to specialise; I've spent hundreds of years with flesh and blood magics, for example. That shitbag Silvai tends to use storms, electricity, that kind of thing. Each different discipline is quite demanding."

Huh. Interesting. "Thanks," I say, thinking about that.

A jogger approaches us, silencing our conversation. The lycra-clad woman stares at us oddly but passes a moment later.

I find myself walking alone as Melusine abruptly turns down a set of steps leading to the river's shoreline and I come to a halt quickly. I turn back and, seeing Melusine waiting at the bottom for me, tentatively make my way down the slimy stone stairs.

The shingly beach, if you can call it a beach, is pretty grimy. Beer cans, small laughing gas canisters and discarded food packaging litters the shore alongside some kind of indeterminate river filth. Everything is damp, and despite the bright sun of the midsummer day, it feels cooler down here.

"Come on," Melusine says, slowly working her way along the uneven shoreline. "The sooner we get there, the sooner we can leave."

I glance down the river, unsure if my stomach can take another transition to a faerie realm. I follow along, almost slipping on a sandwich wrapper. It's pretty disgusting here, and I say that as someone who was recently in a sewer full of blood.

Up ahead, there seems to be a person sat up against the river wall. I hurry to catch up with Mel to point them out; we'll need to find some way to distract them or get rid of them if we're going through to the faerie world, but Mel is already adjusting her path and heading straight for them.

Hesitantly, I slow down again, watching my step as we approach the figure. It's a woman, dressed in robes not unlike Melusine's conventional 'witch-wear', but very food-stained and grubby. She looks younger than Melusine, maybe in her early forties, but her eyes belie that assumption; they're old and somehow timeless, but also intimidating. There's something in the way she looks up at us that scares me, that speaks of irreconcilable pain, of irrationality.

"Sister," Melusine says, going down on one knee in the filthy shingle. "How are you?"

The woman gazes up, squinting and seemingly trying to focus, an incoherent mumbling issuing from her lips.

"Jamie," Melusine says, fishing a clean rag from inside her robes and gently wiping the spittle from the woman's face. "This is my sister Alizon, the witch of earth and water. Alizon, this is my newest apprentice Jamie. He's completely unskilled at the dark arts but has proved a deft hand at shooting stuff."

I glance around hurriedly, hoping that no-one heard that. People are kind of funny about guns in the UK. I mean, understandably.

Alizon looks left and right, following my gaze, before reaching down by her side and picking up an empty beer can. It drips river water onto her robes and she drops it back down.

"Alizon," Melusine says. "I did warn you not to leave your home. Why are you here?"

I'm not sure what kind of reply she's expecting, but she doesn't get one. Ali pushes her arms up towards the sky, stretches and then collapses down into a small heap. I do notice all kinds of elaborate – mostly green – tattoos on her arms as her robes fall away for a moment.

Melusine sighs and reaches into her capacious bag, drawing out a small parcel that smells vaguely meaty. "Here," she says. "Jamie, do you have any water?"

I find a bottle that I bought at the station and offer it to her. Melusine places both next to Alizon and stands up, bones creaking. "Come on," she says. "There's nothing more we can do here."

With a final glance at the dishevelled, now-snoring woman, she carries on down the shoreline, glancing up at the river wall.

"Is she … actually your sister?" I ask, once we've located another set of steps up, thankfully with a rusted metal handrail this time. "Or you know, your sister in a witchy way?"

Melusine raises her eyebrows. "That's your first question?" she asks archly. "Really?"

I snort. "If you were expecting me to ask 'what's wrong with her?' I think I already figured that out – it's Gaia, isn't it? If she's the witch of earth and water, then a sickness with Gaia would presumably affect her in some way. Am I warm?"

"Very good," Melusine's voice is scratchier than usual, and I wonder if this is hard for her to talk about. "It started three months ago. Ali sent me a missive that she was ill, which I ignored, but then two more, expressing concern that the power of her magic was declining. Her house flooded and by the time I came to visit her six weeks ago, she was a babbling wreck unable to remember how to access her own realm."

We ascend another set of steps up to a bridge over the river and start walking towards Southwark, a trio of runners approaching us. One of them stares at Melusine and recoils in disgust as she passes us.

"You can fuck right off, Lululemon," Mel mutters, her face contorting with anger momentarily. She makes a sharp gesture with her right hand and there's a sudden cry from the girl behind us, who skids to a halt.

"My foot!" she complains, as the other two round back towards her. "I think I've got a blister!"

"Several," Melusine cackles softly as she hurries along. "And more to come, I promise you that."

"Come on, let's get home," I say quietly.

Melusine looks at me and shrugs, nastily. "Modern footwear," she sighs. "They just don't make it like they used to."

"Oh, shut up."

Thankfully, she just laughs.

The train journey home is uneventful, and Melusine seems to have recovered her good temper after an hour with her nose in a large tome of spells. She even suggests dinner with Merovech that evening, and I order pizza to Beckett's bungalow as we draw into the station.

I'm even more amazed when Melusine offers to pay, the delivery driver arriving as we get to the front door. She draws a wad of notes from her bag that gets a bit of a stare, but she tips generously.

It's a warm, pleasant evening, and although I've got mixed emotions about the witch – or ex-witch – that we met, I'm also feeling a glow of satisfaction for actually contributing something to our trip to the Unseelie Court through limbo. Maybe I can't do magic, but I can shoot, it seems.

We ignore Melusine's hut and keep going to Merovech's place, seeing that they've laid out the picnic table outside and are sat on the bench waiting for us. As soon as we round the corner, V jumps up from the table and wrings their hands excitedly then waves.

"Hello!" they call, and I find myself grinning back and waving.

V seems to have ditched their standard burn-spattered robe for a pair of chunky blue jeans and a grey Aran jumper, which seems a bit odd given the warmth of the evening. They hurry over to us, offering to take a pizza but I shake my head – three pizzas don't weigh very much, and instead V runs back to the table and puts a box of dusty wine and beer bottles on the table.

"I don't have parties very often!" they exclaim happily. "This is very exciting! Would you like beer or wine? I think there's another lovely bottle of Chateau du Musar from 2006 that I was saving for a special occasion, or there's some beer that Kopek brewed, or some human beer if you'd prefer, or I can just get some water – what would you like?"

Melusine rolls her eyes, but also cracks a small smile as she sits down at the table.

"Wine would be good, thank you V," she says, and the small inventor pulls out a dusty bottle from the box, pouring out three glasses.

I give it a nervous sniff, but it actually smells great. Still, maybe best to let someone else take a drink first; I glance at Melusine, who is tucking into her pizza contentedly, but I don't think she's taken a sip yet.

"So, how did everything go?" Merovech says. "Because I know you've had such awful trouble with the Seelie and Unseelie Courts before."

"Hmmmf," Melusine says through a mouthful of pizza, so I take over.

"Good," I offer. "A few hiccups, but they both agreed to help. We'll have support parties outside the Gaia site when we need them, although it has to be soon."

"And no sign of Silvai, I hope?" Merovech says, causing Melusine to frown. She swallows and grimaces.

"We did encounter the shitbag," she says acidly. "And Tssirai in the Unseelie."

Merovech recoils, almost falling off their perch. "Oh no!" they warble. "Were there any ... casualties?"

Melusine laughs. "No no, I managed to restrain myself ... this time, but they will both be in the support teams."

"I take it you have some history with those two?" I ask, and Melusine rolls her eyes.

"This isn't some playground spat," she snorts. "And it's a long tale."

"Story," I offer.

"Shut up and eat," she growls in a good-natured fashion, and I turn back to my pizza, taking a sip of the wine.

It's good. Like, really good. Thick and rich and almost spicy.

"This is amazing," I say admiringly. "Really amazing. Where did you get it?"

"Lebanon," Melusine says. "Via Dakyid. It's one of the reasons why we tolerate him. He has rather good taste."

I take another sip, savouring the fine, deep flavour. It's incredible.

"I think I have a case if you'd like one?" Merovech offers. "Although I put my spare cogs next to it, so there might be a broken bottle or two."

"V," Melusine says, waving her hand at them. "Don't give away all of the good stuff. We've talked about this."

"Oh," V says, looking downcast. "I'm sorry. Um, Jamie?"

I grin at the sad tinker. "It's fine, Merovech, don't worry about it. It was very kind of you to offer. I'm glad that I could try some."

"Oh," they say, perking up. "Well, you're more than welcome."

The conversation feels like a bit of a minefield, so I focus on my delicious wine and tasty pizza, trying to enjoy the moment. After the spiders, werewolves, giants and elves I'm kind of glad to be in one piece, enjoying the sunshine and not actively in danger.

"So, what's next?" I ask, trying to recall Melusine's flip charts from one of my first visits. "We've got permission and the support. Didn't we need something else?"

"Ah, yes," Melusine says, finishing her pizza and leaning forwards, interlacing her fingers and resting her knobbly chin on them. "We need to kidnap one of your childhood friends."

Chapter 17

"What?!" I blurt, completely taken aback.

Melusine regards me evenly, removing a spot of tomato sauce from her chin with a napkin.

"Did you think," she says acidly. "That a secret scientific military site would just allow you and I to inspect their goings-on, while two elvish battle-parties scout the area?"

I stare at her, speechless.

"Your friend Sam works at the research site," Mel continues. "You're going to make contact with her and then we're going to kidnap her."

My mind reels; how does Mel know about Sam? I haven't seen her for years, but somehow Mel knows that she works at a secret scientific site somewhere – I mean, I knew she did something sciencey, but this is something else. It's just … well, it's Sam. Is this the only reason I'm here? Was all of this 'training' just a waste of time to get at my old friend? A small sliver of doubt starts to work its way into my mind.

"A…and then what?" I splutter. "Torture her until she tells us what's going on?"

Melusine snorts. "Of course not," she says cuttingly. "We'll hex her, and when she's unconscious, I'll swap bodies with her. Then you and I will go to the scientific site and we'll find out what's going on. We'll return, and swap the bodies back again. She'll wake up in the morning; you tell her she had too much wine and fell asleep on the sofa, and no-one will be any the wiser."

I stare at her, incredulous.

"I remember when you did it with Silvai," Merovech chimes in. "You got all those spell components from the Seelie Court's stores and no-one knew."

"And now one more person knows," Mel says, raising her eyebrows at V, whose face falls suddenly.

"Oh," they say unhappily. "But it's Jamie. We can trust Jamie, can't we?"

Mel sighs. "Of course, V, it's ok. But I think Silvai suspected something, that's all."

"Oh yes," Merovech gives a tinkly little laugh. "You don't wake up in a faery glade with a centaur sleeping next to you and think that nothing has happened!"

Mel cackles gleefully, before regaining her composure and looking over at me.

"We've got some time, Jamie," she says. "Think about it. Go home, take a walk, get some rest. No harm will come to your friend, I guarantee it. She's a convenient entry card, that's all."

Shaking my head, incredulous, I set down my last slice of pizza and get up from the table, trembling slightly.

"Sure," I say slowly. "Sure, I'll be back tomorrow."

There's a beautiful purple sunset as I walk back towards Beckett's place, but I hardly notice. It's like my breadth of vision has narrowed to what's in front of me, and barely that.

I pause in the kitchen, staring out at the Manor gardens before a sudden sound makes me jump. I spin, hearing the front door close, then footsteps in the hallway.

"Lad?" Beckett's voice calls, as he appears in the doorway. "Everything alright?"

I shake my head, not even sure where to begin.

"Everything getting a bit murkier, is it?" he asks, spinning a chair around and sitting down, leaning on the table. "She'll do that. Best of intentions, that woman, but she's been doing this for so long that she's blind to what it does to everyone else."

"Yeah," I admit. "Yeah, you could say that. I mean, I guess I believe her about Gaia and the weather and everything, but what she said just now, it's something else."

"You can absolutely tell her no, you know that, don't you?" Beckett says kindly. "I know she's paid you well, but there's always a way out."

I take a deep breath and nod. "I know," I say slowly. "I guess I just need some time to think about it."

Beckett looks thoughtful for a moment. "Want me to talk to her?" he offers. "See if there's another way around it?"

I shake my head, suddenly wanting fresh air and a walk to clear my head. "No," I say. "But thank you. Appreciate it, seriously."

He shrugs. "Anytime."

Feeling slightly better, I head out and down the lane, the normality somehow providing a kind of safety blanket. Surely, I'm away from the witch's magic in the world of small supermarkets with adverts asking for babysitters? Suddenly it doesn't seem possible that elves and magic and monsters could co-exist with this level of mundanity.

Then I remember the joggers spontaneously developing blisters, the broken figure of the witch on the dirty shoreline and I shiver in spite of the warm summer evening, hurrying along.

I'm crossing the road towards the house when my phone beeps. Silently I curse, wondering if it's Melusine, and almost don't check it. Of course, if the hag can sell drugs on the dark web, then she can do WhatsApp, but on reflection, I don't think she's the type to micro-manage. If she wanted to get hold of me, she'd appear on the doorstep ... or wouldn't have let me leave the forest.

I pull out my phone and see a message from Flic, the estate agent's cute photographer, the normality of it all almost making me stagger.

"Hey Jamie," it says. "Finished some paperwork for Cynthia and killing time at your village pub this evening. Fancy that drink?"

Really, all I want is to get home, close the door, curl up and hope the world vanishes before my head explodes, but I also really want to see this woman again. So instead, I find myself messaging her, doubling back and heading towards the pub, feeling a small pang of guilt that I haven't checked in with mum today. I glance at my watch – it's late, and she's probably asleep, but I do pause outside the pub and message her, asking how she's doing.

I've not spent many of my drinking years in the village, but it's sufficiently small that everyone knows everyone else, at least by sight. Even kids are tolerated in the pub as long as they're either eating or well-behaved – and preferably both. It also hasn't changed hands or layout as far as I can remember, so it's pretty familiar.

But it's also a sufficiently small village that as I enter, it falls silent and everyone stops and stares at me. Thankfully the silence quickly turns into respectful nods, a few people greeting me by name and the buzz of conversation resumes.

I look around and see a grinning Flic sat in the corner, where a pile of camera bags is piled up by the wall. She's laughing, presumably at the very stereotypically local welcome I've received. I mime drinking and she raises a three-quarters full pint glass at me, shaking her head.

I order a local beer, surprised to receive it on the house – another fringe benefit of country life – and head over to Flic. She's smartly dressed in a black blouse, suit jacket and trousers, missing almost all of her earrings.

"Hey," I say, taking a deep pull of my pint. It's smooth and mellow, not like the overly-hoppy stuff that you get in most London bars at the moment. "You're looking smart."

"Yeah," she says, still grinning. "Cynthia's selling a fancy country house a few miles down the road, so I had to dress the part."

"Sounds like a big deal. Did it go well?"

"Well enough," she says evenly. "Lots of rooms to shoot and everything had to be perfect. We came back here to review everything, which took just as long as the shooting itself…"

She sighs expansively and takes a drink.

"Cynthia," I say. "Seems challenging."

Flic snorts. "It's not like you made a great first impression," she says. "She said it was like walking into a student house or something."

I laugh, remembering her upturned nose, my own dishevelled appearance.

"She's not so bad," Flic continues. "She knew about your mum – sorry about that by the way – and she's been pushing the sale pretty hard to give you a good deal. You'll notice that you've not exactly been inundated with queries – that's her, looking out for you in her own way."

"Jeez," I manage. "I guess I had her wrong."

Flic laughs; her eyes sparkling. "Yeah, she's alright. Stuffy, but alright."

She takes another drink and looks at me. "Enough about my boss, how have you been? You seemed distracted when I last spoke to you – and I don't mean the obvious."

"The obvious?" I say, playing for time. How do I explain to a property photographer – however understanding – that I'm helping a witch heal the earth spirit? I mean, I can't. I can barely explain it to myself, let alone anyone else.

"Jamie, I've seen people going through loss and grief before," she says. "Including myself, and none of them looked like you did."

I sigh. "Yeah," I manage, still struggling with how to avoid lying to this woman, but also not wanting to tell the complete truth. "Uh, well, since I've been back, I've been helping a … friend of a friend of the family, and it's not quite worked out as I thought it would."

Flic leans her head to one side, tucking an errant blonde curl behind one ear. She's a good listener.

"I've been helping them, and at first it was strange, but then I actually started enjoying it. Only today, they asked me to do something else and … well, I guess it changed how I saw them, if you know what I mean?"

"And how do you feel about that?" Flic says in a tone that makes me wonder if she's had some kind of counselling experience. I stop staring out of the window and look back at her.

"I know they've got good intentions, but I've not really known them long enough to trust them. But I think

... I hope their heart's in the right place, so I have to keep helping them I guess."

Flic laughs. "So serious, Jamie! It's just an errand, right?"

"Sure," I manage, but I think she sees through my platitude. I have a stab at changing the subject, not really wanting to get into this one further. "Listen, how long have you been working for Cynthia anyway? Have you always been a photographer?"

It turns out that she studied psychology at university, wanting to be a clinical psychologist, but after a few side gigs as a photographer when she graduated, she took it full time.

"I was going to do wedding photography," she says. "But I can't do people. Buildings are much more my speed for some reason."

She glances at her phone. "Aw, sorry Jamie, I've got to be up early for the first train tomorrow. Gotta run."

"No worries," I say. "It was good to catch up. You need a hand with all your stuff?"

"Nah," she says, loading herself up, strapping a variety of bags and pouches about her person. "Practice makes perfect."

Trying not to knock any glasses over, she weaves her way across to the door. "Later," she says. "Next time let's do dinner."

"Uh, yeah," I stammer. "That'd be great."

And she gives me another grin and a look that – after the door closes behind her – has an old guy patting me on the back and giving me a knowing glance. Flushing and grinning sheepishly, I finish my pint and head home.

Where, despite my glib assurances to Flic, I find myself sat by the window, pondering Mel's intentions. She said ... well, she said she'd only be swapping bodies with Sam for an evening, right? I still can't quite believe that it's possible, let alone work out if it's moral. Meeting up with an old friend, only to trick her and sort of kidnap her? Even if she's working on some secret government project to exploit Gaia, does that make her 'one of the bad guys'?

I'm not sure that the end justifies the means at all. Maybe I should give Mel back her money and tell her I'm out. I feel a slight twinge about mum and the possibility of a cancer cure from Gaia, but there's no guarantees and she's already had the drug – powder – stuff from Mel.

Then I wonder what Mel would do to my mum if I backed out now. Would she reverse the cancer drug? Was that part of the deal? Is my connection to Sam all she wants? Or would she just ambush Sam in an alleyway somewhere and do it anyway?

Probably. And I'd spend the rest of my life looking over my shoulder for a pissed-off witch who can turn blood into home-made missiles. At least if I agree to this, then it'll be as bloodless and straightforward as possible.

Ok, I think, taking a deep breath. If I'm in, then I'm in. That said, will Sam even agree to meet me? I haven't seen her for years.

And when we discovered Melusine's hut for the first time, back when we were kids? She wasn't the most receptive to the other world. She wouldn't cope with the truth. I couldn't just arrive and tell her that we needed to get to the scientific site and ask if we could borrow her body for a while. Maybe she believes in their cause – I guess if it's regular people trying to measure magic stuff, then of course they're going to be curious. They're not really doing anything wrong from their own point of view.

Stealth is the only way, I realise. Mel's right. I already believe in her cause, having seen the things I've seen, the elves, the monsters, the erratic storms, the earthquakes. Maybe I've not seen direct proof that it's linked to Gaia, but I've seen enough to believe her theory. And if there's a sliver of a chance that this can help mum at the same time, well, then I'm in.

When I wake up the next morning, I'm resolved. I don't like it, but I'll help Melusine, and we'll have to be really, really careful with Sam's body. I dig out her email address and drop her a note, telling her I'll be in town today, and asking whether she wants to meet for dinner.

As I arrive at Beckett's bungalow in the car, Melusine is already outside with a large bag. Once again, she's dressed in her 'grandma camouflage'; sedate black trousers and a matching roll-neck jumper. It doesn't hide her warty face, long nose or beady, piercing eyes. It doesn't hide the charms; some of which look like they used to be alive, hanging from her bag, or the many rings on her fingers, graven with images and small symbols. But she's normal-looking enough. Just.

"Good," she says. "Are you ready?"

I nod. "All good," I say. "I've messaged Sam."

"We'll be staying in a holiday rental not far from the outskirts of town," Mel says, showing me the place on an unidentifiable but modern-looking phone. "Give her the address and let's be on our way."

I send another mail to Sam, hoping that she replies to my first one at some stage, and then we're off.

The driving is easy on the way up towards the Peak District, although we almost have a few problems at a service station. Melusine is definitely cranky from being shut in a car for hours, but after stopping I quickly regret not buying a car-friendly lunch. Instead, we sit in the forecourt eating Marks and Spencer's best sandwiches, purchased with some of what I assume is Melusine's drug money.

She keeps up a torrent of complaints and abuse about other people as we're choosing, paying for and eating our sandwiches. It's a fairly standard service station; the usual array of coffee places, doughnut shops and over-priced supermarkets alongside arcade machines and a steady stream of people heading to the toilets.

"Vapers!" she says as we eat, her voice scraping along my nerves like nails on a blackboard. "If you're going to poison yourself and become an addict, at least do it with something that doesn't look like you're smoking a fucking

USB stick. You people have no self-respect, that's what it is."

I wonder if there's anything I can do to shut her up when she suddenly falls silent. I thank my lucky stars and focus on gobbling my lunch down. I'm almost finished when I notice what she's looking at, staring over some guy's shoulder at the film showing on his tablet. He's watching a fairly visceral horror film, occasionally glancing around, presumably to check that there aren't any children nearby. Seeing Melusine's icy stare, he flicks off the tablet and leaves the table with a slightly worried glance behind him at the witch.

"Oh, the things you humans do," she says gleefully. "Reminds me of the time when I had a lovely holiday in Virginia a few years ago. Sat outside the CIA building and soaked up the terror. And he was watching that purely for pleasure. You're an ugly species, you know that?"

I shake my head. "Come on," I say, taking the last bite of my sandwich, unsure of whether to be relieved by the improvement in her mood, or disturbed by her affection for torture-porn. "Let's get out of here."

She snickers nastily, but gets back in the car nonetheless. I breathe a sigh of relief as her door closes and I head back onto the motorway.

An hour later, we arrive in the pretty market town of Buxton, deep in the Peak District. I park in front of the house, getting out of the car and stretching as my phone beeps.

"Hey, it's from Sam," I say, and Melusine raises her eyebrows, so I read the message out loud.

"Hey Jamie," it says. "What a surprise! Good to hear from you. Sure, that'd be great, if you're in town, I'd be happy to come over. I hope you're a good cook! I'm joking – we can always order in; we might be in the sticks, but we can still get Domino's here. What time will you be around?"

I look over at Melusine, who thinks for a moment. "Ugh," she says. "She sounds sappy. Tell her seven but eat promptly. We should be at the site before eleven."

I reply, thanking Sam and telling her to come then and to bring a bottle of wine. I wonder if she's changed in the last few years?

Buxton isn't a big place, but Melusine commissions me to pick up some supplies from the nearest supermarket as she starts whatever preparations are involved in the body-swapping spell.

I try to distract myself by focusing on the shopping, but there's still a big part of me that isn't happy with all this. I mean, it can't be right to take someone's body like this, can it? Can it?

"Jamie," Melusine says as I return, dumping shopping bags on the kitchen countertop. I glance over, seeing her fingernails glinting red with something that I strongly suspect isn't nail varnish. "I know you're doubting this. I'd be surprised if you weren't. Most normal humans would have turned tail and run at the first sight of a werewolf.

You've got steel in you, boy, and although this might feel wrong, I think you know in your heart of hearts that this is the cleanest way to do it. Cleaner than letting the Seelie charge in there and slaughter everyone, of course."

I sigh. She's right, and I'm starting to come to terms with it, even if I'm not happy about the means to get there.

"I guess," I say, not really wanting to appear weak before this terribly powerful old woman, but still not feeling good about this either. "I mean, yeah, you're right."

"I'm not going to ladle on the comfort," she says, digging her phone out of her pocket. "You can figure out what happens if we don't do this for yourself and I don't have time to pander to you."

I suppose that if we didn't do this, the Seelie might succeed, but it'd be bad from what I've seen of the faery world so far. And if they failed, then presumably this erratic weather and stuff gets a lot worse? I shudder even thinking about the havoc that just a small group of fauns could wreak in the real world.

"Good," Melusine says. "The Courts are in position and waiting for our go. I think Tssirai sent the note, from the tone, so help me here – what kind of dick pic should I send back? Elephant? Donkey?"

I snigger in spite of myself.

"That's better," she says, spreading a large paper map on the dining room table. "Now, I know we can use the laptop for this, but I want to mark a few points."

She reaches for the salt and pepper shakers from the kitchen, as well as a couple of ugly-looking ornaments from a bookshelf, placing them on the map.

"This is the site," she says. "From Alariel's intelligence, it looks like the barriers start here, with the actual mound a short way down the road. The Seelie will set up to the east, outside a barbed-wire fence at this point, and the Unseelie on the other side here. You and I will enter, find out what we can about why they're investigating, and learn the deployment of any staff still on site. If we can, we'll disable the alarms and surveillance, then the Seelie and Unseelie will enter and subdue the guards. We'll inspect Gaia for any damage and take every single human off the site, closing it down and leave the banshee and the elves to do memory magic. That may take another day or so – it's finicky stuff and I don't have the patience for it. We'll return here and debrief the Courts the next morning. Ok?"

I nod. This is crazily real, and there's not a hint of the human-hating pettiness that I saw in the service station. This is a serious, powerful witch completely focused on her task.

"Excellent," she says lightly. "Now, what's for dinner?"

Chapter 18

We've still got a few hours before Sam arrives, so I take the time to explore the house that we've rented. It's nothing special; a two-bedroom place, thankfully not a stag or hen party house like some I've been to. It's decorated in cream and white and it's spotlessly clean. I silently thank our hosts, Neil and Alison.

Mel's claimed the master bedroom; it's a lot more spacious and I figured she might need it for her preparations, whatever they may be. I really hope the stuff that looked like blood on her fingertips didn't drip onto the carpet.

Although on balance, it's not my money that paid the deposit.

I have to take a minute to just stop and look out of the window as my brain tries to compute both managing a body swap and something as mundane as thinking about holiday rental deposits. I don't quite manage it. Does this make me a proper witch's apprentice now? I suppose I can't really be, because I can't do much magic - and it's only for two weeks.

Dinner. I need to focus on dinner.

So I do. I've already worked out the basics of a home-made curry that I feel fairly confident about making, so I kill time hunting through the kitchen to check out the utensils and frying pans.

At six thirty, Melusine turns to go upstairs.

"Have dinner," she grates. "Enjoy the wine. But once you've eaten, excuse yourself and knock on my door. I'll trip the hex and she'll fall asleep."

And with that, she shuffles off, her joints and the stairs creaking at each other.

I swallow hard and try to focus on weighing out rice, working up the spicy paste for the meat. There's still fifteen minutes until Sam arrives, so I find myself staring out at the small patio behind the house. There's a shed, but not much else; a few plants that look neglected, a large blue pot with the stub of something in it.

I wonder if she'll be prompt. What will we talk about? I try to remember details of her life from after we were kids, but there isn't a lot, only what I heard second-hand from mum.

The doorbell rings and I almost knock the spicy curry paste onto the floor, catching it at the last minute and sliding it into the fridge.

I open the door and find myself grinning; it's good to see her. Despite the warmth of the evening, she's in a light coat and smart jeans, sporting a blonde bob. She's slim, and looks a lot like I remember, although my immediate impression is that she's lost some of the impatience that she had when we were kids. I'm not sure why that comes into my head.

She returns my grin with a smile, raising her eyebrows slightly.

"Hey," I say. "Long time no see!"

"Hey yourself," she says, offering me a polite hug and a bottle of red wine. "Nice to see you."

"Come in," I beckon her into the house and she enters, looking around curiously. I take her coat and hang it on a hook by the front door as she wanders around the lounge. She's well-dressed; I wonder how senior she is in this job if she can afford such good clothes – or maybe she's just got taste. Her floaty, gauzy long-sleeved top threatens to pick up dust from the mantelpiece.

"So what are you doing at the moment?" she asks amiably. "How come you're up north?"

This is a lie that I've practised in my head many times, so it comes out reasonably well.

"My firm wants to sell to the mineral water people up here," I say casually, moving into the kitchen and checking my ingredients again. If she looks me up on LinkedIn, the lie will hold. "They've sent me up to do some research."

"Oh really?" she says. "You should have mentioned it, I could have introduced you. When I arrived here for work, they totally rolled out the red carpet for us."

"Who are you working for again?" I say. "I think your mum mentioned the name but I can't remember it."

She grins. "Same old Jamie. It's a research body, Zephyr. Sort of a hybrid between a geo-tech start-up and a proper research company."

"Oh," I say, trying to sound distracted while logging that name in my head. "So not government-run then?"

"Kind of," she says, rolling her eyes. "There's links with government bodies, but it's independently owned. Pays better that way!"

I laugh and nod. "Hell yes. I thought about public sector stuff after I graduated – great benefits, but pays badly. Still, sounds like you've been climbing the ranks pretty fast..."

Sam cocks her head sideways and looks at me, then grins.

"Well, you know me," she says. "Never could stand waiting around, but you really have to work for it if you want to get onto the best projects, even as a junior."

"That's great," I say, unsure of how much to press the topic. I'm over-thinking; Sam has no idea why I'm really here and no reason to suspect me.

"Mmmm," she says, changing the subject. "Listen Jamie, I'm sorry I didn't get in touch before. I was really sorry to hear about your mum. How is she?"

"Thanks," I manage, suddenly feeling really bad about all this. "She took a bit of a turn for the worse this week, but she's doing as well as can be expected."

She nods kindly, and I think I actually see her tearing up a bit, so I turn to one side and examine the wine. "Want a glass?"

"Yeah," she says. "Thanks."

By the time I've poured two glasses, I've changed the subject to where she lives – on the other side of town, but not too far away – and what she gets up to at the weekends – lots of walking; we're in the Peak District of course.

"And how about you?" she says as I fry the chicken and struggle to find the extractor fan switch. Sam spots it and reaches up to flick it on. "How's life in the big smoke?"

"Ugh," I say. "Job's fine, but the flatmates aren't great at the moment."

"No?" she says sympathetically. "I thought you moved in with a friend from uni?"

I start to explain about Mark and his drug habit, Emily with her messiness and obsession with Mark. She makes sympathetic noises as I stir the curry and almost forget to cook the rice, catching myself and putting some naan in the oven as well.

"That's the good thing about being further north," she says. "No flatshares. Even on a relatively graduate-level salary, I can get a place of my own and still save money. More if I walk to work."

"Walking to work?" I say enviously. "You're living the dream."

She laughs. "Small dreams, Jamie. Small dreams."

I laugh, but there's a barb in what she says. Same old Sam.

"Okay," I say, setting cutlery on the table a few minutes later. "It'll just be a few more moments. Top up?"

She puts her glass on the countertop, nodding, and excuses herself to go to the bathroom. I suddenly panic – what if she goes poking around upstairs and finds Mel? Thankfully, the toilet is opposite the top of the stairs and kind of hard to miss, but I do breathe a sigh of relief when I hear the light go on.

I start putting the mini naans on side plates, serving up the curry as she comes downstairs.

"It smells great," she says, smiling and seating herself at the table. She's got a pretty smile.

"Thanks," I reply. "After my flatmate issues stunted my social life, I made an effort to learn a few recipes properly. Better than throwing myself into work – well, healthier, maybe."

"Know what you mean," she says. "Mine *is* pretty interesting, so I don't really mind doing extra hours that much. You sound like you're not happy in yours – you looking for something else?"

"Maybe," I admit. "I don't know. It's fine. I've got a nice team, it's not too badly paid, it's stable. More than a lot of graduates get these days. Took me long enough to land it, that's for sure. How did you end up in yours?"

"Online," she says lightly, but I get the impression that it's a practiced line. "You move around quite a lot. They do help you find places to stay, and head office is down in London somewhere, but I've only been there once for induction. After that, you're on site, depending on what your project is. Anyway, enough about work – anyone special in your life?"

I manage to avert a surprised cough and swallow my mouthful before I spray chicken tikka all over the table. "Uh, well, I kind of met someone," I say once I've regained my composure. "We ... well, I guess we went on our first date the other night."

"Hey, that's great," she says, giving a warm smile. I try to work out whether she looks relieved or not, but take it at face value. "What does she do?"

I start telling her about Flic as she takes another sip of her wine and starts on the curry. There's not a lot to tell, but Sam seems genuinely interested, which makes me wonder if we are actually friends, rather than acquaintances who were friends a while ago.

"What about you?" I ask. "Must be tough if you're always moving around."

"It's not so bad," she says between mouthfuls. "Hey, this is really good."

I grin and thank her.

"Some of the researchers in the lab are a bit weird, no offense," she says. "But there's a whole load of them, as well as the business team and the applied science guys who are ok."

Despite my best efforts, I'd recoiled slightly at the 'no offense' comment, but I don't think she noticed.

"I mean, no-one I'd call a boyfriend, you know," she says, taking another drink of her wine. "But there's enough going on."

I give a forced laugh and try to think of where to take the conversation next. I glance over at the kitchen clock – it's eight.

"So how busy are you tomorrow?" she asks. "Do you have meetings? Maybe I know them?"

"Uh, there's someone in procurement," I manage. "I can't remember their name."

"There are a lot of them," she says, finishing up her curry and mopping the bowl with a piece of naan. "I mean, actually I think there's only two hundred or so in total, but it's a small town and after the company got bought there was a lot more investment in the area."

I try to hurry up and finish dinner as she sits back and starts talking about the town and how it compares to Nottingham, which is where she was based before. In a suitable gap, I excuse myself and head upstairs, softly knocking on the door to Mel's room before slipping into the bathroom.

My hand shakes as I lock the door and I feel a bit sick.

As I slowly walk down the stairs afterwards, I see Sam slumped over her dinner and can't decide whether I'm relieved or appalled at myself.

"Sam?" I say quietly. "Sam?"

There's no response. Is she breathing? I freeze, panicking until I notice her chest lifting as she inhales – and then she starts snoring.

I let out a sigh and go get Melusine, knocking on the closed door.

"Mel?" I call. "It's me. She's out."

There's a long pause, then I hear a key turning in the lock, the door opening a crack. "You sure?" she says scratchily, and I nod.

"Good," she says, pushing past me and heading downstairs into the lounge.

Melusine checks Sam's pulse at her neck, then holds her hand in front of her mouth – presumably to check that she's breathing ok – before making a small grunt of satisfaction and turning back to me.

"Put her on the sofa," she grates, moving slowly back up the stairs again.

I don't know if you've ever tried to move an entire person on your own, but I didn't realise how difficult it would be. Sam is pretty slight, but she's still incredibly heavy. On my first attempt, I try to pick her up in my arms and move her over, but I end up putting her straight back down again. I eventually resort to a half-carry, half-drag, trying desperately not to hurt her or dip her clothes in the last of the curry sauce. It's really awkward and even pulling her three feet from the dinner table to the sofa leaves me a little out of breath.

A moment later Melusine comes back downstairs with her large bag in one hand and a large knife in the other. I feel my eyes widen as I stare at the bare blade.

"Uh, Mel," I start, but she shushes me.

"Relax," she says, unpacking a variety of items, including two dead-looking mice, white chunky candles, a pack of small sticky dots and a few phials of blue and green liquid. "We require a little blood, but none of it hers. Shut up and help me instead of gawking. As I mark spots on the floor, put a candle there."

Taking a deep breath, I follow her around the room, putting the candles exactly on the centre of the sticky dots.

"Now, clear up the table, but quietly," she hisses. "I don't want to be distracted or spoil my rating on Airbnb."

Shaking my head, I rinse the curry from the plates before putting them in the dishwasher as Melusine removes the battery from the smoke alarm and begins lighting the candles, muttering. I try to listen, but the words don't make any sense to me.

The muttering turns into chanting as I put the last of the naan bread into the bin, and I turn to see Mel daubing mouse blood on Sam's forehead and cheeks, before making identical marks on her own face. I don't know whether to watch or not, so I keep half an eye on it while I finish the last of the washing up by hand.

There's a flash of green light and I almost drop the wine glass I'm washing, whipping my head around to see what's going on. Melusine is kneeling beside Sam, with what seems to be a small emerald sitting at the base of Sam's throat. I swear the room is darker now, and I start reaching for the dimmer switch to turn the light up, but then stop – I don't want to distract her. Who knows what could happen if you interrupt a spell like this midway through?

Mel stands up and steps back to her bag, drawing out something long and gauzy, laying it over the entirety of Sam's body; it's like … like lace or a spiderweb or something.

She stands, spreading her hands like claws and shouts three sharp, angular words. There's a flash like lightning.

I blink, and as my vision clears, their positions have been swapped. My childhood friend Sam is now stood over Melusine's body, which is lying prone on the sofa, breathing steadily.

"Bloody hell," I manage incredulously. "Mel?"

"Naturally," Mel-Sam says, sounding at once like Sam, but definitely with some of Mel in it.

"There's nothing natural about that," I add, giving a weak grin and walking over to the sofa. It's absolutely Melusine's body on the sofa. They're both even wearing the right clothes. It's … well, if Melusine wasn't holding herself like she does – and if there wasn't a knowing glint in her eye – then I would have no idea.

"Shit," I say, staring.

"Flesh and blood, boyo," Mel says, smoothing her hands down her body and looking over it admiringly. "If it wasn't such a difficult spell, I could do this more often. It's been a few centuries since I've worn a body this young."

I feel myself flushing and avert my eyes to the body on the sofa.

"Uh, listen ... if she woke..." I say, concerned.

"She won't."

"But she'd be in your body?"

Melusine still manages to cackle, despite being in the body of a twenty-three-year-old woman. "She would!" she says gleefully. "And what a surprise that would be!"

I shake my head, disbelievingly. "So you actually swapped bodies? It's not just like an illusion or something?"

Melusine ignores me and starts putting out the candles, blowing out each one and pinching the wicks to stop them smoking.

"You'll be careful with that, right?" I say.

She turns around to look at me on her hands and knees, giving me a withering look. I recoil; it's like having the worst parts of Mel and Sam put together in one package.

"We've got work to do," she says seriously. It's strange hearing Melusine's words in Sam's voice – the sound is Sam's voice, but the cadence, the emphasis, it's all witch. "Hurry up. Finish that and we can be on our way."

I glance around the kitchen and make a start on the drying up while Mel - Sam clears up the last of the candles, peeling the sticky dots off the floor. I put the last of the glasses away and check the room, turning on the dishwasher to handle everything else. To all intents and purposes, it looks like an old woman has dozed off on the sofa, rather than the after-party to a dark and bloody ritual.

"Come on," she says. "Stop dithering. Let's go."

I grab my car keys and a jacket, pausing to make sure that I've got my phone.

"Are you sure this will work?"

Melusine fixes me with an icy glare and rifles around in Sam's handbag, pulling out what looks like an access pass. "Bingo," she says. "It'll work."

Checking that the small tattoos on my own hands haven't mysteriously vanished, and that I have a few spare magazines of non-lethal ammo for my guns, I give her a nod and we turn to leave.

Chapter 19

The scientific site is a few miles outside of Buxton. It's a cool, clear night and the roads are quiet – I imagine that everyone else is out in their gardens, enjoying a cold beer or a glass of wine. I'm driving with a body-swapping witch towards a rendezvous with a pack of banshees and elves on a mission to save the earth spirit.

I can't stop stealing glances at Mel, or rather, Sam, but it's noticeably not Sam. It's Melusine's affectations, her way of speaking, the way she's checking through her large bag for spell components, keeping half an eye on the road and giving me imperious glares. There's nothing Sam about her actions, even if it's definitely Sam's body.

"So how does the whole body-swapping thing work?" I ask. "Like, do you know what she knows? Do you have her memories?"

Mel looks up from her bag, straightening her spine, then looking strangely pleased as she manages to sit upright. "There are traces of memory," she admits – and it's still odd that she doesn't sound croaky. "My mind is my own. I know some of the things that she's thought about a lot, or that she does regularly."

I shudder and try to focus on the road; for now, it's a reasonably major A-road, but a few miles further down we hit country lanes and that needs a bit more concentration. The scenery around here is fantastic; rolling hills, dry stone walls, beautiful lakes. A moment later, we're going through a steep-sided valley, the grassy walls on either side eventually giving way to bare rock. I wish I could see more of it, or had more time to appreciate it – actually, I'd love to come back and do some walking. Everything feels so natural and healthy, although having just spent a week in a small village in the countryside, I think I'm getting a bit blasé.

The thought of having to go back to crowded, cramped London is starting to fill me with dread.

A single-track road takes up all of my attention for a moment, especially when a large black Audi comes roaring around a bend, forcing us both to brake suddenly. I reverse back to a nearby passing place, the driver thanking me and hurrying past as I carefully bring mum's car out of the spot and retrace the route along the lane. A moment later we turn onto a broader road and then spot a new-looking sign on the left marking the way to a 'works site'. I indicate and follow it, spying a large hill in the distance, much further down the long, straight road.

Mel glances up from her phone. "That must be it ahead," she says. "The Seelie and Unseelie are both ready when we are. Moaning like prissy little shits."

We're stopped by an automatic barrier with a booth at the side, a bored-looking security guard scrutinising us intently. As we draw up, Mel retrieves a pass from Sam's handbag, opens her window and passes it to the attendant. He takes it with a grunt of thanks, scans it back inside the booth and looks satisfied.

"Uber?" he says, handing the pass back to Mel, looking over at me.

"Yeah," she says, trying to mimic Sam.

"Drop her off and come straight back out," he says, and I nod.

He goes back inside the booth and the barrier slowly raises. First challenge down.

There's a relatively long driveway with thick hedgerows on either side. I look around for signs that we're nearing a major magical site, but there's absolutely nothing to give it away. Unsurprising, I guess, from what I've seen so far.

A few hundred yards down the road is a large, fairly full car park, bays marked off with white paint. A scattering of mobile offices has sprung up; the nearest was clearly the first to arrive and is the most mobile-looking – I can still see bricks alongside its wheels, but the others look more permanent.

I glance at Mel, raising my eyebrows.

"It shouldn't be this full at this time of night, right?"

She doesn't reply, giving me a scowl that reminds me very much of her other face.

I manage to do a perfect bay park and we hop out, Mel briefly checking her bag before we hurry inside.

"Hey Sam," the receptionist says. He's a bored-looking guy with a shaved head in a smart blue shirt. "Back already?"

"Left my bag here," Mel says, doing a passable imitation of Sam and making me wonder whether she spent the whole hour with her ear pressed to the door. "The car wouldn't start so I had to take a cab – and then my phone's contactless wouldn't work in the cab so I need to get cash from my other bag. Just my luck!"

She rolls her eyes convincingly, making the guy laugh.

"Fuck my life," he says grinning. "Some days, eh?"

Mel nods and gives a theatrical sigh, glancing at the desk. "Do … uh, I need to sign in?"

"Yeah, sorry," he says apologetically. "You know what they're like. Everyone signs in, but I can probably make an exception for your cabbie."

I grunt in what I hope is a passable impression of a cab driver's gratitude, and Mel signs in, glancing at the receptionist as she passes the book back to him.

"Busy tonight," she says breezily.

"Yeah," he agrees. "Guess you didn't see the note on the intranet – they think they're getting close to something. There's been blasts every hour or so, although the diggers took a while to clear the last one."

Mel looks alarmed but recovers quickly. "Thanks," she says, then looks back at me. "Sorry, I'm keeping you waiting. Come on, let's get your money."

I try to keep a straight face – that must be the first time I've ever heard Melusine apologise for anything – and we hurry down the hallway. We turn right down a passageway before reaching what seems to be a slightly more permanent space. It's a large, open-plan office with a number of desks, chairs and workstations in it. It actually looks a lot like my office in London.

There are a couple of women working at two of the desks to our right. They both look up as we come in, and Mel nods knowingly to them. One waves back but doesn't say anything, looking back at her screen almost immediately.

Mel looks around, then we try to walk as casually as possible to the desk furthest away. They've got low partitions around them, so I crouch down, trying to stay out of sight while Mel turns on the workstation.

"So how much of this do you remember?" I ask in a whisper. "You seemed to handle signing for her ok."

"Most of it is muscle memory," she admits quietly, tapping at the keyboard. "I've done this a few times before and you've got to trust their instincts. Like typing in a username and password."

And voila, she's in their system. Whoever 'they' are.

It seems to be a relatively standard set-up, so Mel opens up the email programme and starts flicking through Sam's folders.

"Hmmm," she says. "Nothing really useful."

Clicking away from email, she finds the file system and rummages through her bag for a USB stick, dragging and dropping the whole drive into it, then grinning as a pop-up window tells her it'll be done in an hour.

"Excellent," she says, going back to the email again. "They're not tremendously advanced."

I'm starting to regret my crouch, so I switch over to kneeling. "The monitoring, or their progress?"

"Monitoring," she whispers. "You can't just attach a scientific instrument and expect it to work, but they have made some progress. If they'd been further along, I suspect the military would have been involved. At the moment, they're confirming hunches."

Her phone beeps and she glances at it, glaring at whatever the message was and sighing, before turning back to the file system. I hear a few muttered swearwords before she makes a pleased sound.

"Got it," she says. "The security system is run from the HQ in London, so we need a communications blackout."

She turns back to her phone and starts furiously typing messages, pausing to look at her – now shorter – fingernails. "These do make things easier, you know," she muses. "But they're not so good for cutting things. Now, Tssirai is going to handle the mobile connections, while the shitbag cuts the main line. Alariel will be by the entrance, but everything depends on Tssirai. Come with me."

She switches off the workstation monitor and we head back out of the office, returning the way we came, turning left down a different corridor and finding a closed door labelled 'Comms Room'. I try the handle; it's locked. Melusine seems to have been expecting this and is already rifling through her bag, bringing out what seems to be a sliver of bone, gesturing for me to get out of the way.

I stand back and she inserts the … well, whatever it is into the keyhole and a moment later there's a click. She tugs the handle and the door opens into a small room. It's barely bigger than my bathroom back in London, and it's rammed with racks and racks of servers. It's really warm in here, although I can feel some pretty vigorous air conditioning when I get closer to one of the racks.

Mel scours the room for what she's looking for, putting a cheap-looking earbud and microphone in place, dialling someone on her phone.

"Tssirai? Everyone is ready."

She looks over at me. "Take out your phone and the moment the mobile network goes down, let me know. Once it's down and I've removed the 4G backup, we'll go back to reception. Shoot anyone on sight."

Trying to breathe as quietly as possible, I wipe sweaty palms on my jeans, grateful that I won't have to worry about my grip on the guns once this happens, and telling myself that it's ok to shoot people with non-lethal rounds.

Just then, there's a muffled bang from somewhere distantly behind us, outside the complex. I spin around, but Mel gives me a sharp look.

"Focus, boy," she says, dialling another number on her phone. "Alariel? Silvai?"

She listens for a moment, then hangs up and shakes her head. "It wasn't either of them or the advance squads. The scouts are getting closer to try and see more."

I wipe my palms again and set my phone on a server shelf, staring at the mobile signal indicator. I've still got three bars.

Then I don't. The signal vanishes.

"Mobile's gone," I say, and Mel nods. She takes out a wire from a chunky-looking rectangular base unit on one of the shelves, then does the same with an identical one next to it, placing both units on the ground and stamping on them vigorously until they shatter.

She looks up at me. "What, were you expecting magic?"

I stare at her, open-mouthed.

"Come on," she says. "Time's a-wasting. Let's get back to reception and find out how many people are checked in. And remember, shoot anyone who isn't on our side."

Calmly, she shakes the last of the electronic debris from her shoe, ignoring the flashing red lights on some of the servers beside us. She opens the door, glancing around before heading back out into the corridor.

"Entrance guard is down," Mel says quietly as I mutter the words to summon my guns. Their weight is oddly reassuring as I curl my fingers around the grips.

We don't see anyone until we reach reception, the guy in the blue shirt staring blankly at his phone. He hears our footsteps and looks up.

"Oh, Sam," he says. "The strangest thing just happened – is your phone working ok?"

With a trembling hand, I raise my right-hand gun up to chest height and, wincing, squeeze the trigger, feeling it buck in my hand slightly. There's a crash as the receptionist falls backwards into a shelving unit, staggering, then collapses in a heap on the floor.

Mel peers over the counter, and, breathing heavily, I join her a moment later. There's a small trickle of blood running down the guy's neck from where he hit his head on the shelves, but otherwise he seems ok. Seeing my concerned look, Mel sighs and makes a gesture. A second later, the blood flows backwards up his neck and vanishes.

"Happy now?" she asks archly, and I banish the guns, holding my hands up.

"Didn't say anything," I say defensively. She shakes her head and leans over to get the visitor book, looking at his name label for a moment and flicking through the pages.

I glance over her shoulder, seeing a lot of names against today's date – and very few of them have written a time in the 'time out' column.

"All teams," Mel says into her microphone. "There are forty people on site, so log your progress carefully. Alariel, can you sweep the car park and rejoin me and Jamie in the main building? Silvai, Tssirai, please proceed to the main site and approach from the buildings. Jamie and I will handle anyone still inside."

I resummon my guns. Mel pauses, listening to someone on her phone, then gestures for me to head back down the corridor.

Then the screaming starts.

At first it's distant; I can hear crackling and what I think are the muffled 'crumps' of shots being fired. As Mel and I walk into the open plan office that we found earlier, the two women who were at their desks are now standing with their faces pressed up against the windows.

"Sorry," I whisper, shooting them both in the back. They're pushed against the glass by the force of the bullets, then sink down to the floor.

"Three for us," Mel says, gesturing to the far door of the room. "Come on."

Resisting the urge to check that they're breathing, I follow her across the now-empty space and she opens the door for me. Almost instantly, a panicked-looking man in a suit blunders out, losing his balance and bashing into Melusine, knocking her to one side.

"Oh god, I'm so sorry," he babbles. "I thought I heard gunfire! The Wi-Fi is down and my phone isn't working! What's going on?"

I'm taken aback by his appearance and caught between the urge to help Mel and the need to deal with him, but I know what she'd have me do. I raise my right-hand gun and, his eyes widening as he sees me, I shoot him in the chest. His face is a picture of pure panic for a second, then he stumbles and falls to the floor.

This time I do check his pulse – it's fine – before dragging him away towards the wall. Once he's out of the way, I turn back to see if Mel is ok.

She's scowling at me and packing a host of small objects from the floor back into her bag. There's what I think are charms, small pieces of wood and metal, glass vials – thankfully still intact, who knows what's inside – and …

"Mel, is that … alive?"

She continues to wrap the large, prone rat in some kind of insulating material before tucking it back into her bag.

"Don't be ridiculous, of course it's not alive," she says scathingly. "You couldn't keep a live rat like this, it wouldn't be humane."

I shake my head as she packs away the last of her things and looks around, rubbing her shoulder. "Go on," she says, cocking her head towards the door. "That's four."

We inspect the small adjoining room beyond the open-plan office, but it turns out to be a meeting room with just the one door. We're walking down back to the main junction when I hear much louder screaming from the area directly ahead of us, and a dark-haired woman suddenly bursts through a door to our left.

"Help!" she screams. "Help, they're shooting!"

Mel scowls at her and makes a sharp gesture, the woman skidding to a halt as her lips somehow fuse together. She touches her mouth, making frantic impotent noises, looking at us as shock spreads across her face.

I shoot her in the chest as well, telling myself that it's the merciful thing to do.

A figure in black leather steps through the door and I raise my guns again, but lower them as I recognise Alariel, from the Seelie Court. He's dressed like a biker, a black scarf curled elegantly around his mouth, making him look like some kind of gentleman bandit.

"Jamie," he purrs. "And Melusine, I presume?"

Mel nods. "Five," she says, as Alariel steps over the body of the woman I shot.

"Three in the car park and this wing," he says briskly. "I haven't checked any further down the corridor."

"Then we have one area left to check," Mel replies. "And we can be about our business."

We return to the main intersection of corridors, walking down away from reception. It's quiet, although I can occasionally hear a clap of thunder or a muffled shout in the distance.

The walls are plastered with a variety of health and safety notices, encouraging the use of personal protective equipment past this point. We must be getting close now.

I push the next door open and find myself in some kind of seminar room. Chairs are set out in rows, facing towards a large plasma screen mounted on the wall, a small cupboard next to it, which I imagine is full of cables, marker pens and the like. There's a lectern with a notebook still sitting on it, open.

Someone seems to have left a laptop on one of the chairs, and the walls have yet more safety notices on them, some of which I've never seen before – it's not just that you need special shoes and high-vis jackets, but also to hold some kind of safety qualification.

I glance around – it's not a big room, so I start heading for the exit on the other side with Alariel when Melusine pauses. I spin around, starting to say something, but she raises her finger to her lips, gesturing for silence.

Alariel glances back towards the door that we came in through, but Mel points to the small cupboard in the corner of the room. Surely there can't be someone …

But I guess she thinks there is. I move quietly to stand opposite the cabinet as she positions herself to one side of it. Alariel rolls his eyes and sits down on a chair, watching both of us with a bored expression on his face.

Melusine quickly pulls the cupboard door open, a middle-aged bald man falling out, landing on his hands and knees. Melusine pulls him up onto his feet quickly.

"Oh, thank goodness!" he booms. "Sam, I heard gunshots and then there was this …"

I shoot him in the chest, starting to tire of this. He slumps down to the floor and Mel steps back, letting him fall against the cupboard.

"Better now?" Alariel asks archly, raising one eyebrow.

"Thanks for the help," I reply acidly.

"Oh, you looked like you had it all under control," he says in mock-sympathy, standing up. "Shall we?"

Melusine snorts and gives the room another quick look, Alariel already opening the door marked with a green EXIT sign.

"How did you know?" I ask her quietly, and she fixes me with an intense look.

"I could feel his pulse racing," she says with a smirk. "It's quieter now."

"Course you could," I mutter, shaking my head.

Alariel hurries through the door, heading down a gravelled path into the darkness. I start to follow, but Melusine grabs my arm in a steely grip.

"Jamie," she says quietly. "We've got the same goal, but I didn't get this old without being cautious. Load one of your guns with regular rounds. Now."

I whisper *gun dexter*, making my right-hand gun vanish back into my hand, and eject the magazine from my left-hand gun, fumbling around in my jacket pocket until I find the right magazine.

"And keep your eyes open," she says, unnecessarily, then follows the elf into the gloom.

Chapter 20

The path outside runs across the centre of a farmer's field. The gravel has been roughly poured between two wooden tracks, a weak-looking orange plastic fence on either side protecting the field from the many feet of researchers and scientific staff.

It leads to a gap in a hedgerow, beyond which I can see a few floodlights illuminating the side of what seems to be a large quarry. On top of the quarry, I can just about make out a copse of trees.

Melusine hurries across the field, catching up with Alariel and muttering to him in low tones. He glances at her and gives me a quick look over his shoulder before replying. I stay back, my curiosity overridden by my desire not to annoy this prickly but seemingly friendly Seelie elf, or upset the delicate alliance that we've wrought.

I almost walk into Alariel's back when I push my way through the open space in the middle of the hedge. He's staring at the quarry, and I sidestep so that I can see what he's seeing.

It's quite a sight.

The land rises rapidly – or at least, it did – in front of us, but most of the hill is now exposed earth and rock, bare like a quarry. There's maybe a hundred metres of gentle incline ahead of us, the once-grassy slope now churned to mud, covered in bark chippings to try and preserve the surface.

Two small site offices sit ahead of us, along with three diggers and a tractor with a trailer attached to it, filled with rubble. Two fences form an inner and outer perimeter.

Then there's the bodies.

The other thirty-odd staff and workers on the scientific site are strewn around the muck. Three muscular orcs and, in what seems to be an uncomfortable display of inter-species collaboration, two Seelie elves, are hefting bodies into the trailer. Another two orcs, rifles slung across their backs, are unloading the quarried stone and earth back onto the grass so that the others can load the bodies in. It's pretty efficient, although judging by the elves' faces, they'd rather be anywhere but here.

There are three figures in discussion up by the bare face of the quarry, and I squint, trying to make out who they are when I see the doors.

There's a pair of them, maybe twelve feet high, covered in a layer of chalky white dust and set into the hillside. They're bound with what initially looks like cast iron, but on closer inspection, I suspect it's wood. I can see a huge keyhole visible under the glare of the floodlights, maybe twice as long as my hand, and as I look, a sense of disquiet sweeps through me. I feel … rooted … concerned … in need of help. It's fleeting, but leaves me with a worried feeling.

I look over at Mel. "Gaia?" I ask.

"You felt that too?" she says. "She's asking for help."

I let out a low whistle, and we start across the path towards the site.

"I'm not quite sure what's more remarkable," Alariel says lightly, but I can hear a frisson of tension in his voice. "Seeing the doors to Gaia's chamber, or seeing those two talk."

Up ahead, Silvai is talking to Tssirai, the unmistakeable banshee-thing with the white eyes. Silvai is dressed in tightly-fitting clothes and what looks like a bulky stab-proof vest, whereas Tssirai – despite the muck – is still in her flowing white robe. As we approach, the third figure, an elf I don't recognise, walks back over to one of the orc crews, leaving us with Tssirai and Silvai.

Again, I'm not sure which is worse; Silvai's glare as ripples of electricity flow up and down her arms, or the blankly terrifying gaze of Tssirai's pure white eyes and ivory features.

"Ladies," Melusine says patronisingly. "Are we all done here, or shall we sit down to tea?"

"Melusine," Silvai spits. "Your intelligence was accurate for once. Did you engineer all this to do … all this?"

She gestures to Sam's body.

"This weak thing?" Mel snorts. "It'd be worn out in less than a week if I tried more than just low-level magic. I don't know what you sacrifice to make static run over your nethers, but I dare say it can't be comfortable."

"Witch," Tssirai cuts across both of them, her voice deep and slow. "We have purpose here. All the humans are accounted for. Is it still your wish that we enchant their memories?"

Melusine sighs and looks over at me. I nod.

"Yes, I suppose we ought," she says. "Killing them would inevitably provoke an enquiry of sorts. Jamie and I will take a closer look at the damage to the doors, if your teams can make a start."

Silvai bristles. "This will take *hours*," she hisses. "Not to mention making the site inaccessible."

"Once the orcs have finished taking the humans to the front gate, have them set up the beacons and make it look like the site is radioactive," Melusine offers. "Strip the offices and blow them, then enchant the beacons with deterrents. If you don't feel up to it, I think I saw a few orcs in cradles who might do a better job?"

I jump as small lightning bolts fire from Silvai's fingertips into the ground.

"Witch, you test me like no other," she seethes. "But your plan is sound. Perhaps the Unseelie ... muscle ... can return in a few days to re-cover the gate?"

"We will return and cover the earth mother," the

banshee intones reverently. "Once we are sure that the humans have disregarded this site."

Silvai looks relieved, but she's definitely still pissed off. "Fine," she says. "I will make sure that the humans do not wake, and we should be away by noon tomorrow. Our timing so far has been impeccable – the humans had uncovered the door but no more. Another hour and things could have gone very differently. Let us hope it continues."

Tssirai beckons a muscular orc over, his green skin partially hidden by his body armour, but his hairy arms are bare and his right hand never strays far from a bulky handgun strapped to his waist.

"Almost done here," he grunts affably at the banshee, as Tssirai debriefs him. "Human transport won't take long. Stripping the offices, longer. Beacons ain't tough, but you and half the lads can go once we've loaded up the van with the servers."

"Done," Melusine says, grinning at the orc. "Come on Jamie."

Slightly mystified by the exchange, but thankful that Melusine didn't quite manage to spark some kind of intra-faery conflict, I follow her towards the colossal doors in the hillside.

"What would we do without orcs?" Melusine muses as we leave the others behind us.

"It seemed … straightforward," I comment, although what I don't voice is that it also seemed fairly capable of tearing us all limb from limb without breaking a sweat.

"You get what you sign up for when it comes to orcs," Melusine says. "Enthusiastic blood donors too."

I'm not sure whether to ask about that or stay quiet, but in the end opt for the safer – the latter – of the two.

As we get closer to the floodlit doors, I see that there's intricate detailing on them. No wonder this company – Zephyr – had called so many people down here to see the big reveal, it's incredible. Trees, vines and woodland scenes are carved into the wood, curled around the decorative darker material extending across the face of the door itself. As I look at it more closely, I can see small woodland animals, birds and even a unicorn in the wood. The detail is fantastic.

"We should not be here," Melusine says suddenly, making me jump and interrupting my reverie. "This is a sacred place. And earth … Alizon should be here."

It's the first time I've ever heard any kind of trepidation in Melusine's voice, and it makes me take a step backwards.

"Jamie, if I don't move for more than ten minutes, find something metal and use it to pull me away from the door, ok? Do not touch me yourself or use anything organic."

I nod, suddenly afraid.

Steeling herself, Mel takes a step forward and carefully lays one hand flat on the door. For a moment, nothing happens, then she goes rigid and the entire door glows with a yellowish light. She begins muttering under her breath very, very quickly, and although every instinct is telling me to pull her away, I force myself to check the time on my phone and just watch.

The unnatural light illuminates the ornate patterns on the doors, some of which seem to have changed in the last thirty seconds, and I wonder what kind of key fits into the giant keyhole. It must be almost a foot high. When I pause and look away from my phone, I can feel a sense of power radiating from the doors, but there's also something else. There's a sense of profound age, but also life.

I shake my head like I'm trying to dislodge something. *Pay attention, Jamie,* I chastise myself. *You're here to do a job.*

I glance at my phone again. Five minutes. I really hope Melusine doesn't die or get sucked into the door or something. Who knows what stuff goes down in the faery world in situations like this?

With a sharp intake of breath, she pulls away from the door, staggering briefly then catching herself. She blinks and looks around, looking at me vacantly and then seems to recover her focus.

"Good," she says. "All done. Gaia knows that we're helping. I need to tell the orcs to remove some probes, but otherwise there doesn't seem to be any permanent damage. How long were we communing?"

"About seven minutes," I say, glancing at my phone again.

"It felt like a day," she mutters. "And that's quick for Gaia from what Alizon told me. She once spent five years sat here. Barely ate. Give me your arm, would you?"

I offer her my support and like a weirdly dysfunctional couple, we totter back to the site, where the orcs are loading the last of the scientists and research staff into the trailer. Melusine consults briefly with the orc who seems to be in charge, and then has a slightly longer exchange with Alariel. The elf gives her a small wooden token that she tucks into her pocket, then she gestures, leading us back to the main office, checking and retrieving the USB stick from the laptop in the open-plan office.

"Alright," she says, patting herself down. "We're done here. Come on, let's leave them to it."

"That's it?" I ask. "That's all we came to do? That's all you needed me for?"

"Of course," she says. "Although give yourself some credit, boy. We might not have done this quite so bloodlessly if I hadn't been able to wear this body. And you did a reasonable job at subduing the humans here, so you've earned your money. I'll return Sam's property and once we get back to my place, I'll give you the balance. Then you can be on your way."

I grunt, but a surge of disappointment rises inside me. A part of me – a fairly big part, to be honest –definitely wants to stay in this world. I'd hoped that Melusine was serious about me being her apprentice, but given that I don't have any skill at magic whatsoever, I guess I should have known better.

"We didn't find out who did it," I say, trying to keep my voice even as we drive out of the car park.

"This isn't a detective novel," Mel grates, the roughness of her voice sounding strange coming from Sam's mouth.

"Once the Seelies have picked apart the servers, and I've given any difficult bits to some of my dark web contacts, we should have a good idea of what they know, who they are and who tipped them off. There are always cranks interested in the faery, and every few decades a more serious organisation rises up. We'll have to watch them carefully. It'll be good for the Seelie and the Unseelie to have a common enemy, keeps them from sniping at each other. Now if you don't mind, I'm going to get some shut-eye. Let me know when we get back."

Feeling a surge of dejection, I turn my attention back to the road, driving along quiet country lanes in the dark and trying to clear my head. The last hour was – well, it was pretty intense, but I felt *needed*. It wasn't the shooting – that was terrifying in all honesty and if I never have to do it again it'll be too soon – but I find myself admitting that I liked being instrumental, being part of the operation.

And now I'm being discarded like some kind of contract worker. Which, I suppose, is exactly what I am. A fantastical one, but a contract worker nonetheless.

It occurs to me that in the fairy stories I read as a child, it's all too common for humans to become glamoured by the elves and their magic, wandering off and getting lost for years. Is this how they felt, I wonder? Not knowing how deep the rabbit hole goes, and desperately wanting to understand, to explore, to be part of the wonder.

I try to focus on the road. I'm done here. Moaning won't help.

I wake Mel when we pull in at the front of the house, and she stirs quickly. I breathe a sigh of relief when I see Sam, or rather, Mel's body still snoring on the sofa, exactly where we left it. For a moment my mind runs through what might have happened if she'd woken mid-way through the night and discovered her mind in an ancient woman's body. That's the kind of thing that leaves you needing serious therapy.

Mel leans over her own body and presses the wooden token to it. I sit down on a chair heavily and wonder when I can go to bed, suddenly feeling completely worn out.

"I had Alariel enchant this box with a memory of an evening drinking with a friend and watching Netflix," Melusine says. "You won't have to account for the lost hours. Wake Sam once I'm done and send her on her way. And we might as well sleep here, but we'll be away first thing in the morning; I want to check on Alizon."

I nod, grunting. I guess that's actually pretty thoughtful, all things considered.

"Thanks," I say. "You didn't have to do that."

"I know," she says. "But you should treat your tools well."

It takes me a moment to realise that she might not be talking about Sam's body, and I just let my head fall backwards onto the headrest as she chants softly under her breath, setting one candle at a carefully chosen point on the floor. Retrieving a phial of liquid from her bag, she daubs a little on her own forehead and the forehead of the body on the sofa. The pitch and volume of her chanting increases, and once again there's a bright flash of light.

I recoil, blinking, then see Melusine standing in the lounge in her own body and clothes again. I breathe a sigh of relief – there was a small part of me that wondered if she might keep the 'newer model', however flimsy it might be.

Quickly, she extinguishes the candle and looks around the room, also glancing at Sam, still asleep on the sofa.

"Wake her up in the next five minutes," she says quietly. "It's natural sleep but I want her dealt with."

And with that, she turns and heads upstairs, leaving me alone with my childhood friend. Although I don't think that the term really applies. You tend not to kidnap your friends. You tend not to let ancient women steal your friend's bodies because they need the security privileges.

Feeling a spiral of self-loathing starting to take hold, I kneel by the side of the sofa and gently shake Sam. There's a moment where I think she's not going to wake, then she slowly opens her eyes.

"Jamie?" she says slowly. "Oh Jamie, did I fall asleep? I'm so sorry, I'm a terrible guest!"

I feel a surge of guilt as she babbles contritely, slowly sitting up and stretching. "God, what time is it?" she says, looking around for a clock and her phone, seeing her bag nearby and rummaging through it. "Oh, it's late, I should get going! Jamie, I'm sorry about being such a bad houseguest, it was so lovely to see you."

I manage to fake the platitudes; in fairness, it was nice to catch up with her, but it's overlaid with such a sick feeling of guilt that I'm having trouble focusing on the positive parts.

I also manage to fend off most of her questions while we wait for her taxi to arrive: no, I'm not sure when I'll be back up here, no, I'm not immediately going back to London tomorrow night, and no, I don't think I'll have time for dinner again, I'll have work to do after my meetings.

Thankfully, the cab arrives before I have to tell too many more lies and with a final wave, Sam gets into the car and disappears off down the road. Shaking my head, I turn back to the house, heading straight to bed where I steadfastly fail to fall asleep. If I can't fit in with the normal world, but I'm being sent straight back there by the faery world, where do I belong?

Chapter 21

I'm tired and fuzzy-headed when I finally surface the next morning, having tried to shut out the sound of Melusine tramping about the house for the last half hour or so. She's grumpy and short-tempered; I only reply to her questions in grunts as I go about making breakfast, which is fine because most of them are things like 'be ready in twenty minutes' and 'do we need more petrol?'.

We don't technically have to leave the house until eleven, but we're pulling out just before nine.

It's mercifully quiet on the roads.

I still feel like crap, and it doesn't help that my brain starts replaying how all this began. A favour for a woman I barely knew. Money. Mum.

I should call mum. It's been a little while and I don't really know if the first set of drugs from Mel worked. I'll call as soon as we get back.

I drag my full attention back to the road. Melusine

seems to be sitting quite comfortably in the passenger seat, getting regular updates from both sides of the Seelie and Unseelie Courts. She snorts in frustration after half an hour, as Silvai decides that their collaboration is at an end and that it's beneath her to keep the Unseelie informed from afar.

We stop briefly at a service station halfway down the M6, thankfully without incident, although Melusine does take it upon herself to roundly criticise the state of the car when we get back to it. It's too small, it's dirty, it's uncomfortable.

"In fairness," I add, during a pause in her tirade. "Until a week ago, I didn't even know I *had* a car – this belongs to mum, remember?"

That shuts her up for another hour or so.

The landscape around us becomes more and more familiar, and we eventually pull back into the village, driving past the house. Oddly, there's something resembling a traffic jam – by village standards, anyway – as we near the supermarket, and I peer down the road to try and see what's going on. Melusine looks up from her phone and follows my gaze.

"What's got the yokels' attention this time?" she says scathingly, and I give her a sharp glance.

"Looks like there's a police car parked up ahead," I say, spotting Sergeant Michaelson and his vehicle a way down the road. "Want me to stop?"

"Jamie," Mel sighs. "If we stop to wipe the arse of

every fucking villager between here and the Manor, we'll never get anywhere. But if you really must."

I almost ask what's got her into such a grumpy state but decide against it. We're almost done here. This time tomorrow, I'll be concluding the sale of the house and out for dinner with Flic ... hopefully.

As we creep forwards, I can see that the problem seems to be by the antique shop. One of the front windows is entirely gone, lifted out. Distracted, I manage to brake before I run into the back of a BMW in front of us.

Seeing Sergeant Michaelson not far away, I wind the window down, poking my head out.

"Jamie," he says. "Heading out?"

"Coming back," I say, pulling the handbrake up and gesturing to Melusine. "Helping a friend of a friend out. What happened here?"

"The oddest thing," he says, still looking perplexed. "As far as I can tell, someone removed the front window pane at about 3am this morning, just when the CCTV switches over to another tape. I've been telling ... well, it must have taken a few people to do it, that glass is heavy stuff. And they only took one thing, as far as Janet can remember. They must have been startled by something. Still, it's worrying."

I realise that stopping for a long conversation in the middle of the road is also worrying, although less so in the countryside when you're talking to a police officer.

"Strange," I say, hearing an impatient cough from the passenger seat. "Well, I hope you get them."

He nods and I check to see how many cars have backed up behind me. There's only one, and I think it's the guy who works at the post office counter in the local shop.

As we draw away, I glance in my rear-view mirror again, and see that the post office guy is doing exactly the same thing that I did, probably getting the same talk from Michaelson. Hell, it's probably the most excitement that Michaelson's seen for months.

Then I realise that it's not. Melusine's drug sales would have been far more interesting – and frustrating – for the aging policeman. Well, I guess if you're immortal, or near enough, you can afford to wait a hundred years or so for the heat to die down.

Once I've pulled up outside the bungalow, I help Mel with her Mary Poppins bag, putting up with another barrage of grumbling. I figure that we might as well be civil to each other for the last half hour of our time together. Or rather, I might as well be civil and part ways amicably, while she moans and makes acid comments about the state of Beckett's front garden.

"And where *is* he?" she says sharply. "I haven't seen him since he finished Merovech's thatching."

I shake my head; I haven't seen him for a while either, although I think one of the regulars mentioned that they'd seen him in the pub recently when I met Flic there.

"If you're the guardian of an entrance to a faery realm, you should take your job a little bit more seriously," Melusine grates. "There was a time when I could rely on Beckett Andrews, but I'm starting to reconsider."

An elderly dogwalker passes us on the footpath, stopping when they hear Beckett's name. I glance at the old man, his hair greying, his aging jacket clearly in need of re-waxing and corduroy trousers patched at the knees.

"Andrews, did you say?" he says in a slightly warbling voice. I don't recognise him at first, then I realise that he's one of the teachers from the local school – or at least, was. "Bumped into him in the shop yesterday evening. Kind man, always willing to help."

"Hmmmf," Mel grunts. "Well, that doesn't explain where he is now."

"He's probably … in the garden?" I offer, earning a scathing look from the witch.

"Fine," she says. "Come on."

Letting ourselves into his house, we find a note pinned to the kitchen door saying that he's running a few errands in the area but should be back by mid-afternoon.

"I need to make a quick call," I say, getting an eyeroll from Mel, although she pauses and makes herself a cup of tea while I call mum.

My phone rings a few times before mum picks up, but she sounds alright and says she's feeling more human. She hasn't had any more surgery or scans, although she's due to have one tomorrow. That's about all I get – she diverts the conversation with questions about the house and various bits and pieces. I wrap it up as quickly as I can, turning back to Mel once I've hung up.

"How is she?"

"Seems to be doing better," I say. "Thanks to you, really."

Mel inclines her head, then gestures at the door. I do the trick with the blind, the lock and the green tile, then gesture for her to go through the fireplace, following a moment later.

Everything seems a little better and brighter when I emerge on the other side of the small door into the rich-smelling forest. It almost feels like the air is healing me, cleansing me as I take it into my lungs.

Only there's some kind of undercurrent. Once again, I can hear a murmuring; there's no wind, but the leaves are rustling.

"Is something…"

"Wrong," Melusine finishes for me. "The trees are chattering about something. Come on."

We hurry down the path towards her hut.

"A few days ago, I thought I heard something similar," I say, feeling embarrassed. "There wasn't any wind, but it was almost like the trees were … well, I don't know."

She looks at me sharply. "What did they say?"

"I don't know," I say haltingly. "I didn't realise they could speak."

"Of course they can speak," she says sharply. "You just

have to give them time. They don't reckon hours like we do."

I'm about to reply with a quick retort, but then I smell something else – smoke, but it's definitely not woodsmoke. Or at least, not only woodsmoke. It's really bitter, acrid.

Melusine looks around. "There," she says, pointing. "Shit!"

I peer through the trees, seeing her hut a way down the path, but the smoke is coming from where … where Merovech's hut should be.

"Come on," I say, breaking into a run. "Hurry!"

"Jamie!" she says sharply. "Stop! Together. Carefully. If there's trouble, it's serious, and this antique can't keep up with your long legs."

I skid to a halt, wondering what she means, the bitter smoke catching in my throat and her words in my mind.

Antiques.

Merovech's hut.

"Mel," I say, pausing and slowly turning around, thoughts arcing through my head like Silvai's lightning-magic. "I have a really bad feeling about this."

Holidays.

Thatching.

She looks at me, realisation dawning in her beady eyes, her hooked nose quivering with anger. She opens her mouth to reply, but I'm distracted by some kind of stirring in the grass below. I look down, starting to step backwards towards Beckett's house but feel a sharp pain in both my ankles. A coiled plastic wire has wound its way around them and is holding me tight to the ground. I start to lean over to try and free myself, but two more coils wind their way down from a nearby tree and wrap their way around my wrists. They pull me back up, yanking my arms around until I'm in an uncomfortable X shape, unable to move.

I feel like I should be about to fall over, but instead there's pressure as the bindings bite into my wrists.

I look over at Melusine, feeling panic rising in my chest; she's also trapped, but now there's some kind of metal mask covering her mouth tightly.

"Shit!" I manage. "Mel!"

She looks at me, immobilised and – from what I can make out – absolutely furious. Then she looks over my shoulder; I can hear something approaching distantly, but I can't turn to see what it is.

The wire is cutting into my wrists and ankles, getting tighter. Dammit. I try to see where it's coming from, but it seems to disappear into the ground about a metre or so away from me. I can feel it pulling my arms higher, stretching my spine while my feet stay firmly anchored. I'm going to be torn apart by a TV power cable.

The pain is agonising, like sharp spikes jabbing from my shoulders through to my chest.

I try to glance backwards but can't get my head around enough to see what's going on. Maybe one of the forest creatures will come and help us.

"Ypotryll!" I yell. "Kopek! Enutef!"

Mel shakes her head minutely, looking down. I try to follow her eyes. She's … looking at her bag? Neither of us can move – what are we supposed to do with that?

I can almost feel my bones being dragged out of their sockets. The pain is becoming red hot as my elbows and shoulders feel like they're being slowly detached.

Then I realise. "*Gun sinister*," I mutter, wincing at the latest bout of pain coursing through my body, watching the organic gun and half-sleeve flow out of the small tattoo on my left hand. I wonder if the elongated sleeve will impede what I'm about to do, but as I rotate my wrist, trying to aim for Mel's bag, it seems to move with me. I silently thank V for their work, then worry about the small inventor. I hope they're ok.

I don't really have time to be too grateful or worried, instead trying to see exactly where Mel is looking. Her bag is hanging off one shoulder, tilted slightly towards her body. Fuck. I don't want to shoot her by accident. Her face is contorted in agony as the wires cruelly pull her more and more tightly, rendering her a thin, scarecrow outline.

I aim as carefully as I can, hands trembling, muscles screaming.

Melusine closes her eyes as I squeeze the trigger.

There's a bang, and the bottom of her bag explodes in a puff of fabric, fragments of small charms, and part of a large dead rat flying everywhere.

Melusine's eyes snap open. She spies the blood and intestines littering the ground, and gestures sharply. The flesh and blood reforms, hardening in the air, almost looking crystalline as it coalesces into two lumpy circular objects, like sawblades. She gestures again and they spin in the air, accelerating faster and faster, before snapping upwards and cutting through the wires holding her wrists.

Mel falls to the ground, landing awkwardly on her hands and knees, the bloody blades slicing down into the ground and releasing her feet.

I let out a moan as the wires squeeze my wrist bones together even more painfully. Mel looks up from the ground and says a word I don't catch, the sawblades leaping through the air towards me.

I close my eyes for a second until I feel myself falling forwards, landing on my hands and knees a moment later, the pain around my ankles easing as the blades cut through whatever attached the wire to me.

"Shit!" I manage, as I sit back on the grass, trying to loosen the strands of plastic from my hands and feet. "Are you ok?"

Mel has unfastened the weird mask-thing from her face and is working on the ties around her feet, flexing her shoulders and grimacing in pain.

"Wanker!" she grunts. "Stinking filthy wanker. Dickhead. Pig-fucking shitbag. Rancid shitting tosser."

"Are you ok?" I ask again, massaging my ankles. "What the fuck was that?"

I notice the two blood-discs still spinning in the air and hear something behind us. Ties still attached to my wrists, I spin around on the forest floor, ejecting the magazine from my gun and spilling a selection of alternatives onto the ground.

In the distance, I can see one of Merovech's scorpion creatures limping towards us, passing Mel's house. It looks like it's been in an explosion; some of the copper cogs seem melted, although I could be wrong – it's still a long way off.

Mel gestures and her blood-discs accelerate towards the scorpion creature, colliding with it and making a loud metallic clanging noise. Two of its legs fly off and the discs fracture, collapsing to the forest floor.

"Fuck," she curses. "Jamie?"

I look at the variety of sleek magazines in front of me, locating a black one, loading it into my gun and summoning the other one, loading it with another of the same colour.

The scorpion seems to rally and points its weird pyramidal head towards us, moving awkwardly on four legs. Bladed pincers emerge from its front section, and I pull myself to my feet, aiming with hands that tremble a lot more than I'd like.

My first shots go wide and blow a hole in the fence surrounding Melusine's house, but the second volley strikes true and with a loud bang, the scorpion explodes in a cloud of clockwork and sharp metal fragments.

I steady myself against a tree trunk. "Are we safe?"

"Of course not, ridiculous boy," Melusine grates, finally freeing herself from all of the torture-plastic and inspecting the damage to her bag. "Are you injured?"

"I ... I don't think so," I stammer. "Mel, I think it was Beckett."

"Hmm," she says. "Come on. Follow me carefully and tread only where I tread."

Muttering something under her breath, she steps past me, looking around for any more traps. As her spell comes to an end, the forest floor glows slightly, one area showing a reddish glow.

"Stay away from there," she says, pointing, as I try to stand in her exact footsteps. She's a lot smaller than I am, so it's not a problem.

"Ah, Mel," I say, suddenly realising that the rat wasn't her only source of escape materials. "You could have done something hideous with my body just then, couldn't you?"

She looks back at me with gleaming beady eyes and nods, rubbing her wrists. "Must be getting soft in my old age. Mind you, blood is easier to work with than flesh and that fucking mask stopped me doing anything more complex."

I swear under my breath.

A few steps later, Mel diverts to the path around the back of her house, towards the rising plume of smoke. There's a large patch of red spell-light on her doorstep, so we both avoid that carefully, taking our time to avoid touching the house as we walk around it.

We reach Merovech's place a moment later.

Or rather, what's left of it. V's once proudly-thatched house is now a smoking ruin of burnt wood and molten copper, pools of metal cooling and creaking. Mel closes on the wreck, peering inside and softly calling V's name. I step beside her, but the heat is still intense.

"So, the ... the thatching?" I say tentatively, as Mel raises her head and sniffs the air.

"Some kind of extremely hot explosive," she mulls, kicking a small octagonal object around with her foot. "Thermobaric?"

I don't know what that is. All I know is that my knees feel weak and tears are welling in my eyes at the loss of the little inventor. The kind, funny, endlessly enthusiastic inventor.

"Jamie," Mel says sharply, gently prodding me with a sharp toe. "Get it together. We've got work to do before we mourn. Here, take this, but mind, it's hot."

She kicks the small copper octagon over to me. It almost looks like a very small box of chocolates or a music box, but I can't see a latch to open it. Tentatively, I pick it up; it's warm but not hot to the touch, so I put the memento in my jacket pocket.

"You don't think he'd really ...?" I start, my mind making its second round of connections.

Mel looks at me seriously. "Go on Jamie," she says, slowly turning around and limping back up the path towards Beckett's house. "Let's hear it."

"Well, Beckett's comment about holidays," I start. "He's obviously pissed off that he's stuck here. And you said that only the Seelie and the Unseelie Court together could grant you leave for more than two weeks. I guess he wants out – permanently – and maybe the Courts can't or wouldn't do that, but could something just as powerful do the same thing, like Gaia? She's the earth spirit, so surely it'd be within her power to play with the realms. Only, you'd need to get access first."

I stop for a moment to massage my wrists and ankles, gathering my thoughts slowly and painfully.

"But if you could arrange for someone else to clear the way to the door, then another party to clear that first set of people and be gone after a few hours, then you'd be good to go. Am I on the right track?"

"Not bad," she says scratchily. "Although given our reception here, I'm concerned about how 'gone' the Seelies and Unseelies will be. And how on earth is the mouldy shitbag actually intending to get access to Gaia?"

"Didn't you say that artefacts blessed by both the Seelie and Unseelie Courts would do that?" I ask, and she nods, still puzzled. "And I'm assuming that 'access' is meant literally, like a key? Only, it'd have to be a really big key to fit that lock. What if that mace from the antiques shop was actually the key? Mrs Jones once said that her great-grandfather had some magical stuff – what if he had it?"

"Fuck," she swears, starting another torrent of abuse, going back to the Beckett's grandfather and his unlikely and illegal sexual proclivities. "Fucking untrustworthy errand boys. I knew that one was holding out on me, he was never the same after that ridiculous war."

I try not to take her comment personally, and let her swear for a bit longer.

"Come on," she says as her tirade ends, and we get back to the bungalow. "We're going back to Buxton. And I hope you don't mind breaking a few speed limits."

Chapter 22

As I set the GPS for the scientific site in Buxton and tear along country lanes towards the M5, Melusine sews up the large bullet hole in her bag, magicking up the last of the rat's blood into a small pellet and firing it out of the window into a farmer's field. Checking through the bag's contents, she decants some of it into a supermarket bag that my mum had lying around under the passenger seat.

I hop out before we hit the motorway to fill the car up with petrol, Melusine twitching with irritation at the delay.

I try my best to placate her with snacks from the small shop, but she berates me for a solid fifteen minutes until we hit seventy miles an hour on the M5. I stay at seventy, reluctant to risk getting pulled over, but Mel doesn't seem to notice. Instead, she turns back to her phone and makes some calls, her frustration at the Unseelie Court winding her up even more.

"Tssirai and the orcs returned early this morning," she grates, hanging up. "A few of the other dark elves stayed behind to help with the memory charms and ignite the beacons, but Balthamel doesn't see any cause for concern. He had the cheek – the very cheek – to thank me for preventing a clash with the Seelies, but he's still suspicious of them."

Her call with the Seelie Court is short and abrupt.

"Motherfuckers!" she hisses. "Wouldn't even take my call. And I can't raise Alariel or Silvai."

Things must be bad if she's contemplating calling Silvai directly, I think, although if Beckett has hijacked more of those scorpions, then things could go very badly indeed.

Hijacked? He's got the master control widget, I think, recalling my conversation with Merovech. He could just use that and have his own little army of near-indestructible scuttling death-dealers.

It's late afternoon by the time Buxton comes into view, and I hurry around the almost-familiar roads, retracing our steps towards the Zephyr site, Melusine deep in the contents of the USB stick from our raid the previous night.

"Either they didn't know his name," she mutters. "Or he was smart enough not to give it to them. It's definitely Beckett though. He knew."

I pull up outside the barrier where Melusine had 'her' ID checked. It now has a 'site closed' sign in the middle of the road. She gets out and casts the spell that illuminates the way ahead in green.

"Ah, Mel?" I say, seeing the tractor and trailer up ahead as I step out of the car. I can see an arm lying over the side, and bile rises up my throat. What if they're all dead?

"Calm down," Melusine says, directing the spell in front of us. Everything looks clear, so we hurry down to where the research staff are all piled up in the large, dirty trailer.

I'm trembling as we step alongside it, but then I see the blue-shirted receptionist lying there; he suddenly exhales deeply and mutters something in his sleep.

"They're alive," I say softly, relieved, feeling tension flood out of my shoulders.

Melusine, seemingly unconcerned with the research staff, has already made her way around to the front of the trailer, which is still hitched to the tractor.

She pauses and makes a soft noise.

"Ah, grandson," she says quietly. "Rest in peace. You did well when you had to."

The side of the cab has been entirely blown open, and slumped over the steering wheel in a pool of his own blood is Alariel. The front of his biker jacket has been torn apart by … something … and …

I step back, vomiting onto the grass at the sight of Alariel's intestines spilling out over his lap. My stomach empties itself and for a moment I'm paralysed by heaves.

I feel a hand on my back and whirl around, but only see Melusine looking at me with something vaguely resembling compassion. She's holding a bottle of water and a handkerchief, both of which I take gratefully, rinsing and spitting before wiping myself.

"Shit!" I say, swallowing bile. "Fucking hell."

She nods and sighs. "Nothing we can do for him now," she says. "And we need to leave the road."

I look ahead; there's a long, red line from one side to the other a little further down. We climb through a thorny hedge and trudge our way across a mucky ploughed field to get back to the safe part of the road.

"Can't you …" I wave my hands at Mel, who scowls at me.

"Hunter magic," she grunts. "Metal things, dead things. Basic cantrips can see where they are, but it'd take too much time to disarm. More time than we have, anyway."

The rest of the main road is mercifully clear. I'm starting to wonder if we'll see anyone else when I hear a scuttling sound. Melusine whirls around with a speed belying her age, and I follow a moment later, summoning my guns and spotting the scorpion-creature between two cars on the distant side of the car park.

I open fire with a volley of explosive rounds, the noise almost deafening as the petrol in the two cars ignites, the shrapnel of the scorpion twisting and embedding itself in the side of the building.

Melusine nods as a small column of smoke rises from the wreckage.

"Weren't the orcs supposed to blow up the building?" I ask, looking at the very much intact temporary offices, the lights still on.

"They usually leave anything cerebral for the elves," she mutters. "Come on."

We pick our way around the outside, trying to keep an eye out for any further red spots marking Beckett's traps.

"Ah," I say, as we arrive at the rear of the building, seeing the track leading down to Gaia's site. "That's a problem."

The gravel track is illuminated in red spell-light, and the field is criss-crossed with patches of it, as if someone had carelessly tossed miniature floodlights all around.

"Come on," Melusine says impatiently. "Stop dilly-dallying."

Cautiously, we pick our way across the muddy field. It's slow going, and every time my foot gets caught in the muck, I wonder if it's a trap that has somehow eluded Melusine's magic.

Thankfully, her spells prove reliable, and a moment later, we're pushing our way through the hedge, thorns tearing painfully at almost every item of clothing that I'm wearing, scraping the skin.

Then we're through, greeted by a warzone. Or rather, what used to be a warzone.

Dead elves litter the main site.

If there was anything left in my stomach, it would be coming back up again as I see the body of Silvai a few paces away, not far from a dark elf I last saw patrolling the outskirts of the site. They're both cut to shreds, blood puddling in the rough earth.

"Jamie!" Mel shrieks, and I turn my head towards her, spotting a bronze scorpion racing towards us, killer scissor blades outstretched, clicking and clacking as it navigates the rough soil with ease. I remember how easily they shrugged off conventional ammunition outside Merovech's house and wonder whether they're similarly immune to spells; no doubt Silvai's electricity was no use against clockwork, judging from the corpse in front of me.

Raising my guns wearily, I send four explosive rounds into the scorpion, leaving nothing but a steaming pile of metal shards in a small crater.

"Couldn't he have waited until they'd left?" I ask, looking over at Mel. She's got one hand outstretched, and seems to be listening for something – signs of life, maybe?

"No," she grates. "With what he might be about to do, he'd need chaos. The Courts would have taken one look at this and gone to war. And with you and I out of the way, there'd be no-one to say it wasn't the other side that had started it all. By the time anyone worked it out – *if* anyone worked it out – he'd be long gone."

"And all because he wanted to leave? To get out of the faery world for good?"

"He's been in that bungalow for almost four hundred years," Melusine says. "Time enough to get sick of the faery, sick of the same village, lying low every other generation to make people think that you're dead before you resurface. It'd drive a lesser mind batty, but to start resenting the faery world enough to start a war? Twisted."

She's spitting by the end, gobbets of saliva flying out of her mouth, hands hooked into claws, poised to throttle someone. "And everyone's dead," she finishes. "All torn to pieces by V's hijacked monstrosities. I thought they'd be a useful deterrent if Lisilya's eye ever turned to our small realm. Hubris, hubris…"

As we draw closer to Gaia's door, I stop and stare at the landscape around us. The previously bare quarry face is now covered with a light dusting of grass, a thin green coat hiding the bare chalky earth. My reverie is interrupted by Melusine swearing softly, and I look over at the huge door.

It's ajar, a large metal shaft protruding from the keyhole, an object that I last saw, well, last saw properly, thirteen years ago in the front display of the antiques shop. Not a mace at all.

A key.

A giant-sized key.

Once again, I can feel raw power radiating from the chamber beyond, like there's a vast turbine inside, or some incomprehensible machinery. At the same time, tendrils of thought and emotion seem to be working their way into my brain. I can almost feel the world itself turning, leaves flourishing, growing old and dying, a sense of loss and joy and acceptance all at once. I start to get a headache; I don't think that the mortal mind is supposed to hold all these kinds of feelings.

It's a lot.

"Gaia is … fighting," Mel says haltingly. "He's sapping her power somehow but doesn't understand it. Men! It's not like taking money from the bank."

She glares at me, as if I should be able to control other men remotely.

"Do you want me to go first?" I offer. "In case there are more scorpions?"

Melusine's expression softens. "Very well," she says curtly. "The second mouse gets the cheese, after all."

"Is that from…" I start, then shrug as the film reference eludes me, replaced by the image of Alariel's dead body. "Never mind."

Trying not to think about it too much, I slip through the doors into the bright greenish-yellow light of Gaia's chamber.

The huge doors give way to a vast tunnel, gently sloping downwards. The walls should be earth, but instead are covered in moss, vines and creepers, some of which bear yellow and green fruit that glows softly. The bare ground gives way to soft, spongy moss, and I peer ahead in the gloom, my guns resting on my still-aching wrists.

I see a flash of copper and throw myself to the side of the tunnel, pushing Melusine to the opposite wall as I do. Twin blades fly through the air between us a moment later, embedding in the wood of the vast doors with a 'thunk'. I sight, spotting the scorpion creature and fire two rounds from each gun, hearing and seeing the explosion, but somehow also feeling Gaia's distress at such violence within her inner chambers.

Inspecting the coppery wreckage, I dismiss my guns and fall to my knees, sinking my hands into the soft moss.

"Forgive me Gaia," I say, almost feeling the surprise and sadness of the earth spirit in the air. "We're coming to help you."

I feel like a bit of a prat, but Melusine gives me a nod as she reaches me, her danger spell still illuminating the path ahead with green light, although it's almost invisible against the moss.

I stand and look up ahead, seeing another set of enormous double doors, similarly ajar.

"Ready?" I ask, but Melusine only scoffs.

"If you're leading, lead," she says. "And hurry up about it."

I roll my eyes and keep moving down the verdant tunnel carefully, smelling plant life, both alive and rotting, overlaid with the stink of burning metal.

I pause just before the door, waiting for Mel's nod, hurriedly slipping between the two huge doors, not quite believing what I see on the other side.

Gaia's chamber isn't vast; it's perhaps the size of a large conference room in my office, if conference rooms were two-storey and the shape of flattened spheres with mossy walls on all sides.

But unlike a large conference room, there's a torrent of yellow and green light in the centre of the room, a column of brightness that gives the impression of motion, a river of movement constantly seeking the ceiling of the chamber. I can hear a rushing, a whispering, a constant chattering coming from within it, and all around the column is *life*; not just plants, but trees, flowers, creepers, cacti, mosses. As I gaze around, I see animals grazing amongst the plants; deer, leaping frogs, a large badger curled up sleepily, birds singing on the branches of the trees. Everything brims with an incalculable verdant force.

Then I see *him*.

In front of the beam of light is Beckett, arms outstretched, sparks from the torrent somehow pulling away from the central column and infusing into him. Already it's begun to change him; I can see a light covering of moss on the back of his hands as I approach.

"Jamie," Mel says uneasily as I walk, and Beckett turns as he sees us. I break into a run, but when I see his eyes, I skid to a halt a few metres away.

Other than the moss, Beckett looks largely the same as the last time I saw him. He's still a solid figure of a man, muddy jeans and a checked shirt, a large backpack on his shoulders – although it looks empty now, and I wonder if it contained all of the tricks and traps we've navigated. But his eyes … his eyes are now gold and glittering with tiny fragments of green. I could stare at them for days. There's something intriguing, something intoxicating about them.

"Ah, Jamie," he says, his voice deep and slow. I can feel roots of some kind pinning my feet to the floor, branches grasping for my arms, but his voice is hypnotic. I need to listen to what he has to say.

"Beckett," Melusine says. "Stop this. Immediately."

I glance back at her, momentarily annoyed that she's interrupting him, but I can barely make her out. The branches from around the chamber are reaching towards her, trapping her in an almost-impenetrable wall of nature.

I shake my head. Remember why we're here, Jamie.

"Beckett," I say vaguely. "What are you doing?"

The big man laughs, stretching one hand out and making a small yellow light dance on top of it.

"Oh Jamie," he says. "You can't possibly understand. The boredom of a small village for a hundred, two hundred years would be enough for most, but try doubling that and only being able to leave for a week or two at a time without having to scrape and beg to the tree queen or the bad faery king. Then consider – you're a huntsman. That's what you do, you hunt. And that's fine in 1760, but in the late nineteen eighties? The nineties and beyond? You might not have a mortgage, but how do you pay for anything? What do you fucking hunt, Jamie? What do you fucking *hunt*?"

Melusine says something sharply, and Beckett winces as pink goo melts down over his shoes and solidifies, fixing him in place. He gestures quickly, and the ball of light flies through the air and fixes itself onto her mouth, the tree branches nearby trapping her hands and stretching her out into a T-shape once again.

Bile rises in my throat as I realise that the pink goo is probably his flesh. I retch, holding my head to one side and vomiting onto the moss.

"But you could have done it, Beckett," I plead desperately, coughing and swallowing hard. "You could have asked Balthamel. Better than this ... slaughter. Better than turning Mel's sister into a wreck. Better than causing earthquakes and storms and turning this place over to us humans. Surely?"

"You think your witch is innocent of all this?" he rails, crossing his arms and glaring at me. "You think it's fun having your house torn apart by the police because she wants to make a living selling drugs on the internet? Don't you think that's ridiculous?"

I stare at him. This seems ... petty. Incredibly petty to cause such death like this. I can't imagine living for four hundred years, but still, to lose your perspective like this, well, it's both sad and pathetic.

"Don't you think it's awfully convenient that you were in the right place at the right time to help her, Jamie?" he continues. "Isn't that awfully fucking convenient? How easy do you think it would be for her to whip up a nasty little potion to make a few little tumour cells grow inside your mother? Just as easy as it'd be for her to make one to slow them down, right? Wouldn't that be a sure-fire way to bring you back to the village? The slow death of a parent, a little bit more blood on her already-drenched hands?"

I reel, almost losing my balance.

No. Melusine wouldn't. Would she?

"I've seen the CCTV footage," he continues. "She was wearing your friend's body last night. It might have been over a decade ago, but I recognise that girl. Don't you think it's terribly handy that you happened to be back in the village at exactly the right time for her investigation? You're just another body to her, another asset. Did she pay you off yet, or did you not even get the blood money that she promised?"

I glance back at Melusine but she's almost completely obscured by foliage now. I can see one hand and the bottom of a leg; the rest is entirely entangled by plants, branches and vines wound tightly around her body.

"Can you imagine it, Jamie? Can you imagine living through all this, their plots, their machinations, their deviousness. Wouldn't we be better off without it?"

For a moment, hypnotised by his eyes, I think about it. I think about Lisilya's rage, Balthamel's paranoia, Silvai's hostility, Kiriel's creepiness.

But then I think of Alariel. Of Dakyid. Of the tiny elf baby in the Unseelie Court. Of kindly Enutef and Kopek, the beer-brewing troll, whose goods I have yet to taste. I think of Merovech.

I think of the nice staff in my office against the backdrop of Mark and Emily, my coke-snorting flatmates.

It's all the same.

So why add to the pain?

"No," I say slowly but firmly to him, somehow conjuring the strength to resist his glamour. "No. It's not better without it. And it's not better to add more suffering to it, even if it would make it better. And I won't believe that Melusine..."

My voice cracks, and I sniff back a load of snot and sick, tears pricking my eyes. "I don't believe that Melusine gave my mum cancer."

Beckett screams at me, his golden eyes flashing dangerously, green and yellow light flowing faster from the column of Gaia's brightness to his hands, cascading up his arms.

Then there's an abrupt utterance from Melusine behind me, and Beckett raises his hands to fend off an attack, a spray of colour spilling from his fingertips. I feel a hot pain as something fast and sharp skims my stomach and disappears into the column of light. I can feel a wet sensation; I'm bleeding.

And then something heavy falls out of my pocket, bouncing towards Beckett. It's the heavy metal octagon we got from the wreckage of V's house. The last trinket from the happy little inventor.

I was going to keep that, I think, watching it sadly.

It bounces towards Beckett once, twice, three times.

Then Merovech's inner hut, a gleaming chrome and brass shed-like structure, reconstructs itself before my eyes, the apex of the roof springing up and striking Beckett firmly under the chin, knocking him back towards the column of light.

There's a moment when Mel's flesh magic seems to hold him back as he teeters on the edge, but she makes a gesture, releasing his feet and tipping him into Gaia herself.

Chapter 23

I stand, mouth agape, half expecting Beckett to surge out of the column of light as Godzilla or something. He doesn't, and instead I watch as Merovech's hut unfolds right in front of me, eventually standing like it's always been there, errant pieces of thatch still clinging to the shiny metal.

Then, to my absolute surprise, tripping out of the hut and shaking themself like a dog getting out the rain, is Merovech.

"Jamie?!" they exclaim gleefully, as I try to pull my way free of the branches and tree roots holding my hands and feet. There seems to be some give – without Beckett's presence, they've become looser.

"V," I grin, despite the circumstances. "You have no idea how good it is to see you!"

"Oh, thank you!" the little inventor burbles. "I'm *very* glad to see you too. I had an *extremely* scary time. I was in my room and there was a big explosion. Before I knew it, the safety measures had tripped and I was shut in the little panic realm for ages. I even had to pee in a bucket! Me! Peeing in a bucket! How about that? Oh, Jamie – where *are* we?"

V looks around and pulls up their goggles as I manage to free one arm from the tree branches.

"Gaia," I say reverently, ignoring V's question for a moment and realising that I might be able to speed this up a little. "A little help, please?"

Merovech gazes around, wide-eyed and taking in the column of light, all of the plants and creatures around us. Suddenly, all of the other branches retreat, pulling away from my arms and legs, curling back to the wall of the chamber. I spin, suddenly able to see Melusine; she's gripping one of her fingers and seems to be … well, not bleeding but definitely dripping some kind of dark liquid onto the mossy floor.

"Mel," I call. "Are you ok?"

She hurries towards me, nodding at Merovech. "I'm pleased to see that you're alright," she says, sounding strained. "Now get out and tell the Seelie and Unseelie Court that Beckett conspired to cause a war between them and use Gaia's power to escape from our realm. Tell them it was all him. Tell them about the scorpions. Mind the traps on your way out; use the detection charm I gave you."

Merovech looks at her, eyes wide.

"Jamie," she says. "With me."

And with that, she hobbles towards me, then breaks into a run and leaps into the column of light, vanishing.

"Fuck!" I manage.

Merovech giggles. "Jamie! That is *not* a nice word."

"I just … well, I thought Beckett was gone…"

"Oh no," V says, gesturing at the light. "Gaia's an earth spirit. Very old, very powerful. This place is only the outer shell of her being. That's the inner part. You'll need to be especially careful in there. Very few rules that you and I understand. Especially you."

I swallow. "Great," I say. "Well, no time like the present. Do you have a phone?"

Merovech pulls out an identical handset to the mysterious brand that Melusine was sporting earlier. "Oh yes," they say. "Custom made. Melusine got a batch last year when she was on the dark web. Very handy."

I pull up my shirt and see a thin line where whatever Melusine did cut into me. Thankfully, it's not too deep and it's mostly stopped bleeding now. I don't really know what to do with it, making a mental note to keep a first aid kit with me in future. I think there's one back in the car, but that's not that useful right now.

"Then be careful," I add. "Lisilya and Balthamel aren't going to be happy that Alariel and Silvai are dead."

"Oh," Merovech says sadly, looking like they're about to shed a tear. "I liked Alariel. But Jamie, I think it's really you that needs to be careful."

"Yeah," I say. "Yeah, I think you're right about that."

I glance around one more time, and steeling myself, take a running leap into the column of light.

There's a flash of green light and a weird sensation of shrinking and growing again as I pass through the outside of the column. Suddenly I'm stumbling on spongy moss, coming down to my hands and knees quite painlessly, but it still knocks the breath out of me.

If Gaia's chamber was a riot of growth, being inside Gaia herself almost defies description. As I kneel, my shoes start taking on a greenish tinge, and a moment later, tiny plants begin sprouting on the tongue near the laces.

Gaia's realm is a thick fog of life, flies and tiny winged creatures drifting past lazily. I almost don't want to breathe in for fear of inhaling one of the small dragonflies.

There isn't a single patch of ground that doesn't have some kind of life erupting from it. Small silver birches spring up next to grand old oaks. Creepers and brambles grow between trees, drooping and dying as new ones rise up to take their place, all in the course of a few seconds.

Birds sing and squirrels chatter, and I can hear hooves somewhere in the distance. I peer towards the sound, but I can't see more than a few metres in any direction; everywhere is vibrant with life, thick with mist and sound. It's almost swamp-like, the moss and grass beneath my feet moist like an overgrown, out of control glasshouse. It's kind of incredible. I could spend hours here just wondering at it all, except for the nagging feeling in my gut that this isn't really a place where ordinary mortals should be.

My hands! There's something ... no, my actual skin is darkening and becoming textured, almost like tree bark. What's happening?

A translucent green sphere drifts lazily in front of my eyes, wafting upwards. I push myself to my feet feeling a surge of panic, thankful to see Melusine standing right in front of me, peering into the lush greenery ahead.

She turns, sees me and holds up one hand.

"Jamie, Gaia's energy will try to change you, unless you channel it," she says, and I look at her hand more closely. All of her fingernails are long and sharp-looking except for one, which is entirely missing, her pink skin torn and oozing a dark fluid.

"Is that what you threw at me?"

She nods, but as I stare, her finger glows green very slightly, a small patch of nail appearing, then growing upwards until it matches the others. She gives me a triumphant look, and I try to concentrate and imitate what she's done. There's so much weird energy buzzing around that I don't really know where to start. I try to focus on the discolouration of my hands, feeling something else there that isn't me. I push that energy to the wound on my stomach, feeling a surge of wellbeing.

Cautiously, I lift my shirt, seeing bloodstains, but no actual cut. If it can heal a cut, then maybe it can help mum too? Later Jamie, I tell myself, survive first, then think about that.

I glance downwards, seeing that the tree bark on my hands has faded.

"Come on," Melusine says. "We can't linger."

She starts to walk – or really, it's more like wading – across the soft, spongy moss.

"Gaia," I murmur, awkwardly feeling like I'm praying or something. "I know it's a bit of an ask, but if there's any chance I could get some of this essence to keep for a few hours, I'd really appreciate it. You see, it's for my mum."

"Jamie!" Mel says sharply, turning to look at me. I fall silent, hoping that she didn't hear, hurrying to catch up.

"So, this is ... this is the earth spirit?" I ask, trying to sound casual. "Or is this the realm that she lives in? Like, will we meet Gaia?"

Melusine pauses to look back at me briefly, looking a bit less haggard than normal.

"Gaia is a spirit," she says quietly. "Spirits rarely manifest in our world, and when they do, it's more of a tendril, a root of their being than the whole of them. All of this *is* Gaia. Or at least, what our eyes can comprehend."

I'm not sure I really understand, but I've got other things to think about right now.

I see moss reaching the top of my shoes and starting to move up my legs. I pause to try and feel the energy-sense again, wishing that I'd brought a bottle or something. Of course, even if I could store it somehow, who knows how long the effect would last.

My shoulders slump and I keep walking, until I'm reminded of Gaia's influence and the moss tickles my knees. I start concentrating to find something that ... well, that isn't me. I think I have it, but I'm not really sure what to do with it.

I imagine myself a bit more well-built, channelling the life-energy into that image. I feel a tingling across my body and it's almost like I'm expanding. I'll have to check whether that worked once I'm back, but something feels different and the moss seems to be gone.

Mel forces her way through a thicket of brambles and I step to one side to avoid being lashed in the face by the springy branches.

Then we see Beckett.

He's in the centre of a clearing, but the trees are starting to encroach on it. Mossy boulders litter the space, ferns sprouting all around and there's suddenly an eerie silence. I can hear birds in the distance, but all of the other noises have become very faint.

He's not in a good way.

Where his booted feet used to be, hooves now show. His regulation corduroy trousers now resemble chunky tree trunks. His torso is still human, but is covered in a greenish moss that extends down his arms, which are sprouting irregular growths. As I look, one bursts and a small kingfisher flies off into the undergrowth.

His face is a picture of confusion and pain, as yet untouched by Gaia.

"Melusine," he screams. "This power! I had no idea. I ... can't control it."

She looks at him, his hooved feet slowly vanishing under a network of tree roots.

"Beckett," she says sadly. "Beckett, the harm you've done."

His face narrows into a rictus of hatred. "Fuck you all," he spits. "Fuck you and all the faery. Fuck pretending that I give a shit. Fuck being the nice guardian of your realm, day in, day out. But most of all, fuck you Melusine."

Mel snorts and focuses for a moment, a slim, crimson blade materialising in her hand. It's the same dark colour as the ichor she was bleeding earlier, and I wonder if she's recycling what she lost. She really doesn't waste anything.

Beckett sees it, his eyes widening before his expression becomes triumphant.

"That's it!" he says. "That's how!"

He concentrates for a moment and I jump to the side as a small swarm of wooden spikes fires from his hand, narrowly missing impaling me.

I feel a stinging sensation on my arm and look down. They didn't quite miss me; there's a large slice in my jacket and a cut on my bicep which is bleeding freely. Mel glances over and gestures, the wound sealing and the blood flying over in a stream to curl up the sword, lengthening it and settling as a spiral of red on the long, dark blade.

She tosses it over to me and I manage to cancel my guns in time to catch it by the hilt. I grip it tightly in my right hand, re-summoning my left-hand gun, not quite sure what to do next.

I look back up at Beckett, whose tree-trunk legs are wobbling as their bark darkens, the roots over his feet seeming to tighten. He looks down, staring hard, the roots starting to recede gradually.

"Quickly, Jamie," Melusine says calmly, but there's an undercurrent of strain in her voice.

She's also looking at his feet and concentrating hard. When I look more closely, I can see a small stream of green particles flowing from her feet to the roots around his. She must be channelling her energy into making it grow as he's trying to dissipate it.

I remember Merovech's burning hut. I remember Beckett's traps, cruel wire pulling my body apart. I remember Alariel, Silvai and Alizon.

I think about a future where the paranoid Balthamel orders a strike against the Seelie, or one where the Seelie attack humans with no thought for stealth.

I take three strides towards Beckett, channelling the energy from the leaves that have started to sprout along my right arm into the moss beneath my feet, making it surge and flow towards Beckett. It briefly startles him, but he quickly recovers, diverting it to one side and laughing at my weak effort.

"Jamie, you'll never be a part of this world," he smirks,

looking down at his hands and summoning another handful of wooden spikes.

I step closer and he looks back up, just in time to see me draw my hand back and swing the ichor blade at his neck with all my new-found strength.

The sword hisses in the air, slicing through his neck with a faint popping noise like hot oil in a frying pan. I gag as his severed head drops to the ground, rolling to rest against the base of a tree and slowly sinking into the moss. There's a fountain of blood from the stump of his neck, his body falling backwards onto the ground, the wood of his legs splintering and cracking.

Then I retch yet again, bringing up what little is left in my stomach, my vomit gradually being reabsorbed by Gaia. I drop the blood blade, resting my hands on my knees and panting and spitting out sick for a moment.

"Jamie," Melusine says softly. "We mustn't linger."

Slowly, I pull myself back up to standing, wiping my chin with my shirt.

"Can we ... can we leave him like that?" I manage, not wanting to look at the headless corpse.

Mel nods, slowly, looking tired. "Gaia knows life and death," she says. "His energy won't hurt her, but you should keep that. It's been made somewhere completely unique, and there's power in it."

She extends a weary finger at the blood blade. I would have been pretty happy to leave it here and I'm not really sure where to put it, so I just hold onto the hilt for now, which is oddly warm to the touch.

Aching and tired, suddenly feeling the adrenaline fading, I stagger over to Melusine and she slings one arm over my shoulders.

"Come on," I say. "Can we get out the same way we came in?"

She shakes her head, and for a moment I want to lie down on the grass and stop. A tree branch tenderly brushes my hair, and I laugh. I guess if we're going to be stuck here, at least I seem to be getting on ok with Gaia.

"Well, maybe," she says. "Let's see."

It's incredibly hard to retrace our footsteps when the landmarks around us are constantly growing and then dying off in the space of minutes. I'm also continually distracted by having to pause and focus Gaia's magical energy so that I don't come out of this with moss growing up my neck. This place is incredible and I do feel an odd sense of being at home here, but I'm not particularly willing to become part of the landscape just yet.

"Gaia," I mutter. "It's been fun, but you know we don't belong here, right?"

Another branch tickles my hip, and a moment later, the silver birch trees in front of us part, leaving a V-shaped gap towards what seems to be a curtain of light.

"Well shit," Melusine grates. "Perhaps I should apprentice you to Alizon next."

"Next?" I say, raising my eyebrows at her. "Next I'm going to go home, have a bath and sleep for a few days, ok?"

She laughs, which turns into a hacking cough. "Fine," she says, spitting phlegm into the bushes. "I suppose that's fair."

As we step towards the gap, light fills my field of vision. It's bright yellow now, with flashes of green that make me blink. It's almost painfully bright, and I shoot a panicked glance at Melusine, who takes a deep breath and pulls me into it before I can open my mouth to argue. There's a sensation of falling, shrinking then growing again, before we're unceremoniously deposited on the mossy floor of Gaia's outer chamber on our hands and knees, staring at the wood of Merovech's shed and several large pairs of feet.

"You've got some telling to do," Balthamel's deep voice echoes around the chamber as I look up at the giant tiredly. "What happened with the huntsman? Why are so many of the Seelie and Unseelie dead? And why in the name of all of that is unholy is there a fucking *shed* here?"

Chapter 24

It takes over an hour to explain Beckett's plot to Balthamel, longer still when a mean-looking genie and a centaur arrive from the Seelie Court and we have to start again. It turns out that Merovech managed to rouse both courts, and quickly too. I suddenly realise that the little inventor is probably almost universally well-liked, although if it ever gets out that they invented the scorpions that slaughtered everyone, well, that might change.

I wonder where V is now, and I hope that they're safe.

Unexpectedly, it's Tssirai and the commanding orc from the Unseelie Court's side of the raid who help to corroborate our story. Balthamel gives a grunt of pleasure when Melusine relates my decapitation of Beckett with the blood blade; apparently it's got both ceremonial importance and also didn't run the risk of damaging Gaia with human-made weapons, however adept at re-growth she is.

As we stagger back up the tunnel towards the surface, I can't quite unpick my emotions. Beckett taught me to shoot, gave me the run of his bungalow, drank at the local pub. He seemed like a nice guy; he *was* a nice guy.

I guess a lot can change in four hundred years.

Suddenly I'm glad that I'm mortal. Everybody dies, and despite the circumstances, it makes me feel a bit better about what's happening to mum.

I break off that train of thought before I tear up in front of the various Seelie and Unseelie creatures who have arrived.

"Jamie," Melusine says scratchily. "I can handle things from here if you'd like to go home."

I shake my head wearily. "It's ok," I say. "You might as well get your money's worth."

Resting one hand on the bare earth wall outside Gaia's main door, watching as the last of the Seelie and Unseelie cross out to the slaughter ground, Melusine turns to face me. There's an angry red sunset, and it occurs to me that time must have passed differently in Gaia's realm. Is it even the same day?

"Forgive an old woman, Jamie," Mel says slowly, flushing with embarrassment. "I may have been hasty. You've done much more than I could have expected and handled yourself well, especially for one with little magical aptitude. Let's ... let's talk again once we've both rested."

I nod wearily, watching as Balthamel pushes the huge door closed, turning the key in the lock and strapping the mace-like object to his back once he's done. I feel like I should be elated that this is all done and over, but all I can muster over and above the exhaustion is relief.

Together we help the Seelies and Unseelies gather up their dead, lifting them carefully into two unmarked trucks. As I bend, I feel something in my pocket, and wonder if my wallet has leaked some loose change or something.

I'm distracted by a contingent of orcs finishing with the beacons, which will show a fake, wide-spread radiation leak to anyone in the area with a Geiger counter. Then the genie, along with Tssirai and her twin sister, Tssirak, consult with each other before casting some kind of levitation spell that causes tonnes of earth from the surrounding fields to rise up and cover the doors to Gaia's chamber once more.

"I don't think I've ever seen two banshees work with an earth elemental," Melusine says, as the last section of the huge door vanishes under the soil. "Perhaps all of this wasn't for nothing after all."

I shake my head. An earth elemental, not a genie. I should know better by now than to judge the faery courts by my experience of Disney films.

"Can I give you a ride home?" a faintly familiar voice says from behind us. I turn around slowly to see Dakyid, the dark elf that we met in the Unseelie Court. "Much as I hate to remind you that I was right about your presence portending disaster, I'm reasonably sure that you've used up your quota of horrendous occurrences today."

I fish the car keys out of my pocket and toss them to him. "Sure," I say. "If you don't mind driving a beaten-up antique, I could use a break."

Dakyid gives me a mocking half bow. "I assure you, unless your car bites me and shits on my boots, it won't be the worst thing I've ever ridden."

I have a momentary flash of panic as I wonder whether he can actually drive. Thankfully, he gives me a grin, climbing into the car and adjusting the seat and mirrors with an easy efficiency that says otherwise. He pulls on a beanie hat that matches his biker jacket and conveniently hides the tops of his pointy ears.

Dakyid gestures and mutters a few words, the windows of my mum's car gradually tinting and becoming opaque from the outside.

"They're activating the radiation field now," he says as an array of trucks and people carriers stream past us. "They're going to send out a message from the communications centre that one of the experimental pieces of equipment has malfunctioned and they're evacuating the site. The staff will wake up shortly with memories to validate this, and anyone getting close to the site will register high but contained levels of gamma radiation for some time."

"Thanks Dakyid," I say, leaning my head back on the car seat. "Appreciate it."

I glance over at Melusine, but she's already got her eyes closed and is breathing deeply. A moment later, she starts snoring and as I look out of the car window, I feel my own eyelids becoming heavier.

I don't resist, only waking when we pull up outside Beckett's bungalow.

Melusine has already woken, and hearing my waking snort, turns to me, proffering two large padded envelopes.

"Here," she says. "As we agreed."

"Thanks," I say, rubbing the sleep from my eyes and slipping the envelopes into a yet another stray carrier bag from under the passenger seat. "See you in a few days?"

"Drop by whenever you're ready," she says. "Dakyid, are you coming?"

"Very well," he says. "But only for a day, mind you. I've seen enough of what happens when the witch of flesh and blood rears her head."

"Aren't you sweet?" she croons. "Come on, I'll cook something and tomorrow we can go and help Alizon get back on her feet. Jamie, you rest and maybe you can meet Ali when you're next over. I should check on Merovech; the Unseelie Court dropped them off, but I'm sure V will have found some way of getting into trouble by now."

I smile at the witch as she walks down the path to the house. She gives me a wave before heading inside, the elf trailing behind her, grumbling all the way. I slip back into the driver's seat and watch the familiar village slip past me on either side as I head back to the house. I'm completely exhausted, but this is all starting to feel oddly normal; I can't decide whether the thought of going back to my office job is oddly comforting, like a worn old jumper, or whether it'll be too boring after these last few days. Or maybe I belong somewhere in the middle?

It's late when I carefully pull up in the driveway. I briefly wonder where to stash the blood-sword, eventually wrapping an old dustsheet around it and putting it in the boot.

I stagger into the house, desperate for a shower and a good night's sleep. I drop my keys into the bowl by the side of the front door, and am about to do the same with my wallet when I feel something else in my pocket. Must be that loose change.

Only it's not loose change. It's a small vial of translucent stone – probably crystal – and I can just about see tiny green spheres drifting around inside, exactly like the ones inside Gaia.

Suddenly I'm filled with wild hope and a surge of energy. I pull off my filthy shirt and tug on a new one, making a quick coffee and rooting around for a travel cup. I grab a couple of cereal bars from the kitchen and set my phone's GPS for Bath hospital.

The roads are quiet, and I make the journey in under half an hour. As I pull into the car park, I wonder how on earth I'm going to accomplish this, although I suppose that hospitals – or at least, parts of them – do stay open all night.

Clutching Gaia's gift, grinning as I remember the brush of a tree branch against my hip, I hurry into the brightly lit hospital foyer, trying to retrace my steps. The purple strip ends at a locked door, and I start to lose my nerve a little as I spy a security guard giving me a suspicious look. I make a point of looking at a sign and following the signs towards A&E, expecting a rebuke at any moment.

It doesn't come, and I pause after the second corner, catching a glance of a red strip behind another – mercifully unlocked – door. Passing a tired-looking old man walking with a stick, I suddenly find myself in front of room 110.

There's a water cooler a few steps away, so I fill a clear plastic cup and take out the vial, wincing as I uncork and upend it. The green spheres bounce downwards in an almost leisurely fashion, but they don't burst when they hit the surface of the water; rather, they sink halfway down, then burst, releasing a cloud of green ... something as they do.

As quietly as I can, I open the door to my mum's room, breathing a sigh of relief when it's not locked. She must have forgotten. I guess she's got other priorities. Closing it behind me, I take a step towards her bed and she stirs, looking up at me muzzily.

"Jamie?" she says, her voice croaky with sleep.

"Mum," I say quietly, proffering the cup. "Here, drink this and concentrate on getting better. Concentrate really hard, ok?"

She takes it and drinks, then looks at me strangely. I hold my breath, not knowing whether she's quite awake or not, desperately hoping for the latter. Then she takes another drink and finishes it all, looking like she's about to ask me a question.

"That's great," I say softly. "Go back to sleep now. I'll see you tomorrow."

"Sure," she says sleepily. "Love you, Jamie."

"Love you too, mum," I say, stepping backwards and slipping out of the room. It's only when the door clicks shut behind me that I swallow hard and wipe my sweaty hands on my jeans. I'm well overdue being in bed, and I can feel the post-adrenalin tiredness starting to hit me hard.

There's a coffee machine in the foyer of A&E, and I gulp down an espresso, feeling a very brittle kind of energy that I know won't last. Wishing I'd had time for a shower and wondering how badly I smell right now, I get into the car and carefully drive home, double checking every single turn and junction. I miss the road into the village, but thankfully there's no-one around to see my sloppy U-turn.

I collapse into bed less than a minute after I walk through the front door.

Surprisingly, I don't even dream.

It's noon the next day before I wake to the insistent beeping of my phone. Wiping the sleep from my eyes and taking a gulp of the stale water in the pint glass next to my bed, I sit up and unlock it.

The first message is from Flic, saying that she's got an assignment in London, but am I free to have dinner there at the weekend? Taking a deep breath – I'd really rather have had breakfast before doing this – I message her back saying yes, and asking where in town she'll be.

The second and third are both from my mum, within a few seconds of each other, asking me to call when I can. I dial her number and she picks up a moment later.

"Jamie, hi," she says, her voice clear and strong. "Listen, I'm just going into another scan, but can you come and see me as soon as possible? I … I think I have news. Good news."

"Sure mum," I say, trying not to sound too hopeful. Could it have worked? "That's great. Anything you can tell me now?"

There's some background noise, someone saying my mum's name a couple of times. "Got to go, Jamie. Maybe be here in two hours? Three?"

"No problem," I start to say, then there's a louder scuffling noise and someone says 'Ms West' more insistently. I hear her placate them and then hang up. I feel a surge of hope, but it's muted by the fatigue of the last few days, however long I've slept for.

I put the phone down and wipe my eyes. I'm not sure I can wait three hours to find out if it's worked.

I suppose if it can regrow a fingernail, there's no reason why it can't heal someone.

Then I remember the other part of my experience with Gaia and spring out of bed, heading for the bathroom mirror. I'm definitely looking a bit broader, and my arms are a bit thicker and more muscular. Well, saves on a gym membership, I laugh, thinking of Flic again.

I shower quickly, closing my eyes and letting the spray wash over me. My mind flashes back to last night – Alariel, Beckett, Silvai. I feel a surge of sickness rising in my throat, and suddenly I'm dizzy. I put a hand out to steady myself and pause for a moment.

When the dizziness passes, I step out of the shower. It's a relief to feel properly clean again, and I dress, eat breakfast and spend a while just sipping coffee and staring out of the window. Time creeps by slowly, but before too long, I'm getting back into the beaten-up old car and driving to the hospital.

When I arrive, my mum is in her room with two doctors standing by her side.

"Doctors," she says firmly. "Could I have a moment with my son?"

One of them fixes me with a stern look. "Mr West, your mother has shown something quite remarkable. Unprecedented even. Please do not tire her," she says firmly.

I nod, but as they walk past me, the same one leans in and pauses. "We don't usually allow guests in the small hours of the morning," she says quietly. "But under the circumstances I think we can make an exception."

I don't say anything, mentally castigating myself for forgetting the CCTV. I suppose that with any luck, it'll just show me coming in to visit and getting a drink of water before seeing my mum briefly. People have probably done worse.

The door closes behind the two doctors, and I turn to mum, frowning.

"So…?"

She smiles, then takes a deep breath. "They still want to do more scans, but as far as the first two can tell, the cancer has completely gone, overnight. It's a bit of a miracle."

I grin, feeling a surge of relief and joy. "That's amazing," I manage, rushing in and hugging her tightly. When I eventually pull away, we're both crying a bit. "That's incredible."

She nods, not speaking for a moment.

"They don't understand it," she says. "It's completely impossible."

She pauses. "Jamie, they said that you came to see me last night. I remember it, but I'd taken pills, so it's a bit fuzzy. I don't know if you prayed, but if you did, thank you."

I take both her hands in mine, feeling completely wrung out. It was all worth it, after all. Thank you, Gaia, I think to myself, thank you. I'm not religious, but I suppose I did pray to the earth spirit a little.

Mum looks down at my hands and sees the two small tattoos on them, narrowing her eyes for a moment.

"Jamie," she says quietly, fixing me with her steeliest gaze. "Did you get something from *her*?"

I freeze.

Printed in Great Britain
by Amazon

62368459R00188